A C**BOOK OF THE YEAR**

**N
A
T
I
O
N
A
L

B
E
S
T
S
E
L
L
E
R**

"Necessary!"
MARGARET ATWOOD, via Twitter

"*The Circle* is a window into the lives of unforgettable characters, families, and community. . . . A masterful work."
DAVID A. ROBERTSON, author of *The Theory of Crows*

"Like Orange's *There There*, *The Circle* is a polyphonic masterpiece."
ERIKA T. WURTH, author of *White Horse*

"*The Circle* draws us back into the lives of characters who we've come to know so intimately that their heartache is our heartache. . . . Distinct and vivid."
AMANDA PETERS, author of *The Berry Pickers*

Praise for
THE CIRCLE

National Bestseller
A CBC Best Fiction Book of the Year

"What a gift we have been given. *The Circle* is a window into the lives of unforgettable characters, families, and community. The nuances, the crescendos, thrum like a heartbeat that hurts and heals, bends and breaks, that mends, always with care through prose that is as beautiful as it is raw and unflinching. vermette has written a masterful work, one that challenges us with an intricate structure, as the circle forms and finally connects. If this is the end of the story, the gift we have is to hold these characters, and live with them long after the last page has been turned."

—David A. Robertson, author of *The Theory of Crows* and The Misewa Saga

"A perfect companion to *The Break* and *The Strangers*, katherena vermette's *The Circle* draws us back into the lives of characters who we've come to know so intimately that their heartache is our heartache. With each new perspective as distinct and vivid as the last, *The Circle* acts as an unsettling reminder that the systems designed to help the most vulnerable too often end up betraying them. This is a stellar finale with an ending that will leave you both heartbroken and hopeful."

—Amanda Peters, author of *The Berry Pickers*

"Like its sisters in this trilogy, every page of *The Circle* is a steady and rhythmic observation of our humanity as Indigenous people. It asks what restitution and justice could possibly feel like when we, as Indigenous people, are all subjects of this unjust empire called Canada. This book is truth in all her fluid forms. It is an altar of love, hope, and grief amidst the relentless torment of settler colonialism. katherena vermette, in her distinctly elegant style, offers a glimpse into the devastating beauty of our people and our capacity to keep moving forward, one foot at a time, guided by the love and strength of our ancestors. It reminds us that, in the end, all that's left is the stories we carry with the people we loved."

—Elle-Máijá Tailfeathers, filmmaker and actor

"Like Orange's *There There*, *The Circle* is a polyphonic masterpiece. Brutal at turns, and tender at others, it's about the tremendous impact one person can have on an entire community."

—Erika T. Wurth, author of *White Horse*

Praise for
THE STRANGERS

#1 National Bestseller • Winner of the Atwood Gibson Writers' Trust Prize for Fiction • Indigo's #1 Book of the Year • Finalist for the Carol Shields Winnipeg Book Award, the Margaret Laurence Award for Fiction, the First Nation Communities Read Award, and the McNally Robinson Book of the Year Award • Longlisted for the Scotiabank Giller Prize • A *Globe and Mail* Best Book of the Year

"A potent, audacious intergenerational saga that explores race, class, inherited trauma, and the strength of matrilineal bonds."
—*The Globe and Mail*

"*The Strangers* . . . speaks, starkly and eloquently, as if directly to the community of readers it creates."
—*Winnipeg Free Press*

"vermette offers up a beautiful, raw testament to those living on the margins. Brilliantly weaving the lives of the Strangers into stories within stories within stories, vermette's confident, understated prose walks the reader through the unforgiving reality of the descendants of those who stood with Riel and Dumont, grasping for survival in a world committed to a long-established campaign of dispossession. Cathartic and disturbing, *The Strangers* offers vital insight into the colonial brutality that still haunts the lives of the Métis."
—2021 Atwood Gibson Writers' Trust Fiction Prize Jury (Rebecca Fisseha, Michelle Good, and Steven Price)

"A deeply moving story of how colonial institutions continue to bear down on and disrupt the lives of Indigenous women and girls. It is a powerful collective portrait of struggle and resistance, of what it's like to be in an Indigenous body in twenty-first century Canada. In the end, it adds up to an engrossingly written ode to another kind of care, one against the grain of suffering. A brilliant follow-up!"
—Billy-Ray Belcourt, bestselling author of *A Minor Chorus*

"*The Strangers* is a unique and essential triumph of a novel. It is revelatory in its artistry—in its constellating of family against violent separation, in its austere poetics of voice and consciousness. katherena vermette has proven once again that she is among the most gifted and relevant writers of our time: someone with everything to teach us about the telling of necessary stories, about grieving the fallen, honouring survival, and revealing the fiercest beauty."
—David Chariandy, award-winning author of
Brother and *I've Been Meaning to Tell You*

Praise for
THE BREAK

Winner of the Amazon First Novel Award, the Burt Award for First Nation, Inuit, and Metis Literature, the Carol Shields Winnipeg Book Award, the Margaret Laurence Award for Fiction, and the McNally Robinson Book of the Year Award • A CBC Canada Reads Selection • Finalist for the Governor General's Literary Award for Fiction and the Rogers Writers' Trust Fiction Prize

"Poignant . . . a story of great depth and compassion. This masterfully written narrative shifts among the intergenerational voices of the women of one extended Indigenous family. *The Break* is a powerful, persuasive novel about the strength and love that bind these women to each other and to the men in their lives. The traditions and wisdom of a community are honoured, as is the exquisite individual humanity of each character. Although this is a novel of social importance, it transcends politics, taking the reader on a journey to the heart of what it means for one person to care about another, survive trauma, and endure."
—2016 Rogers Writers' Trust Fiction Prize Jury (Lauren B. Davis, Trevor Ferguson, and Pasha Malla)

"The lives of the girls and women in *The Break* are not easy, but their voices—complex, urgent, and unsparing—lay bare what it means to survive, not only once, but multiple times, against the forces of private and national histories. katherena vermette is a tremendously gifted writer, a dazzling talent."
—Madeleine Thien, author of *Do Not Say We Have Nothing*

"vermette offers us a dazzling portrayal of the patchwork quilt of pain and trauma that women inherit. . . . These are the stories our mothers, sisters, and friends have told us—the stories we absorb into our bloodstream until they might as well be our own. . . . A stunning debut—a novel whose ten voices, Greek chorus-like, span the full range of human possibility, from its lowest depths to its most brilliant triumphs, as they attempt to make sense of this tragic crime and of their own lives. *The Break* is an astonishing act of empathy, and its conclusion is heartbreaking. A thriller gives us easy answers—a victim and a perpetrator, good guys, and bad guys. *The Break* gives us the actual mess of life."

—*The Globe and Mail*

"vermette is a staggering talent. Reading *The Break* is like a revelation; stunning, heartbreaking, and glorious. From her exquisitely rendered characters to her fully realized world and the ratcheting tension, I couldn't put it down. Absolutely riveting."

—Eden Robinson, author of *Monkey Beach*

THE CIRCLE

ALSO BY KATHERENA VERMETTE

Fiction:
The Strangers
The Break

Poetry:
river woman
North End Love Songs

Illustrated Books:
The Girl and the Wolf
The Seven Teachings Stories

Graphic Novels:
A Girl Called Echo Vol. 1–4

THE CIRCLE

KATHERENA VERMETTE

PENGUIN

an imprint of Penguin Canada,
a division of Penguin Random House Canada Limited

First published in Hamish Hamilton hardcover by Penguin Canada, 2023
Published in this edition, 2024

1 2 3 4 5 6 7 8 9 10

Copyright © 2023 by katherena vermette

All rights reserved. Without limiting the rights under copyright reserved above, no part of this publication may be reproduced, stored in or introduced into a retrieval system, or transmitted in any form or by any means (electronic, mechanical, photocopying, recording or otherwise), without the prior written permission of both the copyright owner and the above publisher of this book.

Penguin and colophon are registered trademarks.

Publisher's note: This book is a work of fiction. Names, characters, places and incidents either are the product of the author's imagination or are used fictitiously, and any resemblance to actual persons living or dead, events, or locales is entirely coincidental.

Excerpt from "Blind Justice" by Lee Maracle in *Hope Matters* © 2019 by Lee Maracle, Columpa Bobb, and Tania Carter. Used with permission of Book*hug Press.

LIBRARY AND ARCHIVES CANADA CATALOGUING IN PUBLICATION
Title: The circle / Katherena Vermette.
Names: Vermette, Katherena, 1977- author.
Description: Previously published: Toronto: Hamish Hamilton Canada, 2023.
Identifiers: Canadiana 20230144500 | ISBN 9780735239678 (softcover)
Classification: LCC PS8643.E74 C57 2024 | DDC C813/.6—dc23

Book and cover design: Jennifer Griffiths
Cover art: *Birch Bark Technology: Morning Star* © KC Adams
Typeset by Erin Cooper

Printed in the United States of America

www.penguinrandomhouse.ca

For my kids,

and all the other warriors out there.

Still, I am not tragic
Not even in my addicted moments
A needle hanging from the vein of my creased arm
I was not tragic
Even as I jump from a boat
In a vain attempt to join my ancestors
I am not tragic
Even in my disconnection from song, from dance
I am not tragic
Even in seeing you as privileged
As an occupier of my homeland in my homeless state
Even as men abduct us as we hitchhike
Along these new highways
To disappear on this long colonial road
I refuse to be tragic

—LEE MARACLE, "Blind Justice"

RELATIONAL CIRCLE

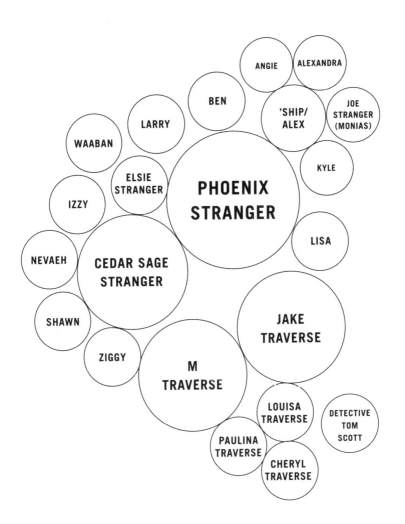

ered that the sensor can be integrated into a microfluidic device for monitoring changes in solute concentration as flow rates change. Considerations of the sensor stability are covered in Section 2.11.

In Chapter 3 an improved version of the sensor is designed to overcome the limitations of the first model. This new model involves fewer optical parts which are optimized to perform at a working wavelength of 850 nm. A model based on thin film theory is developed to characterize the sensor response as a function of the gap formed between a gold coated prism and a mirror. This model also includes an optimization of the sensor sensitivity with respect to all the parameters that define it. It was found that, for a fixed bandwidth, only the working wavelength, the thickness of the gold coating and the distance between the prism and the mirror could be used as tunable parameters. The chapter is completed with an analysis of four different methods to assess the operation of the sensor so the one that is the most effective is identified.

A method to fabricate the sensor is proposed in Chapter 4 along with the tests performed to validate it. Here, the sensor response is mainly characterized under aqueous conditions showing great response to changes in refractive index and good mechanical and temperature stability. Furthermore, when coupled to a microfluidic device, the sensor is shown to be able to monitor changes in solute concentration with a relatively fast response time as the flow rate changes. Finally, a deeper understanding of the limitations of the sensor and strategies to overcome these are presented.

Finally, Chapter 5 presents an overall discussion of the proposed sensors together with the achievements obtained in this project. Additionally, as the work presented in this thesis represents a proof of concept, the possibilities in which the proposed technology can evolve are also discussed.

PART ONE

CEDAR SAGE STRANGER

When I hang up, I want to cry.

I stand there a minute, phone in hand, middle of the long front hallway, and don't move. Can't move. Can't even think.

My thumb slips across the screen and my saver flashes on—me, Zig, Wynn, and Izzy the day we moved into this big old house. I was so happy. Buzzed on that sparkling rosé we used to drink every weekend and half-stoned. Our housewarming, we called it, even though it was just us and a YouTube dance playlist.

So happy. Then. Now, I only feel dread.

It's all my own damn fault. Not like I didn't know this day was going to come. Not like I didn't have an actual countdown to the date. My sister told me so many times. Phoenix was counting the days 'til she got out, of course she was. She was looking forward to it as she should be. I used to look forward to her getting out, too. This is not fair on her. Not her fault. Not this anyway.

I hear the creak of the second step as Wynn comes down the stairs. "Hey," she says and I almost jump. "You look like you seen a ghost." She laughs. I don't say anything so she adds, "You didn't see a ghost, did you?"

I try to laugh or scoff but it only comes out halfway, so I shake my head instead.

"Oh thank god. Phil was watching ghost vids last night. Those things creep me out. Especially since moving in this house." Wynn keeps talking as she crosses the kitchen and over her shoulder while she pulls the oat milk out of the fridge. "Come sit down, you're freaking me out."

I slide my phone in my pocket and go to my chair at the table.

They're all mismatched wooden chairs we thrifted last fall then painted as our own. Mine is curved and round and yellow. Zig painted a red beaded flower motif across the top. "Michif are the flower beadwork people," she said with a smile. Her chair is dark purple, tall and lean with two rows painted like long beads across the seat. "I wanted it to look like wampum but it didn't quite turn out."

We sit around here for house meetings, all of us in a circle, and take turns to talk. Say our feelings and how things are for us. A check-in, Izzy calls it. "So tradish!" Ziggy said that first time, with a laugh, like she does. I smiled, like I do. Not really sure what's funny but wanted to seem like I knew.

"Wanna talk about it?"

I check myself. Sit straighter. I've always seen Wynn as a really self-assured kind of person. She seems so laid-back and only talks when she needs or wants to, not one of those people that have to fill up the space all the time. She told me last year she suffers from pretty serious anxiety and has been on and off meds since she was twelve. I was shocked. Would have never thought.

"Naw," I say slowly, quietly.

"Okay." I can tell she's looking at me but I don't look up. "Want some eggs?"

"Sure." I pull my knees up in front of me and hug them close. Scrambled eggs are the only thing Wynn knows how to make but she makes them so good. She knows exactly how I like them.

What am I going to do?

We've been here almost a year. All four of us in this big old house. Well, five now since Phil, Wynn's partner, never seems to go home. We talked about it and are fine with them moving in officially, but Izzy said we shouldn't try and push them into a commitment they might not be ready to make. Zig said that was stupid and they should pay something at least. I said nothing because I didn't really care either way.

Zig found the place at the end of last summer. A bunch of hippies had rented it for years. She had been to parties here, back when they had parties, and thought it was the most beautiful house. She pointed it out one time, on one of our walks to the Village. I could see what she liked about it. Painted three different shades of brown with stained glass at the top of all the tall windows, on the first floor anyway. A long porch that wraps around the side. One small rowan tree in the front yard. I looked up what kind of tree it was because Zig liked it and I wanted to tell her what it was. It has pale green leaves and white berries in spring that deepen colour until they're bright red in the fall.

Back in the dorm, we had talked about getting a place all together. Something near school, Zig said. As long as it has character, Izzy added. We were all back at home for the summer when Zig found out it was available. They had all been in the dorm too long and were determined not to go back. I didn't mind it and didn't feel super ready to live on my own, but I really wanted to be with all of them. Really wanted to live in a big beautiful house with my friends. My real true friends. So, I grabbed it. I barely have enough for food after all the bills but Dad gives me money whenever he takes me out for lunch. I don't even ask but he does, so I manage.

The house is actually a bit of mess on the inside. It has old wiring for the lights that Dad says is a fire hazard, the rads never work properly so I have to run two space heaters in my room in winter and a big fan in summer, and those beautiful windows are probably as old as the house so they don't even open. We have to put plastic over them all winter. The plaster walls are cracked and even falling off above the stove. One time Izzy stomped around upstairs and a big block of plaster fell into the soup Zig was heating up. It was her mom's soup. The best soup you'd ever tasted and it was a huge pot of it. Ruined. Izzy was super sorry but it's not like it was really her fault. Now there's a hole in the ceiling there with the wood slats underneath. You can see the water pipes and hear whenever someone is on the toilet upstairs. Not the greatest thing when you're trying to cook or eat. The landlord knows about it, I think he even came and looked at it one time, but he still hasn't gotten it fixed. It's been months. It broke at Christmas.

But I love this old house. I love the dark wood panelling in the living room. The curved stairs that are so worn they curve down in the middle. The second one creaks and the banister is so wobbly I am pretty sure it's going to fall off but I love it all. My room is the smallest. It's long and narrow and the window looks out onto the back lane. I can see the cars stuck on Broadway at all hours and even as far as the corner store where we do most of our shopping because none of us has a car. Zig is the only one who even has a licence. It's been the best ten months of my life.

"I think Phil's going to break up with me," Wynn says, sharply swooping her toast over the rest of the yolk on her plate. She likes her eggs runny.

"Why would you think that? Phil loves you! They love you!" I've been trying to avoid using Phil's name instead of their pronouns because they told me that's something they notice people do when they're not comfortable with non-conforming pronouns. I was mortified because I know I did that when I first met them and thought maybe they meant me. I've been working on it. I've been reading about it. Trying to be a good ally and not just a clued-out kid from the suburbs.

Wynn pushes her plate over like she's disgusted. "I don't know. I was reading this article about being demi poly and like, mentioned it, but I totally offended them."

Wynn reads a lot of articles. Her major is gender studies and she started working at the Rainbow Resource Centre. She's really into everything right now.

"I mean, it's not like I'm definitely into that. I think it's interesting, you know. But they said it felt traumatizing to even talk about."

I make a neutral sound like mmmm. And make a mental note to look up what demi poly is later.

"They were the last person I thought would be so judgmental about stuff." Wynn sighs and rubs her eyes. "Oh I don't know, maybe I fucked up."

"I am sure everything will be fine. Talk to them," I try, but I'm not sure this is the right thing to say, or even what she wants to hear.

Wynn sighs again. I hope I've gotten better at this comforting thing. When Phil first moved in, Wynn thought they were gonna break up all the time. They fight a lot. Passionate, Zig calls it. Fucking nuts, Izzy says.

Izzy has a boyfriend too but he lives in Calgary so we've never met him. He's taking some fancy science degree and won't be done for another year. And Zig, well Zig always has at least someone. Zig likes to date. She says it's natural.

I don't have anyone. Not that I haven't tried, a bit anyway. Online. During the lockdowns when everyone was online. I even put that I was into boys and girls because sometimes I think I don't even know. But the guys got gross and the girls never seemed to have anything in common with me, so nothing happened. I figured I'd wait until the world opened up and I could go out in real life again, but even then, nothing much has happened.

"You'll find your love when you're ready, CC," Zig has told me more than a few times. She always says it with her trademark wink. A wink that makes it easy to blush and makes me realize how she always has a girlfriend. I like that she calls me CC. Sometimes I think Zig is my person or meant to be my person. Sometimes when I'm brave or drunk I lean in too close and dare her to kiss me. I want her to. If only to see if it's true. But she never does. She looks at me like she feels a little sorry for me. She still holds me, hugs me. We've held hands while we watched movies or when we've been sad, and this one time when we were skipping down the river walk. Swinging our arms between us and laughing so hard I lost my breath.

She's my best friend and I know everything about her and she knows almost everything about me.

I know that her first girlfriend was a girl named Cora and they dated for her whole first year and then Cora broke up with her so she could date a guy, and Zig was so mortified she went home and didn't talk to anyone all summer.

I know that her Moshoom, her dad's dad, is the best person she knows and her brother, Sunny, is learning their traditional ways by being his skaabi, but Zig is actually really offended she was never asked to be his helper too, and she doesn't know how she feels about all the binaries in her traditional ways but doesn't know how to talk to her Moshoom about that.

I know that when she was thirteen she got beat up so bad she was hospitalized and her best friend was brutally raped. There is no other word for it: she was raped even though it was girls who did it.

And I know it was my sister, Phoenix, who did that. I knew even before Ziggy told me the details. I knew by the way the wind was blowing that night, one of the first cold nights we spent together at the dorm. We bundled up under our bedspreads in front of the common room's tall windows and watched the storm grow. The snow whipped up and swirled in the streetlights. The bare tree branches bent so far I thought they would break, and Zig told me her worst story. I knew it was what my sister did even before she said it all.

"My mom told me *girls* did that to her, to M. Can you believe it? I couldn't understand it at the time. How can girls do that?"

I didn't say anything. Couldn't.

"I mean, I know. I know. But it was still . . ." She sighed deep. The wind howled and the glass rattled a little. I remember it like that but it probably didn't even move. "I read once about these girls, down in the States somewhere, two of them, and they like, did that to a girl. Tied her up and did that. I hate thinking girls can do that to each other."

"It's . . . horrible." I couldn't think of the right word. Maybe there wasn't a right word.

"Sorry." Zig had looked at me, then down. "I know it's such a trauma dump."

"No," I said and thought better of it. "No. You can talk about . . . you can tell me anything."

"I'm sure you don't need to hear about all the rough stuff. You're so lucky. You didn't have to grow up like that."

"Yeh" is all I said to that. I hadn't told her anything much about my life yet. I have told her a bit more since.

"I try not to think about it," she said with a long exhale that seemed to try and push it all away, and then cuddled closer to me under the blanket. I remember feeling the weight of her arms against mine, her knees against my thigh, her hand limp on my lap.

I had never felt so warm.

Couldn't tell her then.

Never told her since.

At first, because it seemed too raw. Then, because it felt too scary. Now it feels like it's been too long, is too late.

After I clean up the kitchen and Wynn goes up to shower, I try to call my mom. I wonder if she's heard about my sister or what she knows or thinks.

There's no answer at the one number I have for her. The other one is still out of service. It's been out for a while but I still try it every now and then thinking that might change. I think it has changed before. Or maybe it's that I like the sound of the automated operator when it goes. Almost as good as my mom's actual voice.

I don't think I've seen her for a year. I talked to her a few times. Here and there, now and then. Sometimes she calls, even, but mostly it's me calling her. It's not like how she said it would be once I got older, once I lived on my own like living with my dad was what was keeping her away. We don't see each other all the time like she said we would.

I was still in the dorm last I saw her. She met me at the door, didn't want to come in, and we walked to a coffee shop. Her hands shook as she paid with coins and shook again as she pulled down her mask to sip her plain black coffee. I ordered an almond milk frappuccino but immediately wished I hadn't. They're so much more expensive. I offered to pay but she waved my card away. We sat on a park bench by a playground. She looked over as if studying the kids playing and I felt sorry I came.

"I get so sad about it all sometimes, my girl," she said to like, no one. I don't think it was really to me.

I wanted to say something like "it's okay" or rather I thought of saying something like that, but I didn't want to. I wanted to tell her I'm here now and I've been waiting for this for so long and could she please love me, but I didn't. I sipped my frap and watched the kids play, too.

She didn't hug me for a long time that day. It was brief. One arm. Her bony shoulder to my shoulder. "Love you," she said. Again, I didn't think it was to me.

When I've talked to her, she says she's doing okay. "Figuring it out" is what she usually replies to my "How are you?" Sometimes I'm glad she doesn't pick up. It's easier to leave messages. Sometimes they sound worried. Sometimes I try and sound upbeat. Today I don't try either:

"Hey. Mom. It's me. I was wondering if you heard about
Phoenix or if you heard from her. I'm, I don't know. She's getting out tomorrow. It's Tuesday if you're not getting this 'til . . .
I mean it's Tuesday today so she gets out tomorrow,
Wednesday. I thought. Well, I guess I thought you should
know, if you didn't. Love you."

I say the "Love you" like an afterthought, or a prayer.
Same difference.

I sit on the couch by the big window for a long time. This is my favourite room. The living room with the dark wood panelling and the fake fireplace where we put a bunch of candles. No one has lit them in a while so they are dusty and look blurry from here. I feel like I've been waiting for my sister to get out of prison my whole life, and now that it's here I don't want it. It's not fair. Not for Phoenix, who has waited for this, not for me, who has managed to build up this new life, one I never thought I could ever even have, just to lose it all in not even a year.

I didn't know lives like this existed.

I've learned so much since I started university and most of that not even in class. When I met Zig, I wanted to be like her, had never met an Indigenous person like her. Then I met Wynn and Izzy and didn't know I could be like any of those Indigenous people either. They're so lucky and special and different from each other. Zig's full name is Zegwan, which means "spring" in Anishinaabemowin, which is her language that she speaks and everything. Her Moshoom is a Traditional Knowledge Holder and leads the Sundance in their community. Her mom's a social worker, her dad owns his own business, and they all live in her home community in the south. Wynn's parents are both doctors. Doctors! Only her mom is Métis, her dad is white, but doctors! I went there for dinner once and they acted like normal people. Their house was amazing. It was in Charleswood, where Wynn grew up. I hadn't even ever heard of that neighbourhood before. Izzy though had the most amazing growing-up because she has two moms, both Métis, and was home-schooled in Wolseley until high school. Her bio dad lives in New Zealand but is from here, and we're all going to go there and visit once we've saved up enough. Well, they will probably still go, but I doubt they'd let me go with them to Aotearoa, not after they know.

Even Phil is Indigenous—Anishininew from way up north, but they've lived down here for years. They came down in grade nine all by themselves and lived as a boarder in other people's houses so they could finish high school. It sounded a lot like foster care to me, when they told me.

I started majoring in Indigenous studies right away. I like English well enough but the dead-white-guy stuff bored me so I decided to only study work from BIPOC authors from now on. I like the history most of all but even took a special land-based course last summer. There is so much to know. And, it's not like I am using my roommates to study or anything but it's something more than that, something I will miss so much. I think it's called community but I'm not sure.

I really don't want to move back home. I've been avoiding going there for weeks. I still get texts from my stepmom, Nikki, every other day, still see my dad for lunch when he's in town and it's a weekday, when Nikki is working and he can get away, but I haven't gone home in a long time. I felt stuck there last summer. After a whole year in the dorm then to have to go back to the empty streets and nothingdays of Windsor Park. I wish I had stayed in the dorm like some kids did, and was even grateful to get my dollar-store job back, so I had something to do. I barely spent any money, which worked out, really, as that was how I could afford to start living here. How I was able to say "I can!" when Zig sent the post about renting the house in August.

I know they can find another roommate no problem. I am fine to pay until then, even though I'm sure Zig will want me to move out as soon as she knows. I'm not worried about them, only me. What am I going to do without them? Without all of this?

I stare out the window and think of it all for a long time. I think of not telling Zig at all and wishing she never had to know. I could avoid it, but for how long? Until my sister wants to know where I live or Zig learns my sister is out? Until she puts it together from the few things I've let slip out here and there? When I've been high, mostly.

Two sisters, now one. (It was a long time ago. I'm okay.)

Jail, jail, jail. Out soon. Maybe soon. I don't know why, some gang stuff, I think. (I never slipped a name. Never never never.)

Mom is MIA always. (I'm okay with it. I haven't been with her since I was so young.)

Foster care. (But I barely remember, right? So that doesn't really count.)

Dad. Nikki. Faith. Alberta. (Of course I love them. They're great. I am so lucky.)

These used to be the only things about me. The only things that mattered.

Funny how none of them are really about me at all.

My stepsister Faith is doing great. She's still in Alberta and a supervisor at a Tim Hortons now. She sends me cat videos instead of texts.

Sometimes I think she's making fun of me with them but I still like them. She has a boyfriend, of course. A nice-looking guy who always wears those big plaid hunting jackets. Dad had one for a while but Nikki hated it so I think she gave it away. This guy though, he wears it in every picture, and smiles big. Faith looks like she's drowning in him, probably is. Everyone has a person but me.

Even my old foster sister, Nevaeh, lives with someone. Well, sort of. She had a baby last year, too. A little girl, Evangeline. They're not far, so I visit them all the time. I've never met her boyfriend. He works a lot and doesn't live with her for some reason to do with housing or something. Nevaeh is like me and doesn't share much. Not like the girls I live with now who seem to share everything. I guess if I had lives like theirs I'd want to share everything, too.

I'm still on the couch staring out at the tree and nothing when Izzy bounces down the stairs. She's sweaty from yoga, does vinyasa every morning and doesn't eat until noon. She's holding a half-drunk recycled bottle of kombucha I can smell from six feet away.

"Why so glum, chum?" Izzy is very awake.

I make a sound instead of an answer. My usual mmmm that means anything and nothing.

"It's finally nice out, hey?" She puts her bottle on the side table and reaches her long arms up, stretching in perfect half moons.

I've done yoga with her a few times but really can't keep up. She likes flows and hard poses and kept correcting me all the way through. It was too much. I like the simple videos of easy beginner stuff. I told her that once, when we were all sitting around, but she sighed and said it's not even worth it because you're not burning any calories, and then Phil said that yoga isn't about burning calories and called her a brainwashed dieter. It got bad actually, because Wynn had to come in and tell them both to take a step back. I didn't mention yoga again.

"I'm going to go for a walk by the river, if you want to come?"

It feels like a pity invite, and she has a pity look on her face. Wynn must've said something to her. I've noticed they do that sometimes when I look sad, which is really always, because I must have that kind of face. Zig started it, but now they all do it. I don't like it, so I square my shoulders and sit up as if that makes me look okay, and shake my head.

"Naw, I think Zig and I are doing something when she gets home."

"Okay. But you should get out, you're looking pale." Izzy is not bossy on purpose, just out of habit. Not rude—efficient. She is an only child and her moms seem to worship her. She told me once she'd never been grounded or even been in real trouble. I could say the same but pretty sure we acted very different. Her moms aren't far either and come over all the time, bring food and little gifts for all of us. They even brought me a present for my birthday. I was really surprised because that was when we first moved in and I didn't think Izzy even knew when my birthday was. Zig must have told her.

Izzy disappears into the kitchen, and when the blender starts, my tears come. I am so used to fighting crying I barely notice anymore until I actually do. I think I've always been this way. Nikki once told me I always look like I'm about to cry, even when I'm smiling. Resting sad face, she calls it. I don't want to go live with my stepmom and dad again. Maybe I can go back to the dorm in the fall, that way I'd only have to be home for the summer. I was really looking forward to summer. Zig was going to rent a van and we were going to drive out to Calgary to see Izzy's boyfriend. Wynn really wants to see all the dinosaurs in Drumheller and I want to see the mountains. I've been saving up for months. Well, in relative terms. I limit myself to one coffee a week and pocket everything my dad gives me that I don't need for bills.

But no, this is what I deserve. I should have told Zig when I had the chance, when I first knew, when she first told me about her and her friend.

But if I'd've done that I wouldn't've had any of the last two years. Not last year when we were all stuck in the dorm during that long lockdown winter. We watched all the John Hughes movies over and over and went on long walks through the almost empty streets. I wouldn't've had any of the last ten months in this old house or learned anything about coffee, culture, yoga, or anything. I would still be the boring old suburban kid, so needy and sad. Even my depression is dull.

"Want any of my smoothie? I got lots. It's blueberry, flaxseed . . ." Izzy's in the room before I can wipe my eyes. "Hey, are you, hey."

She sits next to me, looks with a smile. I usually hate pity. "Do you want to talk about it?"

I shake my head and can't stop. Shaking or crying. I think of something stupid: "I, I want you to know I really liked having you as a roommate."

"What? Are you moving out? Why?"

I shake my head again and feel so stupid. "No, I." I take a deep breath and say the rest as an exhale. "I have to tell Zig something and then I know she'll want me to move out."

"I can't believe, I don't think there's anything you could do to make Ziggy want to kick you out!" She leans back and has this look I can't read.

"No, no, she will."

"Aw, chum," she sighs. "Ziggy's a pretty forgiving person. I mean, remember Allie? She forgave that chick more times than she deserved, holee!" She smiles so big I want to smile too.

But then I hear the door open.

Zig comes in still wearing her barista T-shirt. She must've really wanted to get out of there because she usually changes at work.

"What's up?" she says warily as she puts her bag down.

Izzy nods at her, and gets up with another smile down at me. I usually hate when people are being patronizing.

"What's up?" Zig says again and sits down where Izzy was.

I cry harder. It's one of those ugly cries where you can't stop and can't keep your face from scrunching up. I feel gross and embarrassed and then start to hyperventilate.

"Hey, hey, slow down, breathe."

I pucker my lips and let air out in huffs. I try to bring air in through my snotty nose, but have to wipe it with my sleeve.

I can't take it. "Phoen, Phoenix is my sister," I say as fast as I can.

"Phoenix?" It takes her a minute, and then I see that she can see it.

I keep huffing, afraid for a minute I couldn't breathe. Then afraid that I could.

I really liked living here.

"Your sister? The one in, jail?" she says, putting it together.

I nod and squeeze my eyes tight so they'll stop weeping, or maybe because I'm embarrassed. I wish I could close my eyes and not be here. I want to leave. I wish I could leave. I don't want to leave.

"I'm so, I'm so sorry, Zig. I didn't know . . ."

"You didn't tell me."

I shake my head.

"Why didn't you . . ." She stops. "She's getting out soon."

I know what I've told her. What I've let out ever so small. Sister in jail. Grown up in jail. Sister out soon. Never using her name. Never giving too much away.

I nod.

She leans back. She leans as far away from me as she can get. "When?"

I say it with a wince. "Tomorrow."

JAKE TRAVERSE

Jake's gut wrenched when he saw Phoenix's name on the list. He immediately wanted a smoke. The person who had hurt his cousin was finally getting out and the first thing he thought of was a smoke. Hadn't smoked anything in over two years, but man, that muscle memory was strong.

He squirmed in his seat awhile, looking and re-looking at the email on his screen, then finally leaned over and asked his co-worker, "Hey can I bum one?"

"What the fuck, you don't smoke!" Dakota said, looking up from their phone for once while drumming their fingers on the desk. They were like that, always doing at least two things at once, always moving. Not like an addict but like a super-energetic person.

Jake was never an energetic person, less so these days. But seeing that name on the list made him twitchy, so twitchy. He shrugged, or tried to, like it was no big deal.

"All right, all right." Dakota, maybe sensing his mood, maybe being good like that, got up. Maybe just wanted one themselves. They rubbed their newly shaved head and put their phone in their shirt pocket, and led the way. "Break time," they said to the kids in the hall, motioning to their other co-worker, Musky, with finger guns. Musky nodded and grumbled but continued to clean the counter from supper. A couple kids looked up from their conversation on the couch, another sat at the landline and didn't even notice. They buzzed through the door, and Jake gave his automatic look around. The sidewalk was empty. It wasn't that late yet and still light out.

They rounded the squat brick building and Dakota bounced up to the side of the cement planter to sit, kicking their legs out as they dangled. Jake leaned against the mural that stretched the whole side of the youth drop-in centre—an Elder holding up a pipe with eagle feathers off it. It needed a touch-up but was otherwise clean. No one so much as carved their initials on that wall. No one ever would think to tag it.

"You all right?" Dakota said, handing one over. "Who died?"

Jake lit up and shook his head. The smoke hit his lungs like burning. It never tasted good after so long. Never like how you remember it.

"Wanna talk about it?" Dakota said like right out of the training. Always ask and be available, never assume and pry.

"Not really." Jake smoked quick. He always smoked quick. Muscles remember. "Got some bad news is all."

"Yeh?" Be open and attentive but not imposing.

"Yeh."

Reluctant but willing. Dakota waited, even looked away but still looked attentive.

"Got the release list. Someone's on it I don't want to see."

"Someone bad for the kids?"

The drop-in centre gets a list of the recently released every week or so. There were a couple halfway houses nearby and it was good to know who was back in the neighbourhood in case someone would be related to a kid or a risk to the kids. They called them kids affectionately, but they were officially youths. Under-eighteens and knowing too much of the world already. They, as workers of the drop-in centre, were supposed to give them a safe break from all that. Sometimes even they did.

"Maybe. Don't know," Jake said. "She's been in awhile. Like six years. I think," he added, even though he knew exactly.

"Who dat?" Dakota said, running their hands over their head again.

"This chick, Phoenix," he started.

"No! Shit. Phoenix Stranger? Fuck." Dakota got so animated, their hands all over the place. "Shit, I was in the C with her awhile. That bitch is crazy. Like TV show crazy. Man. What that bitch do to you?"

"She . . ." He didn't want to say too much. For the sake of others, for the sake of himself. "She hurt people."

Dakota's hands kept waving. Hand to mouth in shock. Hand to air to emphasize a point, to act out the words. "No shit she hurt people. That bitch is certifiable. I saw her beat the shit out of this one girl with a food tray. Fucking plastic food tray broke on this other chick's head. Blood everywhere. Broke that girl's nose. She had to have surgery. Shit."

Jake butted out right at the filter and put his hands in his pockets. He still felt twitchy. He still like, needed to do something.

Dakota looked at him. Was almost still. "Who she hurt?"

"My cousin."

"Didn't know you had a cousin. I mean, I figured you did, like doesn't everyone? Never heard you talk about them though."

Jake sighed. "She's, she's not around much."

Dakota stuck their chin out, eyes squinted in the setting sun. "She know?"

Jake shook his head. Realizing what he needed to do.

Jake likes the work at the drop-in. He'd been here two years now, was shift supervisor. The ED wants him to get more training, get his degree, but Jake doesn't think the world needs any more social workers. He likes the trainings though. Non-Violent Crisis, some counselling, CPR of course, and they work with these Elders and go out into the bush, do Ceremony. He likes that. And he's good at the job. Good at talking to people, good at talking with the kids. His mom, Lou, who is a social worker, says it's because he's so quiet. People like to talk to quiet people, especially kids. She also says, all flippant, that he comes by it honestly, as if she too was good at it because she's quiet. And she is, but not in the good way. Not in the calm way Jake likes his quiet.

In school, he took Electronics. He went to a tech high school and got his ticket along with his diploma. That's what he thought he wanted to do, fix things. Don't have to talk to anybody. But his first job was up north for weeks at a time and all those guys did was party. Him and a bunch of old white guys high on coke all the time. He hated it. Way too much testosterone in small rooms. Being around the same people for weeks. Hating them from the start.

He quit and moved back in with his mom. Took this job at the drop-in for something to do. She got it for him. Made him. He made half of what he did up north. Liked it way more though.

Dakota's cool. Musky's a bit of a diva but a good guy. There's a bunch of others he gets along with and they have community people come in all the time to talk to the kids, musicians and artists. Even Adam Beach one time! He likes that. Meeting people doing cool things. His ED's all right. For an old guy.

What he hates is seeing the kids that didn't get out. Seeing the kids that are so much like him, exactly like him, but got so far into it that they can't see any other way. Gang life. Hood life. Like a disease they're sick with. What's the word—indoctrinated. Like they'd been doctored to be like that.

He knows it's not all bad. He knows some of them, the older ones mostly, they can get a little balance. But most of these younger kids still think everyone's out to get 'em. That they have to fight everybody, and do right by their crew no matter what it costs. Think their crew's their family and not just out to make money off 'em. You can't convince them otherwise. Can't compete with the love they're running to.

He was like that. For a while. And no one could convince him either. Until he convinced himself.

He's back behind his computer updating his notes when his mom calls.

"Hey, honey, how you doing?"

"All right." He waits for it. "You?"

"Pretty good. Pretty good."

Her voice is too singsongy. He says nothing, waits.

"Can you watch Gabey tomorrow night? You're not working, are you?"

"No," he says and smiles. Knowing she won't know which he means.

She waits a beat. "Well, can you?"

"What time?"

"Well, I'd love to go for drinks after work so if you can get him from summer program that'd be great."

He makes a noise in reply.

"I'll e-transfer you money for pizza or burgers."

Jake goes back to his notes, knowing their conversation is basically over.

She goes on so she can feel useful. "And don't let him stay up too late. Or have more than a big gulp of pop."

He starts typing so she can hear him typing.

"And don't just be on your phone all night. You know he wants to hang out with his big bro so bad. Spend time. Play a game."

He types louder.

"I love you, Jakey."

"Okay, you too. Bye." He hangs up and throws his phone to the desk. Fucking Lou.

Jake knows she has a new boyfriend. And that she's more checked-out than usual.

Fucking Lou.

Musky picks that exact time to come be annoying.

"Hey, boss, any chance I can take off early tonight? I got this chick..."

Jake doesn't look up from his screen. "Did you clean the bathrooms?"

"Naw, boss, ain't it Dakota's turn?"

"No, it's yours."

"Seems like it's always my turn." He tries to laugh like an ass.

Jake says nothing.

"I'm not saying it's like that but it kind of feels like that," Musky goes on. "Sorry, man."

"I mean it's never your turn..."

"'Cause I'm boss. When you're the boss, it won't be your turn."

"Well hell, guess I gotta get to be the boss then."

"Guess so."

Musky leaves, and Jake can hear his exaggerated sighs from across the hall as he gathers the mop and bucket and spray and cloths. Jake does not like to call anyone lazy, thinks the stereotype is fucked and he doesn't want to contribute to it, but man, that guy is fucking lazy.

Dakota comes back in from talking to this young girl who had walked in.

"Everything all right?" Jake asks, clicking on a new file.

They lean on the other desk. Start fidgeting with a pen. "Yeh, she's eating now. Going to call and get her a bed."

"How old?"

"Thirteen."

"Fuck."

"Fuck." Their pen tap-tap-tapping against their palm. "Still has like chubby cheeks." Their hands wave around their face.

Jake looks up at Dakota leaning there. Tears in their eyes. Trying to steady their hands. When you do this work, you gotta develop a thick skin. You gotta make actual layers of yourself to keep your feelings far away from what you see. So it can't affect you. So you don't take it home. So you can come back tomorrow. Dakota has no layers. Dakota has no thick skin. It worries Jake. He worries for them.

"Safe tonight," he says because it's what he tells himself.

"Safe tonight," they repeat. Then pick up the phone to call the safe house.

He lets Musky go home early after all, updates the late shift coming in, and walks the girl over with Dakota. The beds are all full so the poor kid's stuck on a cot. Jake leaves Dakota to sort it and starts walking home. The girl looked too much like his cousin had, when she was that young. When she got hurt that young. So long ago now. Six years. Six years in and now Phoenix is getting out. Now he has to do a whole lotta things he doesn't wanna do.

The night is warm. It's the good time of summer when it's not too hot yet, and light out 'til almost ten. The street is quiet. They're all quiet all the way home. He used to take his bike 'til it got jacked, then he ran for a bit until he realized he hated running, and now he walks. It's about forty minutes if he doesn't care, half an hour if he's late. He sits all day sometimes, so it's good to move.

The night his buddy Dug was stabbed was a night like this. Light out for so long, but hotter though. It was so hot that day and they'd been drinking and smoking and snorting. In that order. He remembers passing out for a bit in the sun and had a burn on the side of his face. Then got so fucking high they were running down Waterfront laughing their asses off even though they were running from these Central bangers.

Jake went 'cause Dug said it'd be okay. They usually stuck to their turf for obvious reasons, but Dug had an even bigger one. A girl.

Dug had been in the gang longer, was older, and Jake looked up to him. A lot. When his buddy Sunny left for the rez, Dug was all Jake had. Dug and the other guys, mostly way older. Threat was their like, leader, if you could call him that. They mostly hung around, partied, did some dealing. Made a little money. Jake was what, fifteen? It was nothing for him to say he'd have given his life for them. What did he know about life? Or the value of his? It was either that or nothing, as far as he was concerned. All he knew was he was making money. He got the stuff he wanted, even got his little bro some stuff he wanted. Tried giving his mom money too, but she wouldn't take it. He was being smart about things most of the time. Thought he had it made.

He and Dug knew better, they shoulda known better. They took the bus, middle of the day, thought no one saw. They clocked the streets but it was nothing but office people. Dug's girl lived in this building with her mom and it was so sick! A loft, she called it, and it had a full bar and large balcony that looked over the river. They were there all afternoon. Jake lay on a what she called a lounger and watched the river and across to St. Boniface—the old fort and more fancy apartment buildings, the odd boat or even jet ski on the water. He fell asleep he felt so good. Got a sunburn but didn't even feel it at the time.

Dug woke him saying they had to bounce. Chick's mom was coming home.

They walked out there without thinking, at least Jake did, half-asleep. They started down toward the bridge and Jake was looking at the river, not knowing where he was, when Dug offered him a rail. They hung out in the park awhile, Dug feeling himself 'cause he got a rich girlfriend. Jake feeling fine. They didn't see the other guys until they were right on them. Didn't even notice it was finally getting dark and they were in the trees down by the river. It was fucking dumb.

So they ran. Jake felt like he was floating they were going so fast. They thought they lost 'em but they were really fucking high and got jumped from behind.

Jake threw a couple punches but they took his lid, the one he loved and saved up for. He kicked but they got his new kicks. Dug was giving it too and Jake thought he was doing okay too until those bangers started shouting and took off. Dug was lying on the sidewalk, rolling around funny. Crying out. Some lady was screaming from a window or someplace Jake couldn't see. Dug holding his stomach, moved his hands and they were all the way red. Not red like on TV but darker. Jake didn't know what to do so he put his hand there too, pushed it in like he thought he was supposed to, but Dug screamed so he let off. He went to pull out his phone, got blood on it, but then heard the sirens coming close. He knew they were coming here.

"Go, man, go," Dug managed as he reeled.

"No, man. No way," Jake sputtered. His friend's face strained and pale.

Dug gasped and tried to be still and hard. "Just fucking go."

And even though he didn't want to, the urge to stay heavier than the one to run, Jake pulled himself up and ran.

In his socks, his hands full of blood, he snuck down an alley and caught his breath. He saw the light of the ambulance and knew they were taking care of Dug, so he breathed out and tried to think of what to do next. Too heaty to run through downtown and north side in his socks with blood all over him. He wiped his hands on his pants and went to call Threat.

Threat'd know what to do. Jake knew enough to know they'd be able to track his location, so he went down the alley a ways as if that'd make a fucking difference. At least he knew to call instead of text.

"What up?"

His voice shook. "I need a pickup." At least he knew not to say anything.

"What happened?"

Jake sighed deep, thought he was going to cry. He didn't want to fucking cry.

"Never mind. Where're you?"

"Waterfront. By the bridge. An alley. There's a sign for a furniture store."

"All right. Sit tight. Turn your phone off."

Jake sat down beside a dumpster. It stunk but he felt hidden. His heart went in his throat every time a car passed, not sure if it was his friends, his family as they called each other, or the cops.

He sat there two hours. Had dozed off when he heard a whistle. He stood up and saw one of Threat's cars a few feet away. He walked up, checked that they saw, looked around, then jumped in the back.

Stu was shotgun. Threat always drove. He put the car in drive right away, took the first turn to get on the bridge.

"Anyone see you?" Threat said after they crossed the river.

Jake shook his head.

"What happened?"

And Jake told 'em.

He had an awful sleep. Kept waking up, thinking of that thirteen-year-old. Thinking of his cousin. Thinking that Phoenix gets out today.

Phoenix. And all the things he knows about her. She's his age, or older, so early twenties now. Had a kid with this guy Clayton. Kid's gotta be like four-five now. Lives with his grandma down Polson. Near the river there. That Clayton's still around. Still trying to be a badass. Jake sees him here and there. Thinks he stays in the Development somewhere. Heard he had another kid or two. Did some short time.

Jake finally gives up trying to sleep and pulls the blackout blinds up. It was only eleven, he usually sleeps 'til after noon after a later shift. But this was good. He had shit to do. Shit he didn't wanna do.

Two texts waiting for him, one from his little bro talking about plans for tonight. Kid was more responsible at ten than most adults. Planning whether or not to play *GTA* or *Black Ops*.

Jake texted back, "It's cool lil man. Whatever you want. I'll get you from Club."

Gabey replied with a brown thumbs-up.

The other one was from his mom and he didn't respond, reminding him to get his brother, like he ever forgot, and telling him babysitter stuff, like she knew it better than he did. She must be feeling real guilty if she's trying to parent so much.

His mom had always done this. Always ditched him and his brother and run off for any old thing, some drama or some man. She had the worst taste in men. First his own bio dad, that waste of space James or Jimmy, whatever the fuck he called himself. Last time Jake saw him the guy was literally in front of some Main Street hovel getting questioned by the cops. Talk about fucking stereotype. Then there was Gabe, another basic lowlife who took off after not really even being there. He was Gabey's dad, obviously. Jake actually thought they were still sort of together. Sort of meaning Gabe lived up north with his family and came down when he wanted something. But now apparently Lou has a new man. It's been a few weeks. She's trying to hide it but it's too fucking obvious. No one's told Jake anything. He might try Aunty Paul later but doubts she'd say anything if she knew. Harder to crack than a safe, those two.

Jake doesn't really wanna care. Doesn't think this guy would be any different than the last but at least she's keeping him away. And too old to get knocked up again.

Jake thinks she's always been checked out like this, most of his life anyway. Always dealing with something, that Lou, always some crisis she has to deal with. Mostly it's been her job. Social work life is a hard life. It messes people up. Lou was always running to the rescue of someone. Never her kids though. Jake and Gabey got the shit end of all the sticks. That's why Jake never wants to be a social worker. Too much to fucking deal with. So much it changes you.

He lifts weights, watches some YouTube, and makes a bunch of eggs. He's stalling but also knows his cousin wouldn't be up 'til later anyway. M was like him, kept late nights.

Threat said they had to strike back right away. That shit like this can't be left, or else they'd look weak. Made sense to Jake. He was mad, too. He was cold all over. He had to do something. Stu gave him a knife. An old skiv from who knows where. It was a short blade but sharp. The handle rolled over with white hockey tape worn to black in some places. It felt weird in Jake's hand. Like it fit too well.

They knew something of these Central guys from their socials, from other people. They knew where they got to. Next night they rolled down William 'cause someone said one of them lived that way. But it took forever. And they did line after line getting themselves ready. It was after two when they finally saw one of them. Blasted and pumped, Jake started yelling. It was the one guy on his own, wearing Jake's lid. He'd know it anywhere.

He liked to think he was thinking of Dug but he was too fucking high, he was thinking of his expensive hat.

The guy started running, Threat squealed around the corner and Jake jumped out while the car was still going. He stumbled back, got traction, and was on the guy in a second. Don't know where he got his strength, the guy easily had a foot on him. But Jake got him on his back and stabbed before the guy could fight his way over. Jake pushed the blade into this guy's side. Felt it go in, between the ribs. Felt a heat that he didn't even think of as blood go all over his hand. And the guy kind of twisted and looked at him like, what the fuck? The guy stopped fighting, turned over. Jake fell off him onto the grass and sat there. Frozen. Then heard Stu yelling so he got up. Pulled the knife out quick and wrapped it in his sleeve. Guy made this noise like air getting out of a balloon but lay there. Holding his side in with his hands, like Dug had held his stomach.

Jake was shaking when he got in the back of the car. Didn't even close the door, he was shaking so hard. Stu had to reach over while the car was going. Jake kept wiping his hands on his pants, over and over, couldn't stop. Stu smacked him in his face one time, and they were yelling at him, but Jake kept wiping his hands, shaking.

They gave him a smoke to calm him down but it didn't really. He stopped wiping. Acted as fine as he could and Threat called him a little badass.

By the time they got back to some house they went to, they were telling it like a story, like "little fucker flew out the car like whoosh, just started stabbing the guy."

Jake kept thinking that he hadn't grabbed his hat.

He went home in the sunlight. Stu gave him new clothes but he hadn't showered. He stunk with the night and blood.

His mom was drinking coffee, Gabey eating cereal when he came in. Lou had that look on her face she had then. Back then, she thought she was losing her son and didn't know how to keep him home, always mad then, like she gave a shit for once. But still, had given up.

Jake stood in the kitchen doorway for a minute. Watched her face change. From pissed to concerned.

"What the hell happened?"

Jake tried to talk. But fell to the floor crying.

Lou shipped him off to Moshoom's that afternoon. He slept in the car as they went. No one said a thing the whole ride. Not even Gabey who never stopped talking. Jake had had a shower, scrubbed himself long, and wore his favourite old sweats and hoodie.

When they got there all he wanted to do was sleep but Moshoom put him to work cutting wood. His buddy Sunny came around, looking happy and tan, and stacked while Jake took forever to chop. Sunny was in love. Some girl named Sienna, and wasn't that the prettiest name. His friend glowed, and Jake felt his bruises from his shit-kicking the night before, but kept chopping.

Sunny lived with his dad and sister down the road. His mom sort of lived there too but told everyone she lived in an apartment in the town nearby. Jake was going to stay with the old man. He was going to help him and learn from him. He didn't ask how long he was going to stay. It ended up being a year. The old man had a lodge he taught the boys to run. He only spoke Anishinaabemowin so Jake had to learn real quick. He had to get up early and make coffee in an old percolator. Had to always have tea brewing on the stove in case visitors came. And every lunch Jake heated up maple-flavoured beans from a can. Made them with toast and then spent the afternoon smelling the old man stink the place up. It was a long winter.

But the old man taught him things. Taught him in that old way of talking and listening. Telling stories. Taught him how to be a man. How men's work was the same as women's work was the same as everybody's work—to take care of our people. How if we're not doing that we aren't doing anything worth doing. Jake cried some nights, thinking of his dad—long-lost Jimmy and Gabe who took off, too. How they let him down. Moshoom said he didn't know his dad either, he had died when he was young. Moshoom said he was always sad for himself as a little boy who didn't get a dad. But he learned what he could on his own, and was the best dad he could be to his kids and that made up for it some. Jake took that to heart. Took it inside himself and never let it go.

Jake went back to the city at the end of the next summer to start high school. He wasn't afraid. He knew he'd keep out of trouble. He missed the old man and Sunny and everybody but he knew he had to be with his mom, his cousin who'd lost so much already, his brother whose dad wasn't around all the time and not much of anything when he was. Jake went home to take care of them. All of them. And he did.

He got no trouble. Gangs are like on TV—if you wanna leave, you leave. Unless you've stolen from people or know too much or like that, you can go. You lose stuff, sure. You lose everything, really. But Jake had proven himself, as they say, so he was fine. He'd seen Threat here and there. They don't talk but do nod.

Dug was doing okay. Been in and out. Back in now. They talked on Facebook awhile. And the other guy lived too. Someone told Jake he moved to Saskatchewan, Saskatoon maybe. Jake wants to think the guy's doing all right. Glad the guy didn't die.

He still has that knife. Some reason he keeps it in his pocket. Has kept it with him all this time. Took it to Moshoom's, hid it in his stuff when it wasn't on him. Never know when you need something like that.

He walks over to Aunty Paul's around two. Has a good couple hours before he has to be at work, in case things get emotional. This is a counsellor thing. Giving space. Don't rush. M might have a lot of emotions about her attacker finally getting out of prison, so it's Jake's job to make sure he's open to however she responds. She's usually all right but who knows.

Jake regrets wearing his black jacket. It's too hot. He takes it off and throws it over his shoulder. The afternoon summer sun warm on his arms, bright through the trees. The old elms that lean and arch over the street. This place can really be quite beautiful.

It was somewhere there that he decides for sure. Looking up at the colours of the leaves and sun, he knows what to do. What he has to do. Jake has always taken care of his family. One way or another.

Yeh, Jake really doesn't wanna be a social worker. Too many social workers in this world. All the world needs is people to look after their people. That'd do it. It's a fucked-up world that needs that many trained professionals to take care of people. Just got to go and do it yourself.

M TRAVERSE

M is knee-deep in an old-school Twitter fight when she hears Jake come in upstairs. Even after he takes his shoes off, her cousin's got a stomp that could rival an elephant. M laughs for a sec before this guy, person, online shoots her with another one of his stupid-ass reasons why *Supernatural* got the ending it deserved. She hears the scrape of the chair across the kitchen floor as Jake settles in up there, so M takes a couple deep breaths before she fires back to this guy, person, with all the evidence she knows KNOWS about the writers having it in for Dean, the character, and Jensen, the actor. It's a thirteen-point thread. At the end, the guy, person, Stargate6969, gives a grumpy "oh get a life!" like he/they have anything going on that's any better, and M smiles with the satisfaction of having the last word.

M knows Jake'll come down to her room if he wants to talk to her. Her mom, Paul, barely bugs her during the day, thinking she's working on her book, which she should be, but Jake comes down whenever he wants. M knows she's got a bit though. Paul had made a fresh pot of hamburger soup and gets so bored on her days off, always has time to chat.

M looks over to her desk, to her unfinished graphic novel, not even a novel, really, a barely started book, and feels the anxiety rise. She scrolls her friends' tweets trying not to think about what she should be thinking about.

Her book is the third of a planned trilogy. Hardest of all. For some reason she made up a bunch of new characters, stupidest thing she could have done. The world she made broken wide open, scattered about, with no idea what to do with it all. Endings are the worst. M's never been great at endings. The ones she's written so far have been little more than ellipses, pauses before the next chapter, but she wanted something more for this one. She promised something more. Sold the book and is on contract for this unknown something more. She breathes again and mentally checks where her Xanax is. Just in case.

She's not the biggest fan of this process. All her other books were done or almost done before they were bought. This was the first one she sold before she even wrote a word. You can do that, apparently, after you've done a few and they know you can do it. And they gave her a lot of money. She shouldn't have taken it. She should have written the thing first. Planned it better. She drew and wrote the first book on a whim. Was working through her stuff—her emotional education, her therapist called it. She drew the whole thing first and added words after. Not many words, more pictures. It was something her therapist suggested to deal with her PTSD. To process the aftermath of her assault and her sucky life she hated, so she made a new one. A new life, that is. A large-scale high-fantasy world of three moons, and giants and shapeshifters who fight to save being-kind. The character most like herself was a roogaaroo, and the one like Jake was an animikii. They fought bad guys and always won. She didn't do it to do anything, only to play. Her therapist said she should submit it, if it felt empowering to do so, and it did, so she did. The publisher said yes and asked for more. Of course she had more. She had a whole world created, didn't know where to end. What could the end be? How can you end a story when the world is ongoing? When you don't want to leave? M hates endings really. They all suck. Always suck. Endings can go fuck themselves.

She gets a message from her pal Tyrion_Snow, basically commiserating about Stargate6969, who has apparently been trolling all the fandoms lately. Tyrion_Snow manages a bunch of *Game of Thrones* accounts, so can relate to sucky endings. On Tyrion_Snow's advice, she blocks Stargate6969 and tweets a warning about them. Then, still not ready to work, she looks around for content. She runs two SPN fan accounts and a Destiel forum, and also curates an ace information Insta, that's mostly memes but sometimes some real-life stories or information links. It's all a lot of work. Keeps her busy. Keeps her in the know. Keeps her from having to finish her fucking book.

"Emily? Jake's here!" Paul calls down the stairs, as if she doesn't know. Her old people still call her Emily even though she's said she goes by M now. She's given up saying anything out loud anymore but consistently mumbles an "It's M!" that her mom can't hear.

"I know!" she calls up, more aggressive than she meant to.

"Sorry, are you working?"

"Duh!" M finds a funny anime rip-off meme of aces and their love of the colour purple and posts it. It gets ten likes immediately. Her ace Insta is really heating up these days. She regularly talks to a bunch of other influencers about it. Sofia from Columbia and Kit in California, both have like half a million followers. They've taught her a lot about the culture.

Kit in California replies right away with a generous LOL. His profile pic saturated in a deep lilac. M thinks she doesn't have enough purple clothes so starts shopping. Spending the money they advanced her on the book she hasn't even finished yet. She looks over her phone to her desk. The laptop screen's black but some paper sketches and pencils arranged neatly are ready to work. Begging her to work. She slouches down so her phone can block the view.

She came out as asexual last year. It was only to her mom and mom's partner, Pete, and then Jake, but that was a lot for M to do even that. The guys had both just nodded but Paul had a lot of follow-up questions.

"So that means you don't want to date anyone, right? Do you still think of yourself as a girl? Do you think you'll ever want to have kids? I looked it up—are you asexual or aromantic or both?"

Paul doesn't mean to be disrespectful or even overly nosy. M tries to remember her mom is only being protective. Has had to be. For like forever.

But Paul also sprinkles on something like, "You could always change your mind, you know," as if that was helpful or supportive. Even her therapist had said something like "sexuality is forever fluid," which to M is just a woke way of saying it's just a phase. Neither understand, not really. Both think it's 'cause M is traumatized. Both are wrong.

Her journey to understanding herself was typical. Now that she knows a few other ace journeys, she knows hers isn't very different. She thought she liked guys but it was really the idea of guys she liked. She wanted guys to like her. She wanted to be liked and likeable. She wanted the status of being liked by a guy. It wasn't desire. She's never really had desire. Her mom thought maybe something was wrong with her physically and offered to take her to a doctor, or that she was depressed, sometimes it happens when people are depressed, Paul had said, so uncomfortable but at least trying to understand. But no, M had said, sure of herself for the first time ever. No, this is who she was and she didn't need to be fixed. To her credit, Paul seems to have accepted that. For now.

Jake stomps down the stairs and knocks on the door. Unlike Paul, he waits for her to say, "Come in."

He smirks at her. "Working hard?" She's sitting up in bed, still under the covers, hasn't so much as gotten up to pee.

"You know me," she says, waving her phone.

"What's going on?" He's wearing his customary black track pants. He never wears anything else, and has his matching black jacket slung over his shoulder. Must be hot outside if he's actually out of that thing, which he's always wearing too. She usually makes fun of him about this but today she sees him looking at her desk, her sketches there of an oversized animikii, long brown wings she can't get right, lightning striking in below their feet. She feels suddenly shy about it.

"Not much. You?" She smooths her messed hair. She cut it short a few months ago, chopped it to her ears 'cause she felt like it. Still surprises her when she runs her hand over it.

"I gotta tell you something." Jake was never one to mince words. That might be why he's M's favourite person in the whole world.

"Shoot." She puts her phone down on the blanket. Flips it over so she can't see all her notifications ping.

He sits with a thud on the end of the bed. "Phoenix is getting out."

M took a minute. Not having heard that name in a long while. Thinking it could be someone else. Then hoping.

Finally, "When?"

"Today."

M looks at her purple walls. Pete had made this room for her a few years ago. She moved down here when she was seventeen. It's just drywalled. She should have taped the screws and seams like he said to, but she didn't care at the time. She painted it blue at first, a smoky, almost grey blue, and then last year, aubergine it was called. It made her happy, she said when Paul saw it and frowned.

Reluctantly, she acknowledges the conversation she's in the middle of. "Thanks for telling me."

"I thought you'd want to know."

"What are you going to do?"

M doesn't talk about it much. She doesn't have to. Everyone around her knows, even her therapist. After the initial disclosure when she was still thirteen, she has never made M talk about it directly. They talk about her trauma response, or current stress, or how her current stress might be related to her initial trauma response. They all use words like *past* or *before* or even *it* so she doesn't have to say what *it* is. She doesn't have to explain. She's never really had to explain. *It* just is. That's the worst part. *It* feels more a part of her identity than anything else. More than anything that actually should be.

But this was Jake, her favourite person in the whole world. She's more at ease with him, at home with him. She knew she could say anything and he wouldn't dwell or ask questions and look like he was going to cry like Paul does. With Jake it was like it happened to him too, so he knew. It's kind of like that with her old best friend Ziggy too, who she still talks to and texts but never sees, but Jake comes by every other day. He knows why she doesn't like to go out a lot. He still keeps tabs on everyone to make sure she wouldn't run into anyone when she did go out. He's done this forever, even when he was a kid and trying to be a big dumb gangbanger, he still let her know what was going on—where those girls got to. The worst was that year he went away to get all traditional, he was gone for so long. She never went out then, too afraid of who she might see. She was so glad he came back. Once he was home things felt normal. Not safe but safer.

She changed schools, obviously. Went to one downtown for a few months. Until she saw some guy in a red shirt and had a panic attack and had to call her mom to come get her. It was so embarrassing, she never went back. She took online classes, even super-old correspondence classes that gave her pages of paper to read via old mail, did everything she could to avoid classrooms and still get her diploma. The pandemic was actually great in this way because she got to take graphics classes on Zoom and she never had to leave her room. Now she makes actual money and never has to leave her room.

She does though, every once in a while. Her mom makes her go upstairs and sit with them for dinner every night, makes her come up and visit when family comes over. And at least once a week, on one of Paul's many days off now, she drives them to Birds Hill or some other park and makes her take a walk. She's not a total recluse, and despite what people might think, she's actually pretty content, not happy all the way or anything but fine. Better.

When Jake leaves, M checks her twitters again and notices Stargate6969 had snuck in a DM before she blocked him.

"I like your profile pic. What you up to?"

As if that would do it for her. She laughs and deletes. The internet is a strange paradise. People are surprised when she says she feels safe online. No one thinks the internet is safe, but M knows better. Here, this is just a screen. The danger is out there.

She looks over at her desk and sees the wings. She coloured them brown but sees now she needs to give them more texture. He needs new wings. He needs a palette of browns and golds in angles and edges, like Anishinaabe beadwork designs. A large canvas of wings to spread out as wide as the sky, their edges grey to melt into the clouds. That's what she wants to do with this animikii character she based on her cousin, make him like an Anishinaabe superhero or something.

With each line she draws, she sees the story grow clear. All these characters are feeding the centre. There's always a protagonist and he is the main, her Animikii, the Thunderbird, the one like Jake, out there in the storm taking care of everyone—he is the one that matters. Well, they all matter, but he's the one. Arms stretched out playing on an old theme, taking up the whole sky, darkened with strength and might and beauty, he is the hero of this novel. She sighs into the unfolding. Relieved to have found her story. It's as simple as that sometimes.

Hours and lifetimes later, M rubs her pencil-stained fingers and Paul calls her for supper. She can smell the baked bannock and hear Pete come home with his grumbling about the heat and smell of the garage he works at. M thinks she can smell him all the way down here, too. He'll go upstairs to change, like he does every day. He always makes sure he's clean when they all sit down for dinner.

She gives her sketches one last look, a two-page spread of Animikii's new wings, gold and brown and patterned, a grey summer storm behind him. A storm of his making but under his complete control. He is a usually small figure transformed infinite. He is going to make everything right. He is going to keep everyone safe.

Satisfied, she gets up and goes up the stairs, feeling so good all of a sudden. So relieved, maybe? Almost at peace.

BEN

Phoenix's old counsellor Ben is at war with skunks. There must be dozens around his property. Big enough to cause problems. They're getting bold. They're getting closer to the house.

Tensions have accelerated. Drastically. Definitely a war. He said as much to his daughter, Jazz.

"What do you mean, Dad? You're at war with a bunch of skunks?"

"More like they're at war with me!"

"Are you all right?"

It started out harmless enough. He'd smell them around whenever he came up to his place here in the bush. It got worse when he finally retired and moved here full time. Once that happened, they seemed to be everywhere all of a sudden. Kept trying to antagonize his dead wife Fancy's little dog, Porscha. Lured her into the bush more than once to spray her good. Like three times. She stunk for weeks. Kept going back in though.

That last time they got her though, she was on the porch. He took to tying her up, but they still got her. Up on the porch, not three feet from the back door. Bold fuckers.

Now, Porscha's a mean little thing, never backed down from a fight, that one. Scrappy as hell and even worse in her old age. She's a Maltese and those fuckers are feisty by nature, but Porscha's a rez dog, too. Spent her first years in the bush surviving dogs ten times her size. She wasn't going to let some skunks tell her what to do at her own place.

Seems that last one schooled her somewhat though. Now she whimpers when he makes her go out. He has to go with her, watch her shit and piss or else she won't go. Has to, or else she'll do her business inside. Doesn't care much about things like that, does Porscha.

Ben knew he had to do something about it. Those skunks were getting too cocky. Can't have cocky skunks. For one thing, the place stinks.

So this one morning, he was out on the porch, enjoying the sun and his coffee. He still puts it in his old go-mug, like he did for years when he was working. Still likes it in there and then can take it around the yard if he feels like. But that morning he was sitting on his old lawn chair, watching his dead wife's little dog take one of her little shits, and he saw this skunk, bold as hell, strutting down the drive. Not a care in the world, the fucker. Strutting around like he owned the place.

Ben took a rock, one of them ornamental ones Fancy had put in the garden around the porch. Two hundred dollars he spent on Fancy's fancy rocks. It was about the size of his hand, round like a ball, and he threw it at the thing.

To his surprise he hit it on the head. The rock hit it with a thunk and the skunk went down right there. Knocked the fuck out.

He didn't mean to hit it, was never a good shot. More like he just wanted to scare it.

He walked up to it. And its tongue was out a bit and it was making this wheezy kind of sound.

Ben groaned and Porscha whimpered on the porch and went to the back door wanting to be let inside. He hated these fuckers but knew it wasn't right to leave it.

So he went into his garage and got his nail gun. He thought this was the best way, most humane, and wheeled it all the way over the gravel. Popped two in the top of the skunk's head and it was still.

He buried it in the bush next to where he buried Fancy's other dog, Mercedes. That one was a chihuahua. Even meaner than Porscha.

He made the grave shallow though. As a warning to the others.

But he cried that night, he felt so bad. Barely shed any tears for his dead wife but he whined like a little bitch for that fucking skunk. Well, not so much the skunk but because he had to kill it. He hated killing things. Hated that it had come to that.

He was a counsellor by trade. Spent his life talking and listening. Well, this last half of his life—first half was mostly about causing trouble, second half was talking to other people who had caused trouble. He went into it wanting to help, wanting to hold the Teachings he was given and share them. But really, he spent his days with horrible people who did horrible things. He knew the light inside of them was the same as anyone's. Everyone is pure in their truest form. But that never stops bastards like that from doing bastard things. He was no exception, really.

He dropped tobacco on the driveway where there was still blood.

He smudged himself and the whole yard.

He stared into the black night and thought of the people he'd hurt, the things he'd done wrong, the time he spent never quite making amends. For all the good it did. The amends part.

He sang songs to the stars with a voice that cracked mourning.

He sang and thought of everything. His childhood. His regrets. His wife. Her sickness. Her pain. His work.

His old body held so many stories. So much space taken up by people who did bad things. His own and others.

He still holds them.

For all the good it does.

He woke up the next morning knowing he'd do it all again, if he had to. The skunk, that is. He'd for sure kill another skunk, if he needed to.

"Dad, I think we're going to come up this weekend. We'll bring you a Jeanne's cake and have a good visit. You're too alone up there."

"What do you mean? I'm not alone. I go into town every other day. I have coffee at the store."

"Bugging the clerk for fifteen minutes is not socializing, Dad."

"Who says? I talk to other people too, you know."

"Other old-timers?"

"Who you calling an old-timer?"

"You're the one obsessing about skunks."

"Did I tell you they're spraying Fancy's rose bushes?"

"We'll be there before you go to bed on Friday."

Ben goes into town for more supplies but gets hungry so stops by the store first. He goes there for coffee around three most days, can usually count on someone to be around and want a chat.

These days it's this Cheryl. Nice lady. She's fresh in from the city and back living with her old man, a guy named Joe. Everyone knows Joe. Ben's known him for years. Ever since he and Fancy got this place and Joe did their roof. Did a good job and for cheap. Good guy is Joe. Cheryl is good people too. She used to run an art gallery, used to be an artist. But is up here in the bush now, trying to get away from it all, like they all are.

Today she's slumped over her double-double and looking like a cloud is hanging over her. Like something is falling down on her. Shoulders hunched like they can't hold everything they're holding. Ben smiles and sighs but orders his food before he sits down.

He knows a bit about Cheryl's life. She lost a sister young. Her mother not too long ago too. And her granddaughter, Emily, was violently assaulted a few years ago. Violent by the sounds of it. In the city. Horrible. He didn't ask for details. Cheryl worries about her, and the girl's mother, Paul. She worries a lot, Cheryl does.

She tries to smile. "Hey, Ben, how you doing?"

Ben takes a breath. "Good, good. How you doing?"

"Oh, you know."

And he does.

Ben's been like this his whole life. People talk to him. Women. Men. Everyone. His mom used to say he had that kind of face. The kind of face people like to talk to. Ben thinks it's because he likes people and they know he likes them. Sometimes he asks questions but never in a nosy way. Mostly he listens. Or tells stories and then listens. And likes them. No matter what they did. Do. He likes them, and that's why they trust him.

"Bad news from back home, Ben. The person who hurt my granddaughter is out of prison. My poor sweet granddaughter, she's never been the same. I hate that I'm up here. Can't do anything."

"You can do lots of things. Pray. Sing. You could even go home, if you wanted to."

"Naw, I always do that. Always go running to the rescue. Or trying to, anyway. My daughters are grown women. Their kids are mostly grown, even. I gotta start living my own life."

The server brings him his egg sandwich and he eats it in two bites.

"I don't even know what that is, hey?" she says. "How awful is that? I mean, up here, this is Joe's place. His dream. I'm just siting. Down there, I get in the way. How sad is that, a sixty-year-old woman doesn't have a place of her own."

"Thought you said you were on your own a long time."

"Yeh, but not really. I still, like, had my mom, or my girls. Never been totally on my own."

"Who is? Really?"

"I used to think I was going to travel."

"Then travel."

"Ever want to travel, Ben? Any place you ever wanted to see?"

"Naw, not really. Always liked my own territory. I only feel at home on this flat land, you know?"

"Yeh, maybe. I don't know."

They do the crossword together. Or try to. Cheryl's not concentrating very well. And Ben's thinking of the hardware store and the time. He finishes his coffee in a gulp.

"You'll know what to do, Cheryl. Don't you worry. Talk to Joe about it, maybe?"

"Naw, can't do that. Joe gets his back up whenever I bring up this Phoenix person. Maybe it's 'cause he feels helpless or 'cause he wasn't around when it happened. I don't know. Can't talk to him though."

"Phoenix?"

"Yeh. Emily's attacker."

Ben nods. Couldn't do anything else. Couldn't and wouldn't ever say anything. That he knew her. That of course he knew her.

He gets up and waves as he walks away. "See you tomorrow, Cheryl. If you don't take off home."

"Have a good night, Ben."

At the hardware store, Ben gets a roll of chicken wire, some new hinges and screws. He has enough leftover wood at home.

Of course he knows Phoenix. And of course his new friend would be one of the people she hurt. As vast as this territory is, it's really very small, and Ben spent years talking to kids and men in lockup. Kids at the youth centre, men at Stony, people who had done some horrible shit. Some messed-up shit. It's often come back to bite him in the ass in one way or another. Years of his life listening to their stories and giving them space. For all the good it's done. They still did some horrible shit. The people they hurt were still hurt. And most of time, they themselves were still hurt. Half a lifetime of trying to do good and Ben really hasn't done anything at all. He hasn't changed a single thing.

His old co-worker Henrietta calls him on his way home. He always looks when his phone rings, even when he's on the highway. He puts it on speaker at least. Henrietta is still a guard at the youth centre, tough work. She's real good at checking up on him, which he likes.

"Hey, Ben, how you doing!" Her voice trying to be brighter than it is.

"I'm okay. You?"

"Oh, you know, Ben. I'm tired. Baby was up all night. She's in a sleep regression."

"I don't know what that is but it sounds rough."

"Yeh, it is. It is." Her voice falls off, goes to what she really wanted to say. "You hear Phoenix got out?"

"Yeh, I did, as it happens. You okay?"

"Think so. Think so."

Ben waits.

"Some of them get to you, hey?"

"Yeh. Yeh, they do."

She goes on, talking about the baby, talking about people they know. She goes on so long he sits in his seat long after he's home and shut off the engine. Talking long about nothing. The subject doesn't matter but the talking does. It fills the miles between them and makes Ben feel close to this strange person he used to see all the time. He's grateful for the talk.

Ben's lived too long to believe in coincidences. He knows Creator don't roll like that. Creator knows all and does whatever the hell she wants. When she wants you to know, she will make sure you know. When you think you have your shit together, she will make sure and let you know you don't. She will dole out your lessons and laugh at you while doing it. Creator has a sick sense of humour like that.

He lets Porscha out and drops all his supplies in his garage. He makes a coffee before he starts. He fills his go-mug, does a smudge, and sings a quick drumless song.

Ben ran Circles for a while. Restorative justice, they called it. Another rip-off of an old way.

The concept was simple. You sit a bunch of people in a circle—everyone who hurt, everyone who got hurt, all affected—and let them share.

They talk about themselves, say about how they have changed, how their lives are after this thing that happened.

People who harmed others got to hear how they hurt, who they hurt, how bad it was.

Those who were victimized got to hear what the people who hurt them were like, where they came from, what made them do what they did, that they're really people.

Some people, it helped them heal, for sure.

Others went in angry and left a different kind of angry. Learned how the blame belonged on the system, the history, the colonizer, the big things that were harder to change than one bad person.

Some people did good with it, got all radicalized, energized, went out and tried to change the world. Some were empowered like that, but those ones were usually already empowered.

Others though, they hurt. Kept hurting.

A lot easier to put it all on one bad person. Once they're seen though, that's harder to do. The hurt doesn't go away, the hole people have is still there, but they don't know what to do with it anymore.

Those are the ones Ben remembers most. That stay with him.

He never knew what he was doing it all for. Other than to try. Ben has always believed in trying, has always tried. Everyone is always trying. Even when they seem hopeless, people are trying. Even when they're looking like they're doing all the wrong things, they're still trying at something.

Sometimes he thinks he wanted to work with what everyone called the worst sort of people because he related to them so much. He always felt like the worst sort of person. But he kept doing it because he wanted to find that one person he didn't relate to. That one person who'd prove to him they weren't really human after all. The one who was truly bad for no reason, all the way. But he never did.

He remembers once asking Phoenix what her when-I-get-out story was. Almost everyone inside had a when-I-get-out story.

She said it right away. No thinking. No question. "I wanna go see my son. If they'll let me. I want to see him."

Ben knew, like everyone knew, like she must've known, it wasn't all that likely Phoenix was going to be let anywhere near her son, but still. Everyone needs something to keep them going.

"What would you say, you think, if you saw your boy? What would you tell him?"

Here she thought. She was so thoughtful sometimes. "That none of this is his fault. That who I am, what I did, has nothing to do with him."

This was when she was doing good. Digging deep. Ben was proud of her when she did that.

"And I hope he's happy."

"I bet he is."

She was quiet, so he asked another. "And what else? Once you saw your kid, what would you do?"

"I don't even know. I'd like to see the world, you know. The mountains. I've always wanted to see the mountains. Or the ocean."

"The ocean's nice. Mountains, too. Why not both? They're kinda close together."

She laughed a bit. When she was well medicated, she was easy to make laugh.

"I'd like that." She said it like it was the first time she ever thought it could happen.

Probably was.

That was the good times. There were a lot of not-so-good times. Times when he got frustrated, angry, bothered. Phoenix, yeh, she got right under his skin, but he still found something. Maybe it was because she was a young neechie like he was once a young neechie, and goddamn if it ain't hard just being a young neechie in this world. Phoenix was hard and had been so hard done by. You get to hearing people's life stories and you stop wondering why they do the things they do, more like you start wondering how they did as good as they did. Are as good as they are. Phoenix was like that. It was amazing she had any good left at all.

He wasn't wrong. And all the people who hated her weren't wrong either.

He turns on the oldies station and Porscha settles into her spot under his work table. Alert, she looks out the open doorway, watching the bush as the shadows grow. Ever ready is Porscha.

When Fancy got sick, he kept working. When Fancy said she wanted to retire, he kept working. When Fancy got up a dozen times a night to puke and shit all over and cry because she was embarrassed, he cleaned it up and went to work in the morning.

The day Fancy died, he was working. Talking to some old-timer, John, in Stony. John would tell him the same story every time—he had a brother who died like forty years before. A brother who got shot by the cops because John was too high to plan a bank robbery properly. A brother who died because of him. Ben remembers that guy's face. His old face crying like a little kid. Ben patted him on the back. Told him it was okay. He was doing that, and his wife was choking on her own vomit. She was lying in bed by herself because he wasn't coming home for another hour and the care worker had to leave at four.

Some people never forgive themselves.

He makes the box into a frame with a plywood bottom. The sides he fits with chicken wire, and screws the hinges in place.

He has enough to make another, so he does. The second box a bit more sound than the first but both will do. He goes in to get some of Porscha's food and feeds her too. Leaves her safe in the house, looking out the window, ever watchful and checking what he's doing.

He leaves both traps on the edge of the bush, one to the north, one south. Both propped up so they will swing closed with the weight, both with the dog's food in a pile inside.

Fancy loved her dogs, especially this one. Only ever got her hypoallergenic food. He still buys it because the thing's used to it now and would puke up anything else. Fifty dollars a bag! But he does it anyway. The thing was basically wild for the first few years of its life but you couldn't tell Fancy that. Fancy had to get the thing the good stuff.

Fancy found the dog on a reserve she flew into to work for a week. The thing was stinky and matted but she thought it was cute. Brought it home to fight with the other dog and drive Ben crazy. To take it to the groomers and brush her every night like a doll. She did that to both her dogs and both dogs hated him, but Porscha hated him with a special kind of hating zeal. Thing used to poop on his side of the bed, used to bark whenever he'd come home like he was new. He couldn't so much as pick her up before Fancy was gone. And the feeling was mutual, really. Until he found the dog sitting on his dead wife's belly, whimpering but still guarding her. He could respect that.

After he sets up the traps and cleans up his garage he goes in. Porscha greets him like he's been gone a year, like she's been worried about him out there. Like she used to do with Fancy.

Ben begrudgingly pats the dog on the head and thinks of what he could make himself for dinner.

He doesn't know what he's going to do once he traps the fuckers. He could drown them in the dugout. Or take them in the back of his truck and go drop them off at the dump down the road. He could poison them somehow. Or starve them out.

He'll think on it, he thinks. As he makes a baloney sandwich, as he pours a glass of milk and then turns on the TV to catch the bedtime news. As Porscha settles in beside him on the chair.

He doesn't know what he's going to do but knows it'll come to him. He'll sleep on it and his dreams will lead him.

Creator speaks best through dreams, hey. All the time. Even some old man's war with skunks, Creator will know. And pay attention. She's good like that. Any little thing, she'll know.

ALEXANDRA

'Ship's ten-year-old daughter, Alexandra, shouts, "No, Tristan! Don't! You'll mess up my game."

"Dad said I can have the TV now."

Alexandra pushes her little brother in reply. But he's four and dramatic so he falls back. She didn't even push him that hard.

"Daaaaad!" Tristan yells and runs out of the room. He's not even hurt.

Alexandra works quick, knowing she'll have to end her game now. Stupid Tristan.

She finally got all her square pigs in their pen and has to finish her house before the sun goes down. She feels scared and excited. The Endermen give her a thrill when they come out. Black and long-legged like spiders, they scare her. She laughs when she plays but dreams of them at night.

"Alexandra!" Dad yells from the kitchen. "It's Tristan's turn. Get off!"

She knows better than to push it. Dad's been in a mood and just woke up.

Tristan waddles back into the living room all pleased with himself. She saves the game and makes a face at him. Throwing the controller and giving him a final push before she walks out. Doesn't want to watch his stupid Paw Patrol or those baby shows he likes.

She's going to go in her room when Uncle Kyle walks through the front door.

"Hey hey, m'lady. What's shaking?"

Alexandra smiles. Uncle Kyle is the coolest.

"Hey, little man," he nods at Tristan. But then turns back to

Alexandra—"Where's your dad at?"—because she is the oldest and Tristan is stupid.

"In the kitchen," she says, pointing with her chin. "Working." She makes air quotes because she knows he's on TikTok.

Uncle Kyle laughs. Uncle Kyle is easy to make laugh but she still likes to do it.

He takes off his kicks and walks over. She follows at a distance and watches him go get a tea like he does most mornings when he comes over. It's already noon but it's their morning. Her dad and uncle. It's when they sit and talk and work. Mostly they talk. During school, Alexandra hardly ever sees Uncle Kyle or gets to be around when they do this but it's summer so she's here and she's bored now.

"What'd he say?" Her dad doesn't look up from his phone. His name is Alex but everyone calls him 'Ship, as in Bishop.

"Says he hasn't seen her. She went out in the morning and now nothing."

This makes Dad stop and look at Uncle Kyle. "He didn't see where she went?"

Uncle Kyle shakes his head. "She was out by the time he got there."

Dad swears under his breath. "What you think?"

Uncle Kyle makes a shrug and turns to lean against the counter. Alexandra couldn't hide quick enough. "Hey, m'lady!"

"Alexandra, go play," her dad says. Not a yell, not mad.

She moves to the doorway, might be let in. "There's nothing to do!"

"Go outside." He's in a bad mood but not mad.

"I'm still in my pyjamas!" she tries.

"Then go get dressed and go outside." He gets up to get another coffee. She lingers, testing how serious he is.

"Now!"

That was a yell. She stomps to her room and slams the door so he knows how she feels too.

———

She knows what he's mad about. It happened the other day. Wednesday. Alexandra got up early. She's still used to getting up early. She hears her mom get up and shower, so she gets up too and has her cereal with Mom. Then watches her get ready for work and put her makeup on. They talk about all sorts of things they can't talk about around Tristan. During schooltime they do this too, but Tristan is there and they talk about different things. In summers and on weekends, he's like Dad and likes to sleep in so she has her mom to herself for a while.

After Mom leaves for work, Alexandra watches anything she wants. Her dad doesn't care what she watches as long as she doesn't tell her mom. He thinks she's mature enough to handle things, even horror movies. She is. But watches them in the mornings so hopefully she's forgotten about them by the time she goes to bed.

She was halfway through *The Conjuring* when someone knocked on the door. No one ever knocks. Everyone just walks in. But Alexandra wasn't scared or anything. She saw through the window it was only a girl so she opened the door.

"Hey! Alexandra? Oh man, you're all grown up."

Alexandra knew this meant she was supposed to know this person but she didn't. The girl wasn't old but definitely not a kid anymore. She looked pale, which seemed weird 'cause it was summer, and wore a black hoodie and old grey sweatpants. The sweatpants looked dirty and old. And not a name brand or anything. Alexandra knows all the good brands and for sure those were not good ones.

"You were a baby last time I saw you. I'm your cousin. Phoenix."

Alexandra tried to remember all the cousins she knew. Her mom has a sister and two brothers and they all have kids. She thought she knew them all.

"On your dad's side," the girl said like she was reading her mind.

Alexandra didn't know many people on her dad's side. She met her Uncle Toby but he's super old and in a nursing home, and knows her Papa Sasha of course but he lives far away now. Same with her Uncle Joe but she's never met him, only knew about him 'cause he sent her a birthday present this year. It made her dad cry. He tried not to let her see and she pretended she didn't but she did. The gift was a star blanket with different pink flower fabrics and whites and yellows. Mom said it was too beautiful to use and we should send a thank-you card. Or better yet, go visit, Mom had said. Alexandra loved the idea of going to visit. She memorized the return address, written big on the box, in Golden, BC. Mom said there were mountains there. She left the blanket in the box and put it on the sideboard in the living room, so her dad could see it. It seemed so important to him but it was still there all this time later.

"Gonna let me in?" The girl smiled but it wasn't a real smile.

Alexandra opened the door the rest of the way and the girl walked inside. She sat on the couch and looked at the TV and pointed with her chin, like Alexandra's dad did.

"Whatcha watching?" She was trying to be nice.

"*The Conjuring.*"

"Isn't that scary?"

Alexandra shrugged like it was no big deal. The girl smiled again and rubbed her hands together like she was nervous.

"I'll go get my dad," Alexandra said slow. She didn't want to. It was only ten and her dad never got up that early.

Her parents' room has thick curtains that make it super dark. Alexandra opened the door as quiet as she could and walked to his side of the bed. Tristan was lying butt in the air on the other side. Drooling, even, on Mom's good pillow.

"Dad," she whispered. Then "Dad!" a little louder.

"Wha? Wha?" He hates being woken up. "What's up? What's wrong?"

"Someone's here."

That woke him up. "Here? In the house?"

She nodded. Afraid.

"You let them in? What? Who are they?" He sat up. Pushed his palm into his eyes like he does when he's tired. Tristan woke up with a whine.

"It's okay, buddy." Dad pats his back. Stupid Tristan trying to be all upset.

Alexandra looked down and didn't look back up. "She says she's my cousin."

Dad got out of bed. The look on his face serious. He pulled on his sweats and a shirt and flew down the hallway.

Tristan sat up and looked at her. Neither of them knew what to do but knew enough not to go in the living room.

They didn't have to. Dad was talking loud enough and the door was open.

"What you doing here, Phoenix? How'd you—?"

Alexandra didn't hear her answer. The girl talked low.

"When'd you get out?"

More muffled voice. Tristan whispered, "I'm hungry."

"You can't be here. My kids are here."

Alexandra took her brother's hand and tiptoed to the kitchen. She did everything as quiet as she could. Listening hard.

"No, no one's seen Elsie. You get ahold of her?"

Then, "I know that. I know that, Phoenix. But no, man, no. I can't help you."

After that her dad got quiet. Or at least she couldn't hear. Tristan ate his cornflakes with big loud stupid crunching and then started talking about stupid things like everything was normal.

The front door opened and shut and Dad walked into the kitchen. She could see he was stressed.

"I'm sorry, Dad. I . . ." She didn't really know what she was going to say but didn't want him to be mad anymore.

"It's okay, baby," he told her and patted her on the hair like he did.

Alexandra gets dressed quick so she can open the door again but is super quiet and walks slow back to the kitchen. She hears her dad talking again.

"She wanted to see her kid. He's up on Polson. With his grandmas."

"Clayton's right?"

"Yeh. That's where she'll go, if anything. The stupid ass."

"Wonder what Clayton'd do. If he saw her."

"Probably nothing, that useless shit."

He stops, and calls down the hall, "You better get your arse outside, Alexandra. Go play. Be a kid."

Seeing her opportunity, she stands in the doorway again. "There's nothing to do outside."

"When I was a kid, all I was was outside. Climb a tree. Build a fort. Go. And take your brother with you."

She groans. But gets to go turn off the TV on Tristan and tell him, "Dad said you have to go outside."

"What? Why?"

"Dad said."

"But why?"

"Go. Get dressed." She likes bossing him around, and it's so easy when she adds the "dad said."

She waits for him in the hallway but can't hear anything more of what her dad and uncle are talking about.

Finally she leads her brother out with a soccer ball and kicks it around the front yard. Some kids ask them to go to the playground but she doesn't want to leave yet. Something might happen. Tristan starts complaining he's hungry again, always, and wants to go back inside.

"You gotta wait," she tells him.

"For what?"

"For dad to be done work."

"But I'm starving!"

Just for that she kicks the ball down the neighbour's yard so he has to run and get it.

Finally, Uncle Kyle leaves and nods to her with a final "m'lady," touching the lip of his hat. He said he saw it in movies and thought it looked tight.

Then Dad comes out to smoke on the step and watches them play. Alexandra kicks the ball hard and it flies past Tristan. Makes him go chase after it again.

But of course he whines. And Dad says, "Go easy on him, hey. He's little."

Alexandra wants to ask. She knows her dad's stressing and it all has something to do with this new cousin, Phoenix, but she doesn't know how to say it. And it's not like Dad looks like he wants to talk. So she watches him careful instead.

"I'm starving, Dad," Tristan whines.

"Starving, hey?" Dad smiles though.

"Yeh, I'm going to die, Dad. Like right now."

"Okay, then. Why don't we go get nuggets?"

This made stupid little Tristan very happy. "Really? For real? Yes!" He does a stupid little fist pump.

"Let me get my shoes." Dad goes back in the house and Alexandra puts the ball inside.

She sees Dad texting on the couch and tries to look over and read what he's writing.

"Oh you," he says. "Why you all so nosy all the time, hey?" But he isn't mad or that stressed anymore 'cause he pats her on the head as he goes to grab his keys.

"I can't help it, Dad," she says with a smirk. "You're so interesting."

And he laughs. Like really laughs, open-mouthed and loud. Dad is hard to make laugh so she really likes to do it.

ELSIE STRANGER

Elsie got her coffee and went outside to sit on the patio. Wasn't much of a patio really, just a line of chairs and tables along the sidewalk. Something simple they could take in every night to avoid those wandering for a place comfortable to rest. Elsie remembers that. Wandering streets looking for a place to sit or lie down. Most benches that sit out all night are made to be the exact opposite of restful.

The patio chair was flimsy. She settled at the last table, on the end along the fence. A lady came up right away and asked her for some change. Elsie shook her head. She had some, but only enough. Didn't know what her daughter would want. After so many years inside, Phoenix might want something nice and Elsie wants to be able to treat her. She's never forgotten her shame that one time she didn't have enough for her other daughter Cedar's coffee. Elsie hadn't planned on something more than the cheapest. Her face got so hot. She turned away so her daughter wouldn't see her hopelessly counting the not-enough change. Luckily the cashier took pity on her and waved off the coins she didn't have. Elsie doesn't think Cedar noticed. Hoped she didn't. Knew it would never happen again. She had almost ten dollars in her pocket. Phoenix might be hungry. Phoenix might be anything. Elsie didn't know all the things Phoenix could be. She hadn't seen her eldest daughter in over six years.

Not since Phoenix first went in after all that trouble she'd caused. Since Elsie barely got her shit together for a short visit in Remand. Phoenix round with her baby. With her baby Sparrow. Her girl was too young to have been in so long.

A warm breeze blows over her face and picks up a few strays of garbage. Elsie watches an old paper cup roll over the curb. Thinks about how nice it is in the shade. The huge boarded-up Bay building shadowing over everything. The sun on the other side of the street. She's almost chilled, even though it's a pretty hot day. She holds her double-double in both hands and sips it slow.

Phoenix is late already. Elsie should have known.

Portage Avenue stretches on beside her. Seems to grow the longer she sits here. She knows it all by heart. The mall across the street. Its entrances yawning open with people running here and there. Dotted with those who are sitting. Those with eyes up begging for change. Or down looking for butts. She remembers doing that too.

The park is a few blocks up. Even from here she can see the bodies there. Moving slow around the bus shack. Guarding what's going on along the planters and behind. In the back lane. She takes another sip and tries to stop herself. To breathe and stop her thoughts like Waaban taught her to do.

Waaban is her Teacher. And her friend, she thinks, but more her Teacher. Waaban has taught her so many things. Breathing and stopping her thoughts is something she does all the time though. When things get bad. When her addictions pull at her sides and panic sets in. When she feels everything tug at her. When she knows, really knows, there's only one thing she can do. One thing she needs to do. To feel better to be better to do better. She used to give in. She used to think she had to, even though she knew she shouldn't. She did. Now she breathes. She stops and breathes. Tries to remember a thought is just a thought and a mood is just a mood and they both pass. Like the cars on the street here. She lets them pass. Tries. Sometimes it works. More and more it works. Today is a hard one though. She knew she shouldn't meet here. Shouldn't go so close to where she used to get high. Obliterate. She agreed because her daughter said she wanted to see her. Phoenix said they should go for coffee and this was the place Elsie thought of when she said yes. Said yes and got a ride into the city from where she was staying in the country. Where she was camping and setting up for Ceremony and being at peace and almost free. With Waaban. But she left all that behind without even planning how she'd get back. All so she could see her daughter. Have a day filled with smoking cigarettes that were making her sick she was smoking so much. To sip another coffee she really didn't need. To stare down the street at her old hookup place and wait for her daughter who was now really late.

Elsie had stopped counting her days months ago. She used to count every day. Every drug every day. Celebrate when she made it a month off anything. Usually by getting high off something else. First she counted hours, then days, then weeks. After a year she counted months. After a year she was supposed to thank Creator and trust herself a bit more. Or something like that. Waaban had told her to. But she never really got how she was supposed to trust herself. Elsie Stranger who had fucked up everything she ever touched. But she trusted Waaban. She knew how to do that so that's what she did.

She met him at a Sweat. He was doing the Ceremony. She went with some girl she used to work with at the warehouse. He was calm and smart and had these eyes that were almost grey. It was weird. She thought it was weird anyway. Had never seen eyes that colour. He was funny and made her feel comfortable. He said he had a house in the city and she could come anytime.

She did. Probably about a week later. It was a big house on Elgin and he rented out the rooms to those who could help out in some way. Offered the many couches in the long living room to those who needed a place to crash. She moved in within a week. She'd never known quiet like that. Well, not quiet. There was always someone coming or going. But it made her quiet in her head. That was last spring. And when the weather got better, Waaban went to set up his Ceremony grounds so she quit her latest job and went with him. Not only him, about a dozen or so people. They camped all summer. She did her first Fast that fall. Saw things in the bush she couldn't ever explain. Passed her year-clean anniversary and didn't even notice.

It's different in the city though. Especially downtown. It's like she can't do it anymore. She sits here but wants to be someplace else. Even if her girl is going to be here, Elsie wishes she were someplace else. Phoenix is so late. Should've been here almost an hour ago now.

Elsie should have called Cedar. She was going to. When she got the message from Phoenix. When she logged in to her Facebook for the first time in months 'cause cell reception is so bad out there she usually doesn't bother. But she thought she'd send Cedar a hello so she logged in. She was surprised to hear from Phoenix. Surprised her daughter sounded like she might even want to see her. The message was short: Hi. I'm getting out Wednesday. Do you want to meet? I'm going to be downtown.

Elsie said yes before she really thought about it. Of course Phoenix would change her mind. Getting stood up outside a Tims is the very least of what Elsie deserves.

She's been feeling a lot of shame. That's what Waaban calls it—shame. Elsie calls it truth. She should be ashamed. She was a waste-of-space mother. She continues to be a waste-of-space mother. She used to struggle and count the days until her kids were grown so she could have a relationship with them. But now they're grown and she still sucks. Cedar is different than she was. So happy and sheltered. Elsie doesn't want to mess with that. Doesn't want to get real with this kid who is lucky not to have to worry about what her mom's life has been like. What her life would have been like if she'd stayed with Elsie. Waaban says she shouldn't hang on to the past like that. That each day is an opportunity to be a whole new person. Elsie trusts him and believes what he says. But she's also sure if he knew all the shit she's done he'd agree she should suffer more. She couldn't even be a good mother. And that's basic, bottom-line kind of stuff. Waaban says our parenting has been interrupted by colonialization and residential schools. But Elsie has no excuse. She was raised by her good, decent Mamère and Grandpa Mac. She should have known better.

The sun slips over the mall and everything seems to get even darker, colder. The breeze grows into more of a wind. Elsie swigs the last of her coffee that's now cold, watches the office people crowd around the bus stops. It's been almost two hours. She should leave. She shouldn't let herself be so close to where she could slip up. Especially now that she has to admit that Phoenix is not coming. She should have known she wouldn't come. She tries to breathe. She tries to stop her thoughts. She hates the city. She wishes she'd never left the Ceremony grounds.

A worker comes around spraying down the tables and eyeing her sideways. It's time to go. Elsie turns her now empty cup in her hands as if it's still full so she looks like she belongs. But it's time to go. She needs to stop waiting for something that is not going to happen. And stop her thoughts for thinking all the nasty shit they think. Why would she think Phoenix would want to see her anyway?

Elsie gets up and moves slowly on her stiff legs. Still stiff from years of not taking care of herself. She walks around the patio fence and up and away from where she feels the pull of the park. Its tall planters you can hide behind. The almost ten dollars in her pocket. She'll go back to Waaban's house where there will be more coffee or, if she feels like switching it up, tea. Someone will have a smoke. Someone will be watching something on TV. She should call Cedar, or her Uncle Toby, while she's in the city. But she knows she feels too fragile. Too needy. Waaban says it's okay to have needs. Everyone has needs. It's okay to ask for what you need. Elsie isn't too sure. She's been needy for the wrong things so long. Has been asking for the wrong things so long. Has no idea how to go about getting the right ones.

Instead she walks faster. She gets out from under the shadow of the too-big Bay building and goes down Isabel. Goes the long way around the park. Nowhere near it. Someone at the house must be going back out to the grounds today. Or know someone who is. If she hurries she can be back there with Waaban before the sun goes down. Back to the tent she shares with three other women. The warm quiet of the bush and the super dark, out of the city night.

She cuts over the grass of the north corner of the new square, past the happy-hour concert that's happening and a bar she used to go to. She doesn't even look up. The people around her clink beers but she can't even slow down.

At the end of all the tall buildings the shade seems to open. There's light over there. She jaywalks between rush-hour cars nearly parked on the street. Runs to where the sun is.

LARRY

Larry slouches on the pub patio. Well into his third double, he looks up from his blank laptop screen and sees Elsie Stranger stomp by. He'd recognize that walk anywhere, exactly like her great-uncles'. All the Strangers walked like that, a sort of stomp-bounce motion, like puppies who haven't grown into their legs yet. He told his old pal, Elsie's Uncle Toby, that one time, back when they were pals and he could tell him such things. Toby had laughed, and kept bounce-stomping along.

Toby's brothers had walked like that too, both with their own unique air of confidence and self-importance. Joseph had the swagger of men who knew they were good-looking and thus got away with everything, and John, with a sneer on his face and knuckles permanently scuffed. John was a big man, and by all accounts still is, though age has probably hunched him somewhat. But that's not why no one messed with him or with any of them. No, no one messed with the Strangers because they never gave a shit. That's the most dangerous thing, Larry thinks, has always thought, people act the worst when they don't care. The best weapon is to have nothing to lose.

"Elsie! Elsie Stranger!" But she's too far. The patio is full and the din of the concert in the square is too much. The after-work crowd already hopping. He slumps further in his uncomfortable plastic chair at his usual table, and watches her as she goes down the street. He hadn't seen her in years, would like to think she's looking well. Maybe wasn't as pale and hunched and stompy as last time anyway.

Larry empties his glass and checks the time: nearly five. His wife was going out with friends tonight, so not meeting him for her usual after-work drink. He has the night to himself. He motions to Kate that he'd like another, then leans back and listens to the police scanner through his one earbud. He likes the monotone of this operator's voice. It's strong and female and sounds like nothing would faze her. Larry finds that sort of toughness comforting.

He likes to listen to the calls coming in and out as he works, or, more often than not, doesn't work. "Car requested to Beverley Street." "Shots heard near Pritchard, could be backfire." Incidents made into quick sound bites followed by unemotional replies from the squad cars, droned numbers and a "responding." It's orderly. It makes it sound as if it's all in hand.

Larry puts the other earbud in to block out the noises around— "Alarm activated on Waterfront," "Car 13 responding"—and moves the cursor so his laptop screams the empty white page.

He's been writing this book for years. Ever since he left his job at the *Tribune*. It was more of a pushout into early retirement, as they were laying off almost everyone, but he accepted it. Better him than some poor schmuck with kids still at home, or at least that's what he told anyone who'd ask. More time for my book, he'd add. He's been writing it for decades.

It took him a long time to get the beat reporter shtick out of his system. He still fights the urge to grab his notebook whenever some poor bastard is telling him their life story, which happens a lot hanging out at a pub every afternoon. It's a gift, he laughs, but knows it's really a well-honed skill. A face of non-judgment, an open cigarette pack and lighter, and a buddy-buddy attitude he learned growing up in the North End, back when that meant basically the same thing as it does now but with different groups of people.

In his time the gangs were called the Jew Boys, the Rattlers, and several large families who'd make their own what they called a gang amongst brothers and cousins. There were some Natives, some breeds, that's what you used to call Métis, but mostly Polacks or Jews, some Krauts and squareheads, old names from when distinctions like that seemed to matter. As a kid, Larry held his own but appreciated good pals like the Strangers who had his back. Boy, his mom would whup his ass when he came home after getting beat up, which he always found as hypocritical as it was counterproductive, but his dad never said anything. Larry knew he had been the same. His dad was always telling stories of his rumbles back in Montreal when he first came to Canada as a young man. Larry knows it was the same for his grandpa too, though he never knew him. He was killed when his dad was still a boy, but his grandma used to tell stories of his grandpa being pretty scrappy, the kind of young man who'd always manage to find the fight. Still, he was slaughtered by the Nazis like millions of other people, young men or not, scrappy or not.

When Larry started working for the paper in the late seventies, that's the beat they gave him—the North End—mostly because no one else wanted it. Sure it was good for crime stories but hard to get a foot in with the locals, they'd said. Larry had that already built-in so could really shine, as long as he was decent to people. He started with his contemporaries, who were still out and about then, before they all became old men like him. At first all the excitement was bikers, some loosely knit groups of stick-up gangs, moonshiners and pimps, those were the kind of guys that Elsie's uncles rolled with. Toby worked for those sorts for a long time. John did all sorts too, and moved himself up to a position of authority, by all accounts still is pretty high up there, even as an old man in prison so long. Their sister Margaret, Elsie's mom, ended up marrying a Monias, Sasha, a leader in a halfbreed arm of the Nomads. Those guys were instrumental in bringing hard drugs into the city way back when. Then they were also pretty much the cause of the drug war that lost everyone access to most hard stuff to any of the prairies for a while. But being astute businessmen, as Métis have always proven to be since as far back as the fur trade, Sasha's people pivoted almost seamlessly to meth and opioids and tech merchandise. His son Alex, or Bishop as he's known on the street, Elsie's younger brother, heads up most of the merchandise in the city, or at least that part of the city.

It's an impressive family. He remembers more than once, sitting with Elsie, who always struck him as so young, even though only old men like him call forty-odd young anymore, and talking about her relations.

"Never really thought about it, you know. They went to work like everyone else. I used to think it was weird when people had dads who like, wore a suit to work, didn't get their hands dirty. I thought they must be super rich to be able to do that," she had laughed one night. Larry liked it when Elsie would laugh. She had a great laugh.

Ever the reporter: "How old do you think you were when, you know, you caught on they weren't exactly doing anything legal?"

"I guess I always knew, or as much as any of us knew, never thought anything about it. I mean, my uncle died right before I was born and I knew that story. And Sasha, my stepdad, he wasn't exactly hiding anything."

"It was normal to you," Larry said simply, lighting her smoke for her.

"Yeh, sure. I mean, these things are never like they are in the movies. It's regular life most of the time."

When Larry likes to really wax nostalgic though, he ends up talking about the nineties. By far the most exciting time for him as a reporter, the nineties were the golden age of gangs in the city. Overnight, everything coming in from the States was about street gangs. It seeped into the mainstream, and all the disaffected young Aboriginal men related, like all disaffected young men relate to other disaffected young men's attempts at shirking the system. Overnight there was a gang on every corner, and boy, they liked to talk. Larry spent his evenings wandering in his old beat-up K-car and getting all sorts of stories, and the same story. Young men like to boast, young men like to find something they are good at, young men like to find their place in the world, and then they like to brag, well mostly exaggerate, about it. Larry was there for it all with a pocketful of Bic blue ballpoints and old metal-coiled notebooks. A cliché, but they were all clichés, weren't they? He interviewed the Posse, the Warriors, the Brotherhood. He even got a coveted no-holds-barred interview with an anonymous member of the notorious M Boys in '94. That one got him a National Newspaper Award nomination. But the one he most remembers was the guy they called Dawg who was up in Stony on a murder charge in early '97. Dawg was a great talker. He was young and volatile but a great storyteller. He had founded one of the newer, more powerful street gangs with a group of buddies when they were still in junior high, or more accurately, should have been in junior high but were really wandering Central. Dawg reminded him of his old pals and stomping grounds, their fight-or-die attitude. Dawg didn't give a crap about being locked up, even for a long time. Prison was more a badge of honour and certainly didn't curb activity. He had even said—Larry will never forget the lines—"I come from a long line of prisoners, my whole family was prisoners, only they were locked up in residential schools for being Indian or on reserves they couldn't leave without a fucking paper, or in foster care. They were going to lock me up anyway, at least I fucked things up on my way in." Larry loved those lines, loved how thoughtful and smart that kid was. It made him think of his grandpa, what a scrappy young man he must've been like in a concentration camp. What hell that must have been. Hopefully he fucked up a couple Nazis on his way out.

Elsie's kids got taken away from her. Unfortunately, Larry knew a lot of folks who had their kids taken off them, it was way too common a story, and never not completely tragic. Rarely fair. He never out-and-out asked Elsie about it, but she talked about it often enough. I mean, who wouldn't.

"It was the worst for Phoenix—that's my oldest. I mean, I can't even." The kind of voice crack that breaks your heart. "But then, the system, it was worst for her. The little ones got to go to a home, at least. Got to be together. But her, they put her in a hotel, like basically put her on an assembly line to trouble, all because they said she was older. Older! She was fucking ten."

"That's a baby." Larry nodded. Could only agree.

"A baby. But they didn't see her like that. The system. Same as it always is, makes you into some*thing* instead of some*body*."

It was the kind of line he would have written down in the old days, but he didn't have to, he never forgot it.

"How's Phoenix doing?" This was back when Elsie's daughter had first gotten locked up, after she had had her kid. The grandkid Elsie never saw.

"I don't know. I think okay. How much trouble can you get into in jail?"

They both laughed, knowing a little bit about how much.

Elsie added, "I hope she's good though. She's had to be so hard, you know."

Larry nods, because he does. Hard is the only way to survive in some worlds.

"I hope she can, you know, forgive herself. For everything."

"Think she can?"

"I don't know. I'd never be able to teach her."

All Larry could do was nod, again, pass her a smoke, order her a drink. Some people don't deserve some things that happen in their life, Elsie's never deserved any of it. Phoenix neither, by the sounds of it.

He drains another and waves Kate over. He takes an earbud out to talk/yell over the crowd. The loudness around him suddenly invasive. "I can't decide between the butter chicken or the vindaloo. What you think?"

"Mama made the vindaloo fresh this morning. That's what I'm having anyway," Kate says casually, cleaning out his ashtray and taking his empty glass.

"Gotta love Mama." Larry grins, thinking of the owner's mother, who cooks once a week or so just because she wants to. "Sure thing, but extra naan, hey?"

"You know I take care of you. No wifey tonight?"

"Naw. She's out with the girlfriends. All on my lonesome."

"Working hard though. Even with all this noise."

"Hardly working."

Kate looks out at the rambunctious crowd in the square. "People really party hard, post-pandemic."

Larry scoffs as he lights another smoke. "We're all so happy to be alive."

Kate makes a hmph noise, or at least he thinks that's what it is, before turning her attention to two just-sat-down guys. Young guys, look like college age. Look like they have a few dollars and a very different life than him. Larry's never related to the type.

He puts the other earbud back in—"Anyone report on Beverley?" "She doesn't want to press charges, over"—and turns back to his white page and blinking cursor. This odd, slight, blinking line that seems to make words, swallow words, and mock him all at the same time. He's been writing this book all his life.

Truth is, he doesn't know where to begin. I mean, he still knows a bit of what's going on, still does the odd interview with new folks from old connections, still compulsively listens to the scanner like it's a radio station, but gangsters are so boring nowadays. The bravado is the same but they all seem like babies to him.

Everyone thinks it's the worst it's ever been what with the new drugs and the new exploitation, but it's really the same as it's always been, only with different drugs and different kinds of exploitation. He agrees it looks crazy and no, of course it is not good at all, but he's biased. For him, any generation when the government isn't actively and openly killing your people in mass numbers is a good, or at least better, generation. The Natives he knows relate to this too.

With his byline it would make sense for him to concentrate on the nineties, since he has so much copy on all those groups and what was going on then, but really, those guys only got mainstream. Their dads walked so they could run. The older gangs of Larry's generation really had the most fun, and kept almost all of it under the radar. But there were more, so many more. Every decade had its own style and flavour, every age and era its own things to push against. The fifties and sixties were all about pot, before that, the wars had so many rations, normal things like cream and sugar became counterfeit, and during the Prohibition it was booze, obviously. Even before that, this city had a huge underground market in horses.

   Larry has this theory that the city was built by gangs, for gangs, and that's why gangs thrive here. A gang is defined not just as a bunch of criminals but also as a group of people with a shared identity, shared goals, so if you use that as your definition, then that would include every single Indigenous nation at the point of European contact when, as Dawg had said, being Indians automatically put them on wrong side of the law just by existing. Their rights went unrecognized and most industry was closed to them so most of the things they did to make money or to stay alive were considered unlawful.

   Even the very inception of this city, the Red River Resistance, was technically a criminal activity. A group of organized, mostly Métis, mostly young men took over Fort Garry in 1869, and in doing so took control of the entire Red River Colony, much to the chagrin of, well, pretty much everyone else, including most notably Prime Minister John A. Macdonald. The resistance went on for months and had several leaders but the most famous was Louis Riel—an educated and charismatic twenty-five-year-old Métis man just returned from Quebec. They did all that just to communicate with the incoming government, something the government steadfastly refused. Canada wasn't much interested in talking to the people who actually lived here, particularly if they were brown, so the people that actually lived here stood up and demanded their rights, and by doing so became criminals. The law was unlawful. Easy to get on the wrong side of that.

   So then, according to Larry's hodgepodge theory, the groups today are, in many ways, a continuation of the past. Gangs are a result of past wrongs—colonialism and racism have reduced economic choices and therefore made gang living a viable alternative to the otherwise limited options, but maybe gangs are also a part of the resistance, too. Or can be. Could be? Winnipeg is a city built on the insurrection of marginalized Indigenous people, thus an obvious hotspot of continued protest in many forms. Take away all the exploitation and money-making and you could have yourself a nice bunch of warriors, as so many gang prevention programs and gang survivors have demonstrated.

It's a theory. Arguably not a very good one.

One thing Larry keeps getting hung up on is that he's not the right person to tell this story, or to make these connections. Nowadays a non-Native shouldn't tell a Native story, he knows that much. It's not tolerated anymore. Shouldn't ever have been. Natives want to tell their own stories, and should. He doesn't think he's even been telling any one story, really. He's only taken notes and printed quotes. Sometimes he thinks this story, this idea, is not his at all. That he's only putting some things together, but really, he should hand it all over to someone else. That he's just the schmuck putting things together wrong, making nonsense connections based on his limited knowledge, but really one of these Indigenous scholars or writers is someone who could actually finish the book. That he should give it all away as a gift. It'd be the least he could do, all the times John and Toby saved his sorry ass. Maybe that's what he should do. That's what's missing.

That would also get Larry conveniently off the hook to write the thing.

"All units respond. APB for a Miss Phoenix Anne Stranger. Recently released and didn't report. All units respond. Visual coming through."

Larry sits straight up and listens for responses, but there are none. He didn't know Elsie's girl got out. Well, just got out, as they said.

He Googles the name but nothing comes up. Makes sense. She was a kid when she went in so wouldn't have made the news. Then he Googles Elsie Stranger but nothing comes up either. Why would it?

He considers taking a walk toward where he saw Elsie, see if he could see her around the corner, but she's probably long gone. That, and he's pretty far gone himself. Too many doubles. Nothing to do but sit with the bad news, he thinks. Nothing he's not used to.

So Larry raises his glass to a good night for Miss Phoenix A. Stranger and hopes wherever she is she's doing well. Then he bangs it down, harder than he meant to. Kate looks over and Larry feels sheepish. He pulls the earbuds out of both ears and lets the outside pour in.

The sun slips behind the old bank building and another reggae band starts up in earnest. Larry scoops his vindaloo with his bread and eats it too quickly. He didn't realize he was so hungry. Or so drunk. The food and spice calm him, but when he pushes his plate away, he feels awash with loneliness. There are people all around him, any one of them to talk to if he leans over and starts up a conversation, but he's so lonely for a minute he wants to cry. He lights a smoke and hopes Elsie made it to wherever she's going okay. Hopes her girl is doing okay, too. He thinks of Toby and wishes he had a number to call. He hasn't talked to his friend in years and shooting the shit about old times would be so good right about now. Right about always. But that's what it's like with old guys, those that get to be old, Larry thinks. They never tire of talking about when they were scrappy young men.

PART TWO

IZZY

Izzy is annoyed.

"So what, now you're going to go? You're going to leave?" Ziggy yells.

"You don't even want me here!" Cedar tries to yell back, but the words fall with a pathetic whimper.

Ziggy's so mad. "Oh, so it's all my fault? And I have to live with the guilt of making you homeless, too?"

There's a door slam, then another. Then the sound of someone crying hard. That loud sob that happens when the crier doesn't even care that anyone can hear. Izzy doesn't even know which one it is.

She is so annoyed.

Phil smirks from the armchair. "They really should hook up already, you know? This 'will they/won't they' is getting tired."

"Don't be so insensitive. They're really hurting." Wynn looks up from the game on her phone. The annoying beeps not turned down. "I think they're both in shock."

Phil's hands go up. "Shock is usually quiet, isn't it? I think shock should be quieter. They've been like this for days."

Izzy bobs her head in agreement and plops down next to Wynn on the couch. Fighting gets on her nerves. Especially yelling. And crying. So much drama! Izzy's moms always had a lot of drama, emotions all the time, but that doesn't mean she can tolerate that shit. "Did either of you find out what this is all about?"

"Well," Wynn starts in the tone she uses when she's about to spill all the tea, and puts down her phone. "Remember when Ziggy was beat up, when she was a kid? Turns out Cedar's sister is one of the girls who did that."

"No! The one who's in jail?"

"Was in jail. She got out a couple days ago."

"Oh god, is she going to come here?"

Wynn shakes her head. "Naw. Apparently no one can find her. She up and left or something."

"Damn." Izzy thinks on it a beat. "Does Cedar know anything? Like, has she talked to this sister?"

"I don't think so. She seems worried."

"Hence all the crying," Phil adds. "Messed, eh?"

"So that's why Cedar thought she had to move out?"

They both look at her blankly.

"A few days ago. That day you texted me she was sad again. I went to talk to her and she was all like, 'You're a good roommate, I'm gonna miss you' type thing. All dramatic."

"Yeh," Wynn says. "I thought she wanted to leave, but Zig was all, 'You can't just leave!'"

"Zig's still pining for her so bad." Phil sighs but smiles. "Hoping for a 'will they.'"

"I'm glad you think this is funny," Wynn snaps at them. "It's fucking tragic."

"Oh please. I'm Indigenous. This isn't even the craziest shit to happen to us this year."

"So jaded." Wynn shakes her head, but with one of those lovey looks.

Izzy throws her hands in the air. "Ugh, I'm sick of the fighting!"

"Yeh. Phil and I are going over to my parents' this weekend." Wynn turns back to her game.

"Lucky bastards." Izzy looks at her friends, neither of them super bothered. Izzy is so bothered.

"If you wanna come . . . ," Wynn starts but doesn't even look up, and Izzy knows her heart isn't in the invite. Wynn tries so hard to be nice sometimes, but Izzy can see by how Phil is looking at her that they really don't want a third wheel. Phil and Wynn really love their weekends alone over there, when Wynn's parents are at their cottage. They probably fuck loudly all over the house and walk around naked or something. And right now, they really seem to be enjoying not being the worst couple of the moment.

Not that Ziggy and Cedar were ever a couple, but they all had taken bets that they would be at some point.

So annoyed.

Izzy's known Ziggy since first year. They bonded over being Indigenous and vegetarian. Not an easy combo if you're also trying to do Ceremony and traditional things. They also bitched about skirts and women's roles and Water Keeper binary bullshit but only to each other. You can't tell an Elder that. They got really close through all the Cora drama, Ziggy's first girlfriend, and oh that girl was in love! Ziggy grew up mostly on reserve so was pretty much in the closet when she came to university, or might as well have been.

After Cora, Ziggy disappeared home for a while and then came back for second year refreshed and ready for a tear. After that, she was forever with someone or another, trying to convince the world Cora meant nothing.

That's what Izzy thought this Cedar person would be when Ziggy started bringing her along everywhere. Nothing seemed to happen, but Ziggy definitely had a soft spot for the girl. Cedar was pretty quiet. Izzy can be quiet too, but Cedar was basically silent for the first while. She smiled and laughed but hardly ever had much to say. Reminded Izzy of a cat, comforting and purring but boring. Ziggy, though, looked at the girl like the sun shone out her ass.

It was Ziggy that got them worried about Cedar all the time too. As if Cedar was in need of constant protection or care. When they all moved into the house, Ziggy started texting them like a week later—"It's Cedar's birthday you should get her something," "Cedar's sad today so be nice to her," "She's been pretty sheltered. Pretty sure she's a super-sensitive empath" or some shit. Like the girl didn't know how to self-soothe. Izzy never found it that endearing. Yet another thing she had to do, really.

Izzy still couldn't tell anyone much about the girl. They were friendly, did some stuff together, but Cedar still seemed to be more Ziggy's friend than anyone else's. She's nice enough, if a little out of it, maybe. They had done yoga together for a while but Cedar didn't seem into it. Didn't seem into much except for whatever Ziggy was into. Even fighting, Cedar seemed to be agreeing with Ziggy.

Izzy shook her head at the ceiling. The loud sobs had grown quiet but were still faintly there. "I think I'd feel better if she'd scream back, but she seems to be taking it."

"She's a sad case, that Cedar." Wynn doesn't look up.

"I think Ziggy's right." Phil doesn't look up either. "She's so wrecked. She should get help, go see someone. You should give her some of your Lexapro, babe."

"I'm not going to give her drugs! It doesn't work that way."

"Well it might help."

"Do you understand how these things work at all? She can't just take one. It won't do anything."

"Really? When you take them you seem better right away."

"'Cause I've been on them for years!"

"I'm just saying . . ."

Izzy rolls her eyes and knows what's coming. More fucking fighting. She gets up and slowly walks up the stairs. The second-worst couple of the day's annoying loud voices only go away when she calmly, quietly, like an adult, closes her bedroom door.

She thinks of calling up her boyfriend but is real sick of talking. Forever sick of talking. Izzy was raised by two third-wave lesbians who say they aren't Karens but are actually super Karen about all the shit they care about. And feelings and talking are the things they care most about. Mo and Darlene talk about feelings like normal people talk about gas prices or the weather, and all the fucking time. Izzy's been done with talking ever since she started talking. She puts on her favourite meditation podcast, lies down, and tunes out.

Izzy's been dating Bryce for about six months. Since right before Christmas break when she was so bored and it was so cold she didn't want to even walk home to her moms' house, so she stayed in all the time. Before Bryce there was this guy Dylan in her theatre class but he ended up being stereotypically showy and attention-seeking and hooked up with every cis female in the program. Over the summer it was a med student in Toronto. He was cool, but in the end Izzy thinks she was more interested in the ins and outs of medical school than she was in the actual guy. She likes dating and never thought that much about it. She might even prefer when they live far so she only ever has to see them when she wants to. And then briefly, to watch a show together or talk about school. The sex is clean too. In-person sex can smell so bad, be so bad. You never have to worry about breath or BO or not orgasming on FaceTime.

The next morning she hears one couple, Wynn and Phil, leave, and as the last of their loved-up bickering fades off the front porch, couple not even a couple, Cedar and Ziggy, wake up and start their stupid fight all over again.

"Will you talk to me? Please?" Cedar, downright pleading.

"I don't even know what there is to say." Ziggy, doing a horrible job at avoiding.

Izzy puts her earbuds back in, turns up some ambient sleep music. She even pulls the covers over her head.

When she emerges it's quiet, so she risks going down to make coffee. But on the stairs she regrets it. Cedar is on the couch staring out the window. No phone, no nothing, staring like she does. Looks like she's been crying. Izzy isn't heartless. She does feel for the girl.

"Heeeey." Izzy stands awkwardly in the doorway. "You okay? Can I get you anything?"

Cedar looks down at her hands, pulls her sleeve over both of them and seems to curl into herself even more.

Izzy tries again. "I'm really sorry, to hear, about everything. Is there anything I can do?"

"No, not really." She barely looks up.

Izzy thinks it's one of those moments normal people would go over and hug the other person, but Izzy hates hugs so tries not to give them out to other people as they might hate them too. Cedar probably would take it though, she looks so helpless and pathetic. Izzy can see why Ziggy is always taking care of her. Even Izzy wants to take care of her right now.

Izzy looks around. "Where's Ziggy?"

"Work." She looks out the window again. Reminds Izzy of a dog waiting for its human to come home.

"Oh." Izzy stands there another minute more, not knowing what else to do. "I'm going to go, make coffee, in there." She points to the kitchen for no reason.

She thinks she sees the girl nod before she turns away.

The house is too quiet now. Restless, Izzy goes out for a walk. She puts her earbuds in, and heads through the Village and up Wellington. She's not surprised when she takes a left after the bridge and around the hospital, not surprised at all when she winds up close to home. Her real home, where her moms are. She has a way of doing that. Or maybe it's the house that has a way of doing that to her. One day she wants to live in a different city and not one so close to her moms and their house, but she's not quite ready yet.

"Hey, baby!" 'Nimush, her dog, greets her at the door. Izzy is pretty sure 'Nimush's long, gold muzzle is her favourite thing in the world. It's getting white now. Too white. Dog life is too short. "Hey!" She pulls her earbuds out and calls over the food processor chug, knowing it'll be Mo in the kitchen. Darlene never cooks anything more involved than a frozen pizza.

'Nimush leads her down the hall and resumes her constant hunt for crumbs across the linoleum.

"Heya, love, what you doing?" Mo's back rounded over the cutting board, wearing her usual baggy black jeans with the long wallet chain across her hip.

Izzy's home smells the same—lingering patchouli incense, lemon dish soap, and whatever Mo happened to be cooking up. Today the kitchen is full of cilantro and roasting chickpeas. "Falafel?"

"Damn straight." Mo turns to look at her daughter's face. "What's up?"

"Nothing," Izzy shrugs.

"Lies," Mo says but goes back to chopping too many onions.

Izzy props herself on the kitchen stool, her favourite place as a kid. She used to love to watch Mo cook. 'Nimush leans against it and folds down to the floor where Izzy's feet can still run over her soft belly fur. "Where's Mom?"

"Farmer's market." The processor chugs away again. "There's tea," Mo resumes when it's quiet again.

"What kind?"

"Who knows? She calls it goddess tea? I think there's hyssop in it."

Izzy wrinkles her nose. She's tempted and thirsty but doesn't want to get up. "Ugh, I can't be in that house anymore."

"Lady drama?" Done cutting, Mo puts the knife in the sink and turns the water on.

"So much!" Izzy rolls her eyes and looks down at her already snoring dog. 'Nimush is probably close to thirteen now. They got her when Izzy was ten. Half her life.

"It's as if you've been training for girl roommates your whole life!" Her mom smirks at her as she passes her a fresh cup of tea.

"Har har." Izzy takes it, gratefully, and eventually sighs.

Mo and Darlene are pretty comfy now but they weren't always. To hear Mo tell it, they pretty much invented lady drama in their first few years together. When Mo started coming around, Darlene was a young mom, figuring life out, and wasn't even really out yet. Mo hated that and they kept breaking up. By the time they got settled and bought this house, Mo's mom, a born-again Christian, started causing trouble, trying to save Mo's soul or something. Nowadays, Mo and Darlene are pretty boring, talking about retirement and paying off the mortgage. And of course, doing anything and everything Izzy might ever need. Some kids hate being an only child but Izzy has loved it.

Mo scoops the pasty brown stuff out of the food processor and starts rolling it into balls. "So what's going on in the lady house today?" She doesn't have to press. Izzy always ends up talking. Izzy hates it but does it anyway.

Izzy sighs. "Cedar and Ziggy are at it. I mean, ugh, Cedar's so . . . I can't stand it. It's like she has no fight or anything."

"Not everyone's a fighter," Mo says simply.

"It's actually a really crazy situation. Remember what I told you happened to Ziggy when she was a kid? When she got beat up or assaulted or whatever? Well, apparently that was Cedar's sister. That did all that, her and her friend. Or something. I don't even know all the details. And now her sister like, took off or something." Izzy takes a long breath, her Coles Notes version feeling inadequate and too much at the same time.

"That's intense, love. I can see why Cedar's really sad." Mo is really bad at making Izzy feel better.

"She's kind of pitiful," Izzy tries.

Mo keeps working but her voice changes. "Drama does things to people."

"I, I don't get it." Izzy slaps her hand to her thigh, a quirk she knows she gets from Mo. What Darlene calls the exasperated thigh slap.

"Don't get what?" Mo's listening but also concentrating on rolling. Her two-sizes-too-big T-shirt is white and spotless even though she's obviously been cooking awhile.

"I wish . . . I don't know. Maybe she should move out or something. She's so . . ." Izzy doesn't even know.

"You sound mad at her."

"I'm not mad!"

"Didn't say you were mad. Just that you sound mad."

Izzy thinks again. Tries again. "I think she should have more guts is all."

"Says the girl who grew up very different from her."

"She's from the suburbs."

"But she also isn't, too. She was in care for how many years?"

"That was before."

"Still was." Mo gives her one of her knowing looks. A hard look. "Where's your empathy, Iz?"

Izzy looks away and scoffs. "You're so annoying with your constant contrarian-ness."

Mo shrugs. "It's a gift." She puts the tray of balls into the oven and pours her own cup of tea. "Let's go outside. It's a beautiful day. Come on, old girl." She pats her leg for the dog, or maybe for Izzy, who knows with sarcastic Mo.

Mo has told Izzy the same story in the same way—that she knew she was gay, was born knowing. Mo always knew who she was, full stop. She was mixed but raised by her Mennonite mother who told her she looked white so should be white, but Mo knew it wasn't true. She knew the way the world looked at her and her dark-enough skin, eyes, and hair. No one believed her blond mother was her actual mother. They thought she was adopted. But Mo knew she was like her mother too, headstrong and opinionated, but in the completely opposite viewpoints. She came out the old-school way when she was seventeen and promptly got kicked out of the house. Mo accepted it and didn't talk to her family for years. They reconciled when she settled down and started raising Izzy. That grandma used to babysit Izzy on Saturday afternoons, for a little while anyway. She seemed nice enough, but as soon as her moms were out of earshot, she'd start to tell Izzy about hell and sin and all that shit. Izzy hated the preaching, bible talk was so dull, but they'd make cookies together so that was fun. When that grandma would introduce her to people, it was always as her "adopted granddaughter," an extra word that seemed to physically push Izzy away. Often followed by an overpronounced "In-di-an. Na-tive," when someone asked what Izzy was. Izzy wasn't sad when they stopped seeing her. Even at ten she understood it.

Mo stretches out on one of the twin Adirondack chairs and Izzy sinks into the other, pulling her legs up to her chest. Mo slides on a pair of shades and 'Nimush slumps at her feet for a new nap.

"Did I ever tell you I heard about that? Ziggy's assault. When it happened."

"No." Izzy turns to her and stares. "Think I would remember that."

"Yeh. I'm lying. I didn't tell you. It was too disturbing and you were too young to hear about something like that."

"How did you, like, know about it?" Izzy squints at the sun and can see the wrinkles around Mo's eyes from the side. Mo's might be her favourite face.

"Oh, around." She pulls a bit at the back of her hair like she does when she's uncomfortable. Izzy does this too. "Lisa, I think. You remember Lisa. I worked with her for a bit, at the women's centre, hey? I think she was the one who told me. This troubled girl who did that to another girl. You don't forget something like that. It was devastating to me."

"Why?" Izzy holds her hand up to block the glare and keep looking. Mo's nose red with emotion.

Her mom takes a breath. "Oh, probably 'cause she was close to your age. Felt too close to home, you know? We worked really hard to keep you from stuff like that. Worked our asses off so you didn't have to experience any of that kind of bullshit. Kinda funny though, 'cause it still affects you. You're still in it. It's just life." Mo turns to face her, casually wiping a tear from behind her shades. "But, love, listen. You got to grow up with a lot of support and not an easy life but a pretty protected one. Not everybody had that, Iz."

Izzy looks down with a shudder. Mo is really not good at making her feel better.

"You should give this kid a break, you know. Doesn't sound like she's had what you've always had."

"I know. I know." Izzy hugs her knees closer, and Mo knows to stop.

―――

Izzy doesn't remember a time when Mo wasn't her mom. She knows that Mo wasn't around in the beginning, from pictures and stories. Izzy has a dad, knows how it works and everything, but he's never lived anywhere close, felt more like another uncle that anything else. Someone they'd go visit. Mo was her mom right away. She was the one who looked after her while Darlene went to school and then work. She was the one who homeschooled Izzy after they pulled her out of kindergarten because her teacher insisted Izzy get tested for hyperactivity. "She didn't need medication, she needed to get out of that goddamned institution!" Mo would rant to everyone and anyone. She quit a good job to work crappy contracts so she could stay home, and she never complained because she really loved it. She'd download lesson plans on her old Windows 97 computer and they'd go to the dollar store to get supplies for art projects. Mo organized meetups and field trips with other homeschoolers, and put Izzy in any and every activity she wanted—dance, drama, soccer, guitar—and Izzy always wanted another activity, even though she'd often quit after a few weeks. Mo never said no to Izzy, not for anything like that anyway. Izzy only went to high school because she knew she'd be smarter than everyone else and it would be easy, and it was. She missed Mo though. Never told her that, but she did. In grade eleven Izzy organized her schedule with extra spares in the middle so she could go home for lunch every day. She thinks Mo probably knew but never said anything, for once.

 Darlene's old Yaris pulls into the parking spot as Izzy finishes her tea.

 "Hey, family!" her other mom calls, greeting the dog, who wobbles over first, then pulling a couple cloth bags out of the back seat. She kisses the top of Izzy's head with a loud smack as she passes, and then, when she gets inside, yells a frantic, "Mo! I think these are burning!"

 "Oh fuck." Mo bounces up, her wallet chain dangling behind as she runs in.

After supper, Izzy insists on walking back home. It's almost dark and Darlene wants to drive her but the weather is still nice and it's not far.

"Okay then, you text me as soon as you get in that door." Darlene waves a finger at her. "I mean it. I will drive over there and check. I will."

"I know, I know." Izzy pushes her feet into her Crocs and gives 'Nimush one last cuddle.

Mo hands her an old cloth bag with leftovers in tinfoil, a bottle of her favourite rosé, and a small tin of her moms' new favourite indica. Her mom smiles conspiratorially. "Go make friends."

Izzy takes it all and the beautiful summer air breezes in as she opens the door.

She does text Darlene as soon as she sees her porch. "ND," their code for "not dead," an old joke between an overprotective parent and her protected child.

Darlene, obviously waiting for it, replies with "xoxox."

Izzy can see Cedar through the window, again on the couch. Or still.

"Hey." She makes her voice light as she walks in, determined to be cheery. Or at least not annoyed.

"Hey." At least the girl is doing something this time, looking down at a show on her phone. But something.

Izzy plops down beside her. "Whatcha watching?"

"Nothing." The girl looks outside. Her face reflecting on the glass.

"Where's Ziggy?" Izzy asks, but she regrets it right away as Cedar shrugs an answer.

"Hungry?" She pulls up the old bag. "Or maybe thirsty?"

Cedar gives what could generously be called a half smile. Only half, but there.

The girl picks at the falafel wrap, loaded with greens and tzatziki, as Izzy sips from the bottle and loads her pipe.

"Sooooo, what *are* you watching?" Izzy says, then inhales.

Cedar swallows. "Native TikTok."

"Perfect." Izzy leans over and passes the girl the wine. "Show me."

PAULINA TRAVERSE

Paul often thinks a mother's work is never done. She mulls this incomplete or maybe complete thought as she goes about her life, considering, these days, who she is and what she does. She is always a mother. Always a mother to Emily, M. Sometimes that is her only identity. The only one she thinks on, feels, worries about. Her worry is like a current through the back of her mind, all the time, ebbing a bit and flowing a lot. She wonders if it, that worry, anxiety, dread sometimes, will ever go away. She thought it would now that Emily, M, is an adult, something her daughter never misses an opportunity to remind her of. Twenty, even. No longer a teenager. A young adult, but no less an adult, but to Paul, unfairly, her daughter is forever that baby she held and didn't know what to do with, that child who needed to hold her hand all the way into the classroom, that too-young teenager whose childhood was so abruptly taken from her. She tries to see Emily, M, as grown and capable, which she of course is, so smart and wise and independent. So much more than Paul was at her age, so much better. But whether it's fear or the seemingly constant reminders of her failures to protect her girl, Paul defaults to worry, to nag, to annoying. And her twenty-year-old is, in turn, forever annoyed.

"Mom, you don't need to wake me up. I have an alarm!"

"I was just checking, sweetheart. I know you had your appointment today."

"I can manage my own stuff, you know. You really need to get a life."

"I have a life." Paul fights her defensiveness. "How was I to know you were already up?"

"Um, why do you care? Or notice? It's *my* appointment." Her daughter practically spits at her while shuffling around her bedroom, not looking up from gathering her clothes and things, likely for a shower.

Paul stands in the doorway, arms crossed in front of her, and keeps trying to talk gently. "You missed therapy last week and I had to pay for a session you didn't even have."

Emily, M, stops and turns. "That wasn't my fault! My phone died!"

"Something that would have been fixed if I had woken you up!" Paul's voice goes too loud. Too mad. She doesn't want to raise her voice. She wants to be calm, serene, even, but never is, and her daughter knows it.

Paul stomps up the stairs. Realizing at the top she forgot to put the wash in the dryer, her original excuse for going down to the basement to check on her kid. She's sorry for yelling. She hates to yell. It's one of her many failures.

Back in the kitchen, she can hear M below, doing her own stomping, and then the cupboards in her bathroom shut hard. She's not careful with them, likes to slam when she's angry, and Pete has had to fix them more than once.

M screams "Oh my god!" at what, Paul doesn't know. She wants to but doesn't go check. She turns on the kettle to make some tea instead. Then sits at the table with nothing much to do.

M's been in a mood for days. Paul knows why. Paul also knows there's nothing she can do about it. She's powerless. Can only remind her daughter to make her therapy appointment so hopefully the girl can be okay. At least for today. For now. But Paul knows M's never really been all the way okay. She knows this by the many ways and things her daughter has shown her over the years, but mostly she knows this because she, too, has never been, and likely never will be, okay either.

Her sister's text bings. "Hey are you busy? Later? It's your day off, right?" Paul is so grateful for it, hopeful for a visit. She hasn't seen Lou in over a week, pretty long for them. They still talk every day, or text at least, but it's not the same. Post-Covid has really made Paul appreciate real live visits.

"Yep. Wanna come for dinner?"

"I can't. I got this thing. Can you watch Gabey for a few hours?" Then right after, "I can bring him after program. Pay for takeout."

Paul puts the phone down on the table a little too aggressively. Jealous of Lou's something-to-do.

She doesn't answer. Lets Lou stew a bit. Knowing the something her sister has to do is really some*one*, some guy she's been seeing for a while now. This weird secretive relationship Lou has going on with someone none of them have even met. It's not like Paul would judge her or anything. Lou's baby daddy, Gabe, has been in and out and up and down for years. Spends most of his time up north taking care of his aging aunty and uncle, or at least claiming to. He comes back all the time, but never stays. No one would blame Lou for taking up with someone else. Paul hates that her sister won't even share this with her. All the information she has gathered has been so minimal.

"So what's his name?" Paul had asked a few weeks ago.

"Whose name?" Her sister is awful at trying to look all surprised.

Paul gave her this knowing look, an inviting look. "The guy. There's obviously a guy."

Lou shook her head. Kept eating.

Paul kept at it. "There's obviously a guy. Or a someone. I don't know why you won't tell me."

Lou took a super-long time to chew before answering a frustrating: "There's nothing to tell."

"Uh-huh." Paul smiled, confident in her knowing.

She would never admit she's hurt by it. By the one secret her sister has ever kept from her. That she knows of anyway.

Her mom, Cheryl, told Paul to let Lou be, in an equally frustrating way.

"She must have her reasons. I'm sure she'll tell you when she's ready." Like Cheryl has ever let anyone be.

Paul scoffed into her phone. "Like he's probably a serial killer, or married or something."

"Naw, Lou's not like that. He's probably just white."

"Like we would say anything if he's white."

"Maybe he's a Conservative!" Cheryl's version of being funny.

"She'd never do that! Give her some credit."

Her mom sighed, same way Paul sighs at M. "Oh Paulina, let her be. Give her time."

"I don't know why she would keep it a secret."

"Why do you care so much?"

"I don't know, maybe she's in trouble?"

Paul could feel her mother roll her eyes. "The last thing Lou would be is in trouble. Maybe it's a woman?" Her voice even and playful.

"Why wouldn't she tell us that? I think she would tell us that. Don't you think she would tell us that?!" Paul didn't want to be as annoyed as she was.

Paul did think it was a woman for a while. Looking for all the clues. She knew it had to be someone from work, or someone she met at work, because Lou usually went out straight from her office, if she could get someone to pick up her kid. Paul doesn't think it's anyone from a dating app or something because Lou has often complained about those things. She does frequent a bar downtown, an old pub she goes to after work. Paul's even gone so far as to ask to go there with her, thinking she'd catch her out, but Lou didn't fall for it.

"Why do you want to go there? You don't even drink." It was a text but Paul could tell the tone.

"I do, too. I have a glass a wine once in a while."

"When was the last time you had a glass of wine?"

"Like, I don't know. Christmas?"

Lou waited ages to text back. Obviously too busy, as usual. "You haven't been to a bar in years. You'd only complain it's loud and want to go."

"I can be fun, you know."

"No, I don't." Laughing emoji. Like the thought of Paul getting out of her sweats and going to a bar was so funny.

It was. But Lou didn't have to laugh about it.

Paul also knows they go to hotels. She knows this because she saw a receipt in Lou's kitchen one time when she was dropping off Gabey. The

Lombard. A nice place. Downtown and close to Lou's work. Not a cheap hotel at least. She also knows the guy or person must be pretty healthy because Lou has been trying to eat right again. A good influence at least. And they must be fit because Lou also joined a gym.

"That's so weird. That's not like her at all!"

"That's a good thing," her partner, Pete, had said. "We're supposed to work out. *We* should work out."

She laughed gently. "When have you ever worked out?"

"I never said I did, only that we should. Maybe she can get us some guest passes or something." But he kept watching his show.

"When do we have time to go to the gym?"

Pete shrugged, but Paul knew she did have time, just didn't want to. She also knew Pete was only being kind. He didn't care all that much, about the gym or about who Lou could be dating. And why would he? Paul has wondered why she does so much. It's something about the secret. About it being a secret. It's also about worry. Always worry. A sister's work is never done either.

"Mom, have you seen my purple sweater?" M calls up before stomping up the stairs.

Paul waits until her daughter is actually in the room before answering. "No, why would I? It wouldn't have gotten up here."

M doesn't stop, just goes to the fridge to get some juice. "Argh! Why isn't anything . . . Did you do my laundry again?"

"Nope. Didn't touch it." Paul still sits in the chair at the table, slouching back, hand warm around her mug of tea.

M drinks right out of the carton. "I hate when you do that. You fold it wrong."

"I didn't touch anything." Paul's voice is quieter than she thought it'd be. She feels a million miles away.

"Did you go in my room?"

"Wouldn't do that either."

"Argh, this house! I can't wait to get my own place!"

This is M's new dream, or threat. It scares Paul, to think of her out there on her own. She also gets so worried about all the time M spends alone. In her room. By herself. M has so few friends and reasons to go outside as it is. Paul thinks if she lived on her own she'd never bother. With any of it. She'd grow pale from lack of sun.

"It's not the worst thing in the world," Pete has said to her more than once. "I mean, that's what kids are supposed to do, right? Grow up, leave home."

"Yeh, but if she got an apartment she'd never leave the place. And she's never cooked in her life. She'd have to live off toast and takeout."

"When I first lived on my own it was all Kraft Dinner and instant noodles. I never ate anything else."

"I should have taught her how to cook."

"Still time."

"She's not interested. She's not interested in any of that. She wants to work on her book and fight on the internet."

"It's not the worst thing."

Paul senses Pete's excitement at the prospect of M getting out of the house. She thinks that's what he's been waiting for all along. He's been around all through everything, and knows better than anyone, but has also been left out. She's literally left him to care for her daughter so many times. From not talking to him or paying attention at all to actually sleeping in M's bed for the many years her daughter couldn't sleep alone. He's been on the sidelines, neglected and waiting. She's appreciated the space, the patience, and she's stopped worrying he's going to up and leave one day, mostly, but feels bad at how little she gives him. Their only intimacy is in the shows they religiously watch together, their own special time lying on the couch too tired to go upstairs. He never complains, or rarely complains. He looks on with a pleading sort of look sometimes. Another thing she's not doing right.

"???" Lou texts.

It's almost four but Paul had completely forgotten about her sister's ask.

"Sure fine," she types fast, and puts her phone down. Then takes it back up with another thought. "But we want Thai food."

It's not a burden to have Gabey. She loves having him. Pete too likes to hang out with his one young nephew on her side. They'll play games and Paul will sit at the kitchen table some more. Probably clean something or find a book to read. M will do something in her room and only come up to eat and just because Paul makes her. Told her she can't eat in the basement because of bugs or something like that to scare her enough to actually do it.

Paul would go out. Not that Lou has asked her in forever, but she'd love to go out actually. Remembers nights out when she and Lou would dance 'til close and she'd sip beer until her head got spinny. Been a long time since she did that. It'd be nice. She probably wouldn't last 'til close but it'd be nice to dance again.

M comes up with her face blotchy and eyes red. Paul's glad she agreed to weekly sessions again, with all that's going on. M keeps it all in and pretends like it doesn't bother her, but Paul can see how rattled she is. Since she was thirteen, M has looked over her shoulder, been afraid to go anywhere unknown, never wants to leave the house alone, so scared of being unprepared, being unsafe. And now the person who did that to her is out free, could be anywhere. Could be down the block, could be next door. Paul feels it. Paul feels that new layer of insecurity. Like the safe, locked door between them has opened and who knows what could happen. If Paul can feel it, it must be a hundred times stronger for M. Her dear girl who never hurt a fly. Her dear one who never deserved any of this and has had to make sense of the nonsensical.

Paul's still wrapping her brain around this new part, this next part of the nightmare. That familiar feeling of utter helplessness and failure when her nephew Jake told her that person was out. The look on his poor face. He was so devastated, so scared himself, trying to be all brave and what he thought a man should be like. Little Jake. Paul looks at him and still sees a little boy. A gentle kid who had a broken arm for months, such a bad break. His whole life has been bad breaks.

"It's okay, Jake. Everything will be okay," she told him. She said the words and tried to believe them.

"I know, I know. I wish I could do something." He looked down at his hands. He barely looked up the whole time.

"What can you do? What can any of us do?" She sighed.

He didn't say anything. Jake is like that, pretty quiet, but still full, of thoughts, of worry too, she thinks. But he sat there, holding it all.

"It'll be okay," she said again, and if she kept repeating it, maybe one of them would believe it.

She and M say nothing to each other. Just move around each other in the kitchen. Paul finishes the dishes, M chomps on a granola bar. Paul doesn't even have to touch her child, she knows. She hopes that feeling works in reverse too, but doubts it.

Pete comes home with his gruff motions. His boots hitting the floor, his feet still heavy up the stairs. He's so self-conscious of his garage smells, ever since M once said something about it, about him smelling. For some reason he took that to heart. It was right after, and M wasn't exactly nice about it. She wasn't nice about anything for a long time. But Pete took it, took it seriously, and every day since, he goes and washes up when he comes home so he can please M a little bit. M's never said a thing about it. He still does it though.

"What's for dinner?" he asks when he comes down in a fresh shirt.

Paul sits at the table with M across from her on her phone. "Lou's gonna buy us Thai."

"Sweet!" M smiles.

"Gabey coming over?"

"Of course."

M rolls her eyes, knowing. "Find out anything more about her secret man?" Because she sometimes cares, too. Or at least, humours Paul that she does.

"Not a thing." Paul shakes her head. "So frustrating."

"Maybe she took a second job as a secret agent?" M leans in. "Or a call girl."

Paul laughs. "She's too old to be a call girl!"

Pete's leaning against the counter and almost spits out the water he's drinking. "That's your answer to that!?"

M laughs too. "A dominatrix maybe. I could see Aunty doing that. Bossing people around."

"She is good at that," Pete says over his glass.

"Oy you!" Paul teases. But her sister with a whip would not be the most shocking thing she's ever been.

They're still laughing when Lou walks in, and they quiet but Lou can feel it. "What's up, guys?"

"Nothing, nothing," Paul says when no one else does. "How are you, Gaberoo?"

But Gabey is right up to his uncle asking about cars and talking Hot Wheels and they're off to the living room to look up something on YouTube.

It's Lou who lingers, looking at Paul a little too long. They make the food order and then M says, "Let me know when food gets here," and takes off downstairs again. Paul sighs but notices her sister. Still not leaving.

"Are you staying to eat? Thought you had a hot date."

Lou shakes her head and starts, "Paul, I."

Paul straightens her back. Thinking this is it, the big secret. She's not surprised at how excited she is. She knows she really has to get a life, as M keeps telling her.

"Paul," Lou starts again.

Paul thinks of what would be best to make her talk. She tries a gentle, "What is it? You can tell me anything, Lou. I won't judge. I—"

"It's not that. It's Phoenix."

Paul's stomach drops. That name. "What?" She bites the word.

"She's missing."

"Missing?"

"Like gone."

"I know what missing means."

"She didn't check in, to her halfway house. She's been gone days." And then to clarify, "I only just heard."

"Where do they think she is?" Paul tries to watch her voice. Not too loud. Not too much emotion.

Lou shakes her head. "No one seems to know."

"She took off, then?" Paul slumps down, angry, so angry.

"Or." Lou looks worried though. Enough to snap Paul out of it.

"Or what?"

"Or someone did something to her."

LISA

Lisa is enjoying the morning sun when her daughter Jesse yells, "Mom, we're leaving!" from the kitchen. Lisa's daughter's always yelling like a teenager even though the woman is in her forties.

"Hang on, hang on," Lisa mutters as she gets up slow. Too slow. Her body is still moving so slow. She grabs her empty cup with her good hand and puts it in her near-useless one, then grips her cane to guide her body around the chair. It's a straight line, from there to the kitchen where her daughter and great-grandson, Sparrow, wait for her to see them off. It takes her easily ten times as long as it used to.

They are patient though. Jesse gets Sparrow's backpack on and pretends not to watch as Lisa hobbles and strains. Her right foot still drags, still feels like its fast asleep without the pins and needles. Of course it had to be her right side, she thinks at least a thousand times a day. Her left, she bargains, that would have been better.

"Bye, Granny," sweet Sparrow cries and runs up to hug Lisa's slow-moving legs. He is so careful not to be too hard, so gentle. He's always been like that, but is even more so since her stroke. Such a caring boy.

"Oh thank you, my Sparrow. Have a great day at daycare, okay?" She puts her hand on his head, feels the length of his short, messy braid and fusses over it a bit. Jesse never does them tight enough.

"Try and rest today, okay, Mom. You need rest, especially after all that excitement yesterday. I can water the garden when I get home." Jesse looks tired. Looks like an old grandmother running after her five-year-old grandchild. "Your roses can live without you for a day."

Lisa scoffs but quiet. Then smirks something like a smile. "Go to work. You don't worry about me."

"Hah!" Jesse's own scoff. Then kisses the top of Lisa's head, like she does Sparrow. It makes Lisa feel small, short. She didn't realize she was bent forward so much. She used to be tall. A good inch taller than her daughter. "Now go rest. Only rest today, okay?"

"Yeh yeh yeh." Lisa waves them away and shuffles to the counter for another cup of coffee. They both slam the screen door as they go. Jesse has always done that, and Sparrow follows after his Kookoo Jesse like a shadow. Slam. Slam. Annoying and endearing.

Lisa pours her milk, thankful Jesse left it out, and checks the time. Eight. The whole day in front of her. The whole day and nothing to do. She used to be at work a half hour by now. Would catch the first bus and get the whole office ready for the day. Her boss, James, called her "indispensable," and she knew it. She knew that place like the back of her hand, like the face of her daughter. It's all going to pot, her old co-worker, Janice, had texted her the other day. The new girl doesn't know shit, Janice's words. You wouldn't believe it! Lisa takes more than a little satisfaction in that.

Coffee warm and in hand, Lisa starts back to her chair in the sunroom. It's slow going but she gets a little faster as the day goes on. Peaking around noon like the sun. She has to concentrate, like the physio guy keeps telling her, mindful steps. It's not hard but slow. She's so bored of walking. It's like she's on a bus inching along, and just wants to get there. She's taken to looking around, taking inventory of her house and making lists of all the things she will do when she can move faster.

Back in her sunroom chair, she settles in to watch the leaves and street. She loves this room. Her house is right on the corner so it's a great place to watch the world go by. The school is kitty-corner and the long field stretches out to her side. Her friends all thought she was crazy living so close to a noisy elementary school but it's never bothered her. Or never used to. She was always at work when the loud parts came— the buzzers and the recess-screams. But when she first had her stroke, when they finally let her back home, it was all she heard for weeks. Her naps and once-easy simple tasks like brushing her hair or putting her slippers on, all punctuated by the seemingly relentless noise. She was so thankful for summer's coming. For the buzzer to quiet. The daycare inside still has kids play in the field, albeit at irregular times. That's where Sparrow goes. She wants to learn their routines so she knows when to come out and try and see him. Try and watch her sweet boy play and run in the sun, his long, messy braid bouncing behind him.

To the other side, down the street about half a block, she can see the river. If she goes to the front fence and leans over she can see it anyway, a peak of shimmering brown water through the elms arching over and an old bench once centred in the overgrowth. She loved that when she bought the place. Loved the address too. The lower the number the closer to the river, and hers is 45. So close to Scotia, the fanciest street in the North End. Posh, she called it at first. Overpriced, she learned her first years there when their little house kept falling apart around them. When repairmen would come in and tell her things with stupid tones and patronizing shakes of their heads. Still she worked at it, kept it. Took out loans, a second mortgage, anything she could to keep it up. She was never going to let it go.

Jesse loves it too. Loves being so close to the school. When he gets a little older, Sparrow will be able to run back and forth for lunch, will be able to run down this street to all his friends' houses. It pleases Lisa so much. She was never able to give that to Jesse, or to Clayton, her grandson, but third generation's a charm, or so she jokes. But really it's the furthest thing from a joke.

Her phone startles her. The number says Police, and that surprises her even more.

"Hello?"

"Hello. I'm looking for Lisa Spence?"

"This is she," she says in her best professional voice.

"This is Detective Scott. I'm calling to follow up on the report you made yesterday."

"Yes?" She waits, staring out to the leaves that twitch in the light wind. Detective? It was just a simple sighting. She grips her cup. What the hell has Phoenix done now?

It was yesterday around noon and Lisa was out in her roses. They line the chain-link to one side of her small yard, and she takes great pride in them. Or used to take great pride in them. Before the stroke, she'd spend her whole summer working on them, every evening, every weekend, and it showed. The blooms had grown and flourished with years of care. People would stop on the street and compliment them.

She had wanted rose bushes since she was young. Pink ones. Back in the day Jesse's dad used to bring her pink roses on payday. Lisa loved that. It was the most romantic thing that ever happened to her. She promised herself when she had a house she'd grow them. So she did.

She was at her fence, moving slow as she does and fussing over brown curl in the leaves. They needed water.

She was going to get the hose, make the long trip across her small yard to get it, but then the daycare kids came out into the field to run. She leaned on her fence, looked for the blur that she knew was her great-grandson, and smiled. He didn't see her or look over, just kicked around a ball and ran around like he was supposed to. It was a nice day, a hot day but not sweltering. She stood there propped between her cane and old chain-link and felt well, okay. Sometimes, if she was still enough, her body felt like it used to.

She closed her eyes to the sun and when she opened them, she saw her. She knew it was her even with her old eyes and the sun in them. It was Phoenix. Phoenix on the sidewalk watching Lisa's great-grandson playing in the grass. Lisa didn't see a face, Phoenix's hood was up, but the way she stood, the way she slouched at her shoulders, Lisa knew.

The authorities had told them Phoenix would be out, of course. Had emailed Jesse, and the social worker had checked in. No one else thought Phoenix would actually try and see Sparrow, no one except Lisa. Lisa had visited her in jail. Lisa had seen the way the girl grasped at that little photo of sweet Sparrow. Had looked at everyone else with nothing short of pure hatred. Lisa knew they'd not seen the last of that one.

Just like she knew it was her here now, stood there not thirty feet from her, across the street and near the trees, but definitely. Lisa wanted to move but knew she couldn't go fast enough to be out of sight. So she thought as quickly as she could. The girl didn't know where they lived, did she? Wouldn't think anything of a frail old lady with a cane in her rose bushes, would she? Lisa looked nothing like she had the last time Phoenix saw her. Almost two years ago when Lisa was a professional woman in her prime. Now, here in her yard, she was an old lady, post-stroke, cane, long white roots in her hair, face not done, and wearing an old sweatsuit. No, Phoenix wouldn't recognize her.

Lisa limped backwards and considered her options. She could call the police, call the social worker, call Jesse. Or she could stand here a minute. She wasn't afraid of what Phoenix would do. Not really. She knew the daycare workers all knew about Sparrow's situation, knew his no-contact mother was getting out soon, and she could see three of them stood out around the kids. They'd report anyone lurking too long at the fence. They'd never let her near him.

For a long heartbeat, neither of them moved. The kids ran and screamed and were thankfully completely oblivious.

Then a boy approached Phoenix. Man, maybe, young man, for certain. Lisa couldn't see his face either, his back to her. He must have come from the other side of the street, blocked by trees until he was close. His black jacket and pants out of place in the hot day. But unmistakably he went right to Phoenix and seemed to show her something. In another moment, they turned toward Lisa and started walking. They were on the other side, thankfully, but still, coming closer.

Lisa panicked and turned so her back was to them. She even closed her eyes. She felt silly. Like an old cat they used to have who would run into the corner when she vacuumed. The cat would press his head into the wall as if that would make him able to hide. They had laughed at the old thing, but that's what Lisa did now. She stood there, head bent, eyes squeezed shut, and waited.

She finally opened them when she thought they'd have long walked past. And they were, three houses down, almost at Scotia, still on the other side of the street. It looked like they were headed to the little park. She watched them, Phoenix in front, the boy following. They didn't look friendly. They went past the bench to the river, and one by one disappeared down the slope.

Going off to do some drugs, she thought, and huffed. She knew people went down there to use. When the river was low, the slope went down quite a bit and was completely hidden from the houses and streets. It was actually a nice spot. Or would have been.

But that wasn't the important thing. The important thing was that it was Phoenix, and Lisa knew it.

She settled herself down on the front stoop and called Jesse, FaceTimed her so Lisa could look her in the eye and then her daughter would know how serious she was. How sure.

"It was Phoenix, I tell you. I know it."

"Mom, it's not that I don't believe you. It's just that, you know, your eyesight, and that was a ways away."

"Never mind that, you should call the daycare right now. I know she can't do anything but still, they should know."

Jesse sighed. Looked tired. Her studio noisy behind her. She worked with young artists in an old echoey warehouse. The kind that's cold even in this weather. As if knowing what her mother was thinking, Jesse wrapped her sweater around her chest a bit tighter. "Okay, Mom. I'll call. I'll call the daycare and then the social worker. Do you want me to come home?"

"Ooof no!" Lisa snorted. "I'm not a child!"

She hung up pretty quick after that. Probably too quick. She didn't want Jesse to think she was mad, not at her anyway.

Feeling like things were taken care of, she got up and made her way to the hose. She needed a new nozzle on this one, the spray went everywhere and got her hands all wet, but still she watered her roses generously. She kept looking over as she did, to the little park and the thin, bright slice of river.

She didn't see anything more. Didn't see them come out, but they could have at any time her back was turned, the long, slow way she had to unravel and re-ravel the hose around the hook. But she did know neither of them approached the school again, she could see that much. She was never out of sight of the field, even long after Sparrow and the rest of the little blurs went in.

Jesse called back as Lisa got to the top of the stoop's stairs. She kept the phone away from her mouth, didn't want her daughter to hear how out of breath she was.

"The social worker said you should call and make a police report. They will need a record of it."

So that's what Lisa did. She called and talked to some uninterested young person and listed the things she saw in rote basics—what they were wearing, what direction they walked in.

When she got off the phone, she felt frustrated. She also had to pee, which meant either the stupid plastic thing Jesse had bought and placed in the corner of the kitchen, or going all the way up the stairs to a proper bathroom. She didn't know which of the two things pissed her off more.

A uniformed officer and a detective are there a few hours later. Almost noon again. They knock loud and wait while she moves across the room, fixing her hair as she goes.

The detective is young but not too young. Brown but not too brown. Slightly thinning and grey-on-top hair. She thinks he might be Métis but can never be sure. There are so many Slavic folks and Polish folks around, sometimes it's hard to tell. His name, Scott, doesn't give much away.

"You want to walk me through everything?" the detective says with a smile. He's trying to be non-threatening. Lisa narrows her eyes to see him better. He had held her arm as they went down the stairs but still seems smarmy. As much as he wants her to, she doesn't trust him.

In the yard, she goes over everything one more time, points and says all the details she remembers—where they walked from, where they went. The uniformed officer goes down to the park to "have a look around" and the detective asks more questions that make Lisa repeat the details over again. Phoenix was looking at her son. She didn't seem to know the young man that approached her. He definitely showed her something. They went to the park.

Sparrow and the kids come out into the field as Lisa stops talking to look. Sparrow seems to be looking over, probably sees the police cruiser and a strange man in his yard. He waves, or she thinks he does. She waves back.

"What do you think he showed her?" The detective takes notes on his phone, looks like he's sending messages and not paying attention to her at all.

"Don't know. Probably drugs. She has a history with that, you know."

"And again, you're *sure* it was her?"

Lisa looks at this detective, looks him up and down and up again. He is smiling but just with his mouth.

"Yes. I am sure."

"Do you wear glasses, Mrs. Spence?" He looks down at his phone again as he asks. Doesn't have the nerve to look her in the eyes.

"It's Ms. And yes. But I'm good at seeing things far off. I saw my great-grandson just now. You saw. And she was closer than that."

He looks up and tries one of those fake smiles at her. "We have to check everything, you understand."

Lisa doesn't have to respond. The uniformed officer comes up again, shaking his head as he approaches. "Nothing down there. Some footprints in the mud. Someone was definitely there recently."

"Could have been fishing. People still fish down there, Ms. Spence?"

Still trying to show off, this one. Show her he knows something of the neighbourhood.

"Not here much. The fishers go down by St. John's Park. Better clearings, I think."

"Did you take pictures?" the detective asks the other officer, who nods and looks around.

"It's such a nice street." An empty statement.

After that they say their goodbyes. Add a meaningless "If you remember anything else" and even a "Thank you for your time." But they're talking about something else as they walk to the car. Lisa thinks the whole thing was a waste of time. She feels sore from standing so long. And neither of them had offered to walk her back up the steps.

She goes over to look at her roses again. Their leaves yellowing, curling a little more than yesterday. She curses herself for overwatering. She should have been paying closer attention yesterday. Was too distracted.

She shuffles over to the shed, minding all the cracked concrete and weeds that need pulling as she goes. Thankfully the fungicide isn't on the highest shelf. A generous spray on the soil should do it. She has enough energy to do that much. And time—she definitely has the time. She has to keep these roses looking as pretty as can be. While she can.

ANGIE

Angie walks into her beautiful home and the air conditioning deliciously hits her face in instant relief. Angie loves this old house. She loves the little table at the entryway with the small blue dish for keys. No one ever uses it but it looks nice. She had seen it in a magazine and amazingly the dish has survived her kids so far. She loves the painting above the little table. A Norval Morrisseau print. The colours are perfect. She takes a deep breath in.

Her kids are in the living room. Alexandra's face lit up by the big screen of the TV, and the calming sounds of *Minecraft* fill the small room. Tristan's face is blocked out by his mini-player. The rest of him stretches out impossibly long on the couch. So tall already at five.

"Hi, guys," Angie says, taking her purse strap from where it sat criss-crossed on her body as she walked from the bus.

"Hi, Mom," they chime off-unison, not looking up.

She breathes again, but it's more of a sigh. She hopes they had gone out today. She equally hopes they had eaten something halfway nutritious.

She walks down the hallway painted a dusty greige, into her Chadbury green kitchen. Her partner, 'Ship—everyone calls him 'Ship but the old people—hated the colour but humoured her choice. The table is a light pine. The print on the wall an Alex Janvier.

Angie can tell something is wrong by the way he holds his body. She can always tell when something is wrong with 'Ship. Not like a sixth sense or anything, he makes it pretty obvious by pacing around the kitchen, reeking like he'd been smoking all day. Angie measures her movements carefully before speaking, hangs her purse on the kitchen chair, drapes her sweater over top, long sigh before beginning, calmly, "What's up?"

He slows his circle but doesn't stop, hand to his mouth. "Phoenix." He knows that's all he has to say.

Angie sighs again. It'd been a long time since they'd had some Phoenix drama. One of the benefits of her being locked up. "What'd she do now?"

"Gone. She's, fuck, no one knows where she is. It's been days of this shit." His hands go up and down and all around, his body in constant movement.

"How can she cause this much trouble already? She's only been out five minutes."

"Exactly." He looks out the window, then to his phone. Thinking. No, planning.

"What do you think?" She wants to sit down, but doesn't. She might have to do something, he might need her to do something, so she grips the back of her perfectly light pine chair instead.

"They think that . . . she went to see her kid . . . and they saw her there with this kid. This uppity young kid who works at the drop-in. Kyle found out. Who it was." He parses out the information like he does, leaving out details about how he hears stuff, how he knows, who told Kyle. The things she told him she never wanted to know. The things 'Ship always seemed to know and she didn't ask about.

"And she took off?"

"Or . . ." He looks right at her.

And she sees his thinking. "You think this kid did something to her?"

"I don't know." His fingers text quick now, then back to his mouth. "Or tried to?"

"Tried to?" She scoffs a bit, trying to ease the tense air in the room. "Never known anyone to try something on Phoenix and get away with it."

"Exactly." Back to his phone. "I got to, I gotta go, Ang."

"'Ship," she starts, careful. Slowly. "You know Phoenix . . ." She reverts to an old strategy. "This'll probably all end up being nothing, you know. Phoenix has a way of attracting trouble, but . . ."

"If that kid did something to her . . ." He points. So upset. Angry.

"Phoenix can hold her own."

'Ship's eyes flare. She has all of his attention. "Then where is she? Huh? If she's so tough, where the hell is she?" His voice gets louder, higher, then stops midair.

Angie puts her hands out, calming, stopping. She takes her own breath. "Okay, okay, 'Ship. Everything's going to be okay."

"If that kid tried anything . . . ," he says again. Then gets to it. "She's blood, Ang. Hey? She's my fucking blood."

"Okay." She knows she can't say anything to that. She knows his complicated devotion to his family, his messed-up niece especially, isn't anything to question or criticize. Or rather, she knows if she did, he'd do whatever he was going to do anyway. Better to save her energy for something more constructive. "Anything I can do?"

"Naw, it's, all under control." He says it like it was supposed to make her feel better.

Once he leaves the room, she pulls out the chilled bottle of sauv blanc and one of her mint-coloured wine glasses. Another complementary green to match her kitchen. Everything is green in here, even the window that looks out to the little patch of backyard grass is green this half of the year. The other half of the year, it is white with snow and still matches well.

She sips as she hears 'Ship on the phone in their bedroom, getting ready. Planning. Executing. She tries to think of something else. Anything but wondering what he is going to do. Her exhausting day, maybe. She wanders back to the living room to stretch herself beside her boy, her arm propping up her head so she could sip her wine as she curls around him.

"Whatcha playing?"

"*Mario*," Tristan says simply.

"*Mario*! You know, I used to play *Mario* when I was little."

"Uh-huh."

She tries again. "What'd you guys do today?"
"Nothing."
"Nothing."
Their uneven chorus.
"Oh yeh." She gives up. Sips again.
"'Kay, I'll be back when I can," 'Ship calls but doesn't look at them as he flies out the door. "Love you, guys."

Her mom tells her she should leave him. That she'd hung around too long and men like him never change.

Her sister, too, tells her she should kick him out. That the house was in her name so she should keep it and no one would say a thing. That she should go find someone worthy of her.

Neither of them really know 'Ship, or the fact that he's said the same to her a hundred times. No one's telling her anything she doesn't know. And still, she's here.

Work was a shit show from start to finish. Communications in politics always is. You get right in the thick of it and spend all your time in the fights. Angie loves it. She started working for this new MLA she really admires, Jennifer. Jennifer is a beautiful youngish, outspoken, intelligent Indigenous woman, so naturally constantly in the thick of it too. Today it was another uneducated sad sack of a white man on the other side of the floor. He said something stupid and Jennifer called him on it. But she didn't call him on it the right way. Didn't think long enough about what she should have said and reacted too quick. And now they were criticizing her tone, her stance, her choice of words, her everything. That's what happens when you don't plan what you say before you say it. When you have the audacity to be an Indigenous woman and you don't plan what you say, what you do, how you do it.

As a result, Angie spent the day reading Facebook slags and writing a thoughtful apology. The rage-inducing but necessary work of being a human in this particular kind of body.

"*You* have nothing to apologize for!" Angie told Jennifer, a little too loud but behind a closed door.

"I know," Jennifer says, calm now, cut down a few pegs by the premier, who told her to "sort it." "But we look to the bigger picture, don't we? We catch the flies with honey."

"Always with the honey, hey? No wonder we're so tired! Spending all our time thinking of all this honey."

Jennifer laughed. She was so nice to Angie. Called her "irreverent" once.

"If anyone can do it justice, you can." The MLA beamed. Or was it Angie who beamed at that.

Angie got to work. Angie was very good at her job. Angie crafted the longer public statement, the personal letter to the "affronted" party (fucker), and the short, to-the-point social media posts for the end of the day (fuckers). They went back and forth, her and Jennifer, that beautiful dance of finding the perfect words, "No, not this," "How about this?," "More here," "Less there." Jennifer is as soft as she is hard. Jennifer is someone to strive to be, even if she says the wrong thing now and then. Jennifer seems to have it all together.

At least at work. At home Jennifer has two teenagers and no partner and says she struggles a lot. The rumour is that she's seeing this other MLA who is married and it's a whole thing, but they're discreet about it. Angie doesn't know if she believes it. Or more like, she doesn't care. She doesn't like to judge such things. Who is she to judge?

She finishes her glass and wants another. She doesn't want to get up but her polyester pants are so constricting, her bra chafing. Her stomach growling. "You guys want to order burgers tonight?"

"Yeh."

"Yeh!"

The most emotion she's gotten from them so far.

"Wait, did you have burgers for lunch?" She should have known.

"No."

"No way, Mom!"

"I had an apple before." Tristan knows what she's after and turns to her with his sweet eyes.

Angie thinks fast food twice in one day is a bad idea but decides she doesn't care. She gets up with a smile. "Fine, then. But five more minutes and you're off those things." Then, "I mean it!" to stave off the groans.

She orders the food and changes into her comfy clothes, goes back to the kitchen with her empty glass. Her body feels like it's singing in 'Ship's old sweats and tank top.

The landline rings as she pours. No one ever calls on that except telemarketers and old people, and she picks up ready to swear at someone but hears Uncle Toby's raspy "Hey, Ang" instead.

"Oh hey, Toby, how are you?" She sits down on one of her pine chairs. Toby always wants to talk.

"Good, Ang. Good." Then like he remembers: "You?"

"I'm okay. Hot out there today, holy smokes. You go out today?"

"Naw. Naw. They keep it nice and cool in here so I stay by the window. But they make me walk! They take us up and down the hallways like we're dogs or something. Everything but the leash!" Toby recently moved into a care home. He had been in assisted living for years, in an old run-down building on Main, but it wasn't enough and he was getting on. 'Ship found him a nice place along the river. The old man complains about it so much, Angie knows he must love it.

"They give you treats if you get far enough?" She laughs a bit and sips a bit more.

"I wish. Someone told them about the diabetes, you know. Everything they give me is bland. All this sativa stuff. Don't like it."

"I think you mean stevia, Uncle."

"How the hell do I know? It's not good. I'm not even allowed salt, for fuck sakes. And my cholesterol is good. It's fine. But hear them tell it!"

"Yeh, salt's bad for you."

"And try and go out for a smoke?" She can hear him waving his hands, if you could hear such things. 'Ship's whole family were hand wavers.

"That stuff's not good for you, Uncle. None of it. They just want to keep you around a little longer."

"For what? To watch bad TV with old people? They never got anything good on. Only ever watch *Wheel of Fortune* in here."

"You love *Wheel of Fortune*!"

"Well I got to now, don't I?"

"Didn't 'Ship get your TV set up in your room?"

"Yeh but, you want to watch with other people sometimes, don't you?"

"Yeh, I guess."

Angie drains her glass. Some days it goes down too easy. "Hey, sorry, Uncle, but 'Ship's not around right now. You can probably try him on his phone."

"No, no, I won't bug him. Just wondering if you guys had seen Elsie. I tried calling but she doesn't call me back. Haven't seen her in a while."

Angie can't remember the last time she saw 'Ship's sister. Elsie is a waste of space, as far as Angie is concerned. Or, if she's feeling more compassionate, Elsie is a troubled soul. "I don't know if 'Ship's talked to her but I haven't seen her in a long time."

"I worry about her, you know. She can't stay with me no more. Not here. So I worry."

"Yeh, I know." Angie doesn't know what she can say that would comfort him. "Elsie gets by though, doesn't she?" A vague question? Or was it really a statement.

"Yeh, she does that. She does that." He seems a little comforted at least.

Angie empties the rest of the bottle into her glass. She has to slow down. It isn't even six yet.

After the kids go to bed, Angie goes into the living room under the pretense of watching something on TV, but she ends up scrolling and scrolling through the various things 'Ship subscribes to and doesn't find anything she wants to watch enough. She stops on a decorating show and lets her mind wander. She loves her living room. The feature wall a deep velvety steel grey and the rest a lighter, cooler shade. But not too cool. It was supposed to feel warm. The walls are lined with Daphne Odjig black-and-white prints, the faces series she did in the sixties. All the portraits looking like family. Angie loves the lines on the Elders' faces, the wispy curves of their still-black hair. She leans back on her sectional and rubs her hands in circles on either side of her lap. The couch is new, only a month old, and dark silky black. She wanted leather but thought the kids would wreck it, so it was stain-resistant fabric for now. There is, of course, already a stain.

She finished this room before summer started. She did one room after the other and it calmed her. The bathroom is next. She's thinking yellow.

She texts 'Ship before ten, and tries not to sound worried or nosy. "Hey you ok? Are you coming home?"

He doesn't get back to her. She isn't surprised. She knows when he takes off like this, he's working. She knows she should text her mom to take the kids tomorrow, or plan to call in sick. She should have a plan for the unexpected. She thinks of what she has to do at work tomorrow, what she can get out of, what she can pass along to someone else if she has to stay home with the kids.

As if reading her mind, Jennifer texts her right then: "Great job today. I am so happy with how everything turned out. You truly have a gift with words. Don't know how you do it."

Angie smiles into the empty room. Happy to have a boss who believes in praise. She sure has worked for enough who don't.

But she hates when people say, "I don't know how you do it." Like they are suspicious of her. Like they think it was something she stumbled upon and not a skill she's honed, over years, something she's had to learn.

She gets up and scans the room for any last mess before going to bed, folds the blankets, fluffs the pillows. The package from 'Ship's brother still sits on the top of the sideboard, opened but not emptied. Angie doesn't know what to do with it. It's a beautiful blanket, too beautiful to be a kid's bedspread. She doesn't know what 'Ship wants to do with it, if he wants to keep it or would he be offended if she put it somewhere.

He was so upset when it came. Addressed to his daughter, he knew who it was from and didn't open it. Angie came home hours later and it was sitting in the corner like it was kicked there. Alexandra begged to let her unwrap it, it was addressed to her after all. 'Ship eventually relented but was no calmer when he saw the homemade gift and little note that accompanied it, promising something soon for Tristan. Angie read it aloud. An invitation, a kindness from his long-lost brother, Joey. 'Ship left the room. The box stayed where she put it, for weeks now.

Joey had been a withdrawn, depressed kid, and a little weird. Never said much to her, his little brother's little girlfriend. He'd taken off the minute he turned eighteen. 'Ship hated it when he left, thought the whole weight and responsibility of his family was on him now. He was barely sixteen. He wanted to roam the streets and get high, but suddenly felt like he should help out and be a grown-up. Angie thought it was strange, but it's not like she ever understood his family. His mother was a real piece of work. Angie never met an angrier person than ol' Margaret. No one was surprised when she died of a heart attack. The real surprise being that she had a heart after all, as they joked at the time. His dad a bit better but not by much. Sasha's a good guy, decent grandfather, not exactly on the up-and-up but no one can say many bad things about him as a person. And of course there was crazy Phoenix. She had been such a sweet little kid. Well, needy really, but Angie never thought she'd turn out so hard. 'Ship talks like he had a great childhood, good family, but Angie knows better, just by knowing him all along.

Her mom said, "That family is so messed up. You don't even want to know the stories I've heard. That niece is a piece of work."

Her sister said, "He's going to turn out like his uncles—in jail or dead. My money's on jail. He's going to go in again, only a matter of time."

Angie opens the warm red on the counter and pours half a glass, to help her sleep. She checks her phone as she walks, rereads the text from Jennifer. She feels proud of herself. She likes doing good work, and being told as much.

'Ship still doesn't text back and on reread of her first one, she thinks it sounds a bit needy, so she adds a casual "xoxox nite" to be even-handed.

She crosses the dark room and turns on the bedside lamp, loves seeing the shadows play on the violet walls and upholstered headboard. A large star blanket her Aunty made her hangs over the dark wall. It's a small room but she was able to fit an accent chair by the closet. It's where she sits when she gets dressed in the morning. Also where 'Ship throws his dirty clothes but she throws them right off. It's marigold, tufted, lovely. She never lets the kids anywhere near it.

"I don't get why you need all this stuff," 'Ship had complained, more than once, when she showed him what she was ordering and he was paying for.

"You want to have a nice house, don't you? This is all for you too, you know."

"If it was for me we'd have a cheap-ass couch and big-ass TV and that's it! A king-sized bed and one of those feather blankets and I'm good."

"Well, it's basically that, with some colour."

"That's a lot of money for colour."

"But you love me."

"I do." He had smiled his shy smile. The one she loved. The one that meant he was going to give her whatever she wanted. The one that lets him get away with everything.

And he does. But so does she. He gives her anything she wants. She said he should stay home with the kids 'cause she didn't like the daycare, so he does. She said he should live in the house with them like a proper family, and he does. He always does. He said it was the old way—give the woman everything, let her be in charge. Angie doesn't know if that was true, that it was the old way, but doesn't mind it. Who would?

It isn't easy but isn't exactly hard either.

She leans back on her too-many pillows, opens her book, but she can't read. She can only stare at her perfectly painted wall. She loves being home, in this house he bought her, another thing she wanted. She is safe here and she knows that. Feels it. She knows 'Ship will always take care of his family. Most of the time it makes her so grateful.

But sometimes it also makes her so scared.

She thinks again about all the things he told her, the exact words—"some uppity-assed kid from the drop-in"—and how he said it: furious. How he paced around the kitchen: anxious. The way he looked at her when he thought something happened to Phoenix: afraid. That was the worst of it, when 'Ship was afraid. No one could think straight when they're scared. Angie should know. She's been scared for as long as she'd known him.

Not scared of him. Scared *for* him.

CHERYL TRAVERSE

Cheryl waits for her daughter Paulina to pause her explanation. They both take a breath over the phone, but Cheryl blurts out before she exhales: "I'm coming down!"

"You don't have to come down, Mom. Lou says she has it under control." Her daughter sounds so sad.

"When has that ever been true? Lou can't do this on her own. This is too much now. Did she call Gabe at least?"

"She's not going to call Gabe, Mom. They haven't been together for, who knows how long." Paulina sighs. "Lou's been going through something. You know she's been distant."

Cheryl rolls her eyes, doesn't mean to but does. "Is this about that guy you think she's seeing?"

"No, Mom." But Paulina is thinking. "Well not just that. She seems to, I think she wants us to stay out of it."

"Stay out of it! My grandson's in jail! How am I supposed to stay out of it?!" Cheryl's hands cut the air. She didn't know what to do with herself.

"She says it's all a mistake."

"Of course it's a mistake. Jake would never do anything like that! But still." Cheryl drums her fingers across the counter. Her hands couldn't stop. "We should be there, for her."

"We are there for her. But she's not going to let us be anything right now." Paulina sounds so tired.

"We should still try." Cheryl doesn't want to cry. She's too mad to cry. "How is M?"

"She's, oh who knows." She could tell her daughter was crying. Quietly, but still.

"We should call Gabe."

"Lou doesn't need a man to come save her, Mom."

Cheryl's heart beat faster. "I'm coming down!"

Cheryl's partner, Joe, is out on a job and wasn't going to be back 'til the end of the day. She has to wait. He won't like her taking his truck but her old Colt wouldn't last the six hours south. She only uses the thing now to take her to the lake nearby, to go into the tiny town for coffee, to make her feel a little less completely isolated in the bush. But at least Joe will have that. She will need the truck to make the drive. If she gets her shit together, and Joe gets his ass home, she could be at Paulina's by suppertime.

When she moved out of the city that last time, she had all sorts of dreams of the road and trips planned out. She was going to Batoche to see the graves again. She was going to Edmonton, Prince George, down through the mountains she'd never seen. She wanted to go to the Bear Forest on the coast and do a whale watching tour, then come back home slowly, maybe even going down as far as the Grand Canyon because she wanted to see that too.

But she came up here to see Joe first, her ex at the time. She told herself that it was on the way but really she wanted to see him. She had such a weird love for him that ebbed and flowed since they were kids. She got here, they drank a bottle of whiskey, and things seemed to flow again, as they do with whiskey. It's been five years.

Cheryl can't believe it's been that long. She's slowing, in her age, resting more. She doesn't mind it mostly. She is sometimes restless, sometimes fine, still here. She thinks she wants to be, but mostly she feels like she doesn't have anywhere else to go. There is something so knowing and peaceful about their furious love in old age. Something familiar and exciting enough. Love with lots of naps. Quiet life.

She never was good at getting men. Has never known how to have relationships that aren't clumsy. When she first left Joe, when their kids were small, she'd go out sometimes with her sister Rain, later her old friend Rita, but nothing ever came from those drunken romances she found at the bars they went to. Messy things, and she never got it any other way. So she kept going back to Joe, and for better or for worse, he let her.

They rage and argue a lot, always have. They're both stubborn as each other, but they also get bored. There's only so much you can do in the bush stuck with someone. Sex just goes so far. Fighting is what makes you feel really alive.

"How soon can you get home?" she says as soon as he finally answers his phone.

"I dunno, five? Six, maybe? We just put down the paper." He's so fucking calm.

Cheryl is not calm. "If I drive the Colt to you, can we switch?"

"The truck's full of shingles, Cher." He sounds like he's walking away from the noise. Like he knows. "What's this about?"

"I gotta go down to the city. Jake's in trouble!"

"What happened?" He's doing his breathing, his stupid calming breathing using his calming voice. He's been doing this lately. Since he quit drinking. Even quit coffee. He's been reading up on Buddhist stuff and meditation. Talks about it all the time. Breathing shit. Living in the moment shit. Like that's ever worked for anyone. The moment is usually intolerable. And aren't we all fucking breathing all the time?

"They think he *hurt* that Phoenix person." She can't say the other word. The real one.

"Hurt how?"

"She's gone! Took off. And they think he did something. He's in the Remand Centre!" She's pacing as she talks, goes into the bedroom to pull the bag off the shelf. "Apparently he was seen, or someone like him was seen with her. Another brown kid in the North End, go figure. They all look the same to them, I guess."

"I don't understand. If they charged him . . ."

"Do you really think Jake could do something like this?" She pulls a sweater out of her drawer and stuffs it in the bag. Some underwear.

"Settle down. Settle down." He sighs. His stupid centring bullshit.

"No, I don't, but what do you think?" His infuriating questions.

"I think our daughter needs me. Both our daughters. They need me. I'm going down!"

"Okay, okay, I get that. What do you need?" Always with this need shit.

"I need the fucking truck, Joe!" She hangs up. But does the stupid breathing he told her about too. She doesn't mind it, but would never tell him so.

She hasn't gone down much. To the city. She doesn't want to visit too often and overstay her welcome. They talk all the time. Her and her daughters anyway. She doesn't hear much from her grandchildren directly, but knows what they're up to from their mothers. Jake has a good job, M is writing comic books, Baby Gabey does really well in school. She even hears from her niece Stella now and then, who calls her Aunty all respectfully and gives updates on her kids Cheryl has barely met. It's nice. But also makes her realize she's the matriarch now. Her mother gone and now it's her, for all of them.

She didn't realize how old she got so fast.

When she first left the city, after she quit her job and gave up her apartment, she thought it was for freedom. She had a few dollars saved, wanted to see something new, go make art from new sources, but really she wanted to get out of the way. Paulina had M and Pete, Louisa had her boys, and Gabe, as off and on as they are, he always comes home. Stella didn't seem to want much to do with any of them, other than a phone call now and then. Even Cheryl's best friend Rita moved to the reserve to be close to her kids. They all seemed complete.

It was Cheryl who still had holes in her, gaping spaces where her sister and now mother used to be. No partner. No nothing. She was sixty years old, and packed everything she loved into a new used car and drove it away.

It barely made it to Joe's place, really. He tried to fix it up as best he could but she still didn't trust it to take her anywhere she wanted to go. Not that she knew what she was going to do when she got there anyway.

With no choice but to wait, Cheryl paces the room. Her bag packed and at the door, she goes around the living room in circles, dragging her feet to rub on the carpet. A cool sensation on her toes she likes. Trying to be in the moment maybe. She breathes. She calms. She tries to hold her breath in between breaths. It helps a bit.

Then she knows she has to call Louisa.

"Mom, I can't really talk now."

"I know, I heard. I'm coming down."

"Mom, I can't, you don't have to come down." Her daughter's voice is shaky. She's emotional, too.

Cheryl smiles, knowing she can make it better. "Of course I do. I can look after Baby. You can accept help sometimes, you know."

Louisa sighs. "It's not that, it's just . . ."

Cheryl panics. "What happened? Did something else happen?"

"No, he's still in lockup. They're keeping him in."

"They can't do that, can they?"

"It's a murder, Mom. Or a suspected one." She sighs again. "They can do whatever they want."

"How could they!" Cheryl's eyes dart around the room. She tries to think. Tries to see everything. "I don't understand. No one can believe he did this?" It should have been a statement.

Louisa took a moment before answering. Like she was doing something. Distracted. "They got, well, they said a witness. Who saw him. Identified him. Last seen with her and—"

"And what?" Cheryl interrupts. She doesn't mean to but Louisa isn't talking fast enough. "He's a good kid. And she's, she isn't, is she?"

"It doesn't quite work like that, Mom." More sighs. Worse than a teenager, this one.

"They wouldn't be doing this if he was white. Or anything else. This is racism."

"Maybe. But—"

"No, that witness!" Cheryl is mad all over again. "Whoever says they saw him probably got him mixed up with some other brown kid. Or the cops picked up the first brown kid they saw. Or—"

Louisa breathes. "He had a knife on him."

"A knife!" Cheryl's breath goes from her. "Why'd he have a knife?"

"I don't know. It's not uncommon. But it, it doesn't look good, Mom. There's so much. His lawyer already suggested a plea. Thinks they won't give him bail at all." She still sounds like she's doing something as she talks. How could she still be doing something?

"That's bullshit! What kind of legal aid hack did they put you with?"

"It's a friend, Mom." Her exasperated tone. She seems to put down what she's doing at least. "It's, they're a good lawyer. I've known them for years. It just doesn't look good." Louisa, for all her tough and grit, starts to cry. She's trying not to, and trying to be quiet about it, but Cheryl can tell.

"Oh honey, I'm sorry. I'm so so sorry," Cheryl whimpers. Then takes in a long breath. "I'm coming down!"

"No, Mom, you don't . . . ," she sputters.

"Don't be like that. I know you need me and I'm coming. I can help."

"Mom, I don't need—"

"This is my grandson!" Cheryl's finger points down, at nothing.

"It's not about you, Mom!"

It's a rough, loud statement. Cheryl takes it in like a blow. Then breathes and thinks Louisa probably didn't mean it. Louisa is hurting.

"Louisa," she starts but doesn't quite know where to go.

"I gotta go, Mom. I gotta transfer case files, and I gotta go get Gabey from Summer Club. You don't have to come. Please stay up there. I will call you when I know something different."

Cheryl didn't say anything. She didn't have a chance before her daughter hung up.

After that, and some pathetic, angry crying, Cheryl puts on her old hiking boots and goes out into the bush. She walks nearly every day, switching up her paths and routes and too often making herself get lost in the birch trees. She knows them pretty well by now and can find her way back, eventually, but does still wander off a bit. She takes her phone and a compass on a chain around her neck too. To be safe. She knows where the bears roam and where the berries are best. She even found a little sage patch last year. Enough so that she'd always have smudge. She's dried a bundle to take down with her to the city. Or at least would have, if she was going down to the city.

It's so hot at midday she takes off her shirt and walks in the empty bush in just a sports bra and shorts. There's never anyone around for miles, not that they'd care to see an old lady in her gitch anyway. There's only the rabbits and they don't care.

She cries more as she walks, feeling sorry for herself. Feeling sorry for her kids too, but mostly herself. Her restless not-helping self.

The sky is that forceful blue of summer and there's almost no wind at all. She pants and sweats up the incline, not exactly a hill, more like a big rock. This slight edge of the Canadian Shield up here. She sits at the top of it and looks down over the trees, the lake far off. She can even see a bit of the town from here, the coffee shop she goes to sometimes. Talks to this old guy named Ben who is also a calm man like Joe. Cheryl's surrounded by a bunch of people who don't need her.

She cries some more, but mostly because she has nothing else to do.

Thing is, she's never been anything else. Her mother, her sister, she got with Joe so young, her daughters, her grandchildren. Her life has been about other people. Always. Even her work, her art, that she so painstakingly learned and practised, is all about other people—how they grow, how they change, how she sees them, how she remembers. How much they can be. She used to think it was really about her, somehow. That all these other faces were reflections of her own. And they probably are, but that's not all. They are also about them. More so about them. Her version of them. Her world all filled with other people. They say it's supposed to be like that, surrounded by family, but then why does she feel lonely all the time?

A few years ago, when her mom was still alive, Cheryl had asked her what the meaning of life was. It was supposed to be a joke, but after she said it, she felt bad.

"How the heck would I know the meaning of life? Because I'm so old? That's insulting." Flora had chuckled though. She was so gentle in her waning years.

"You're supposed to be wise, Ma. You're an Elder now."

"News to me."

"Come on, you know you know things. Always knew better than us."

"That's 'cause I'm older than you. You can get away with more bullshitting when you're older. Have more experience at it." She took a long breath. "Really, I never knew much of anything. That's the other thing you realize getting old. You don't know most of it."

Cheryl nodded, agreeing.

"Don't go all nodding like I'm being wise. I'm not. I knew more when I was a kid. Kids know more, or at least think they do, which is like the same thing. You lose that confidence being in the world. Stop nodding! I'm not being wise!"

Cheryl laughed and tried something else. "Well, how about, what's your meaning of life, for you?"

Flora had thought long on that one, chewed on something and thought about it. She was having a good day. She was still there. "You guys, of course. My family."

"Yeh. I think it's the same for me."

"Of course it is. But you should also put you in there. Too often we forget about ourselves. We get all wrapped up in family. But we're family too, hey?"

"How do you mean?"

"Well, you're supposed to surround yourself with loved ones, right?"

"Yeh."

"They forget to tell you that the one person you're supposed to love most is yourself." Flora chewed some more. "When I was with your dad, when I was a kid, I hated myself. Was so mean to myself. No one was meaner to me than I was to myself. Then I had you guys and poured all my love into you, but then you grew up. Even before you grew up, you didn't need me every second, so I was alone again sometimes and still hating myself. I had to fix that. Can't be spending all your time with someone you hate. That's abusive. I didn't want to be in an abusive relationship again and couldn't get away from myself so I had to fix it. I think I did. A bit, anyway. Don't hate myself, anyway. Thing is, you can't be around people all the time, but you're always with yourself. It's a shame to not even like yourself. That's a hard way to live."

Cheryl was quiet for a minute, before she asked, "How did you get to like yourself?"

"I found things I liked to do. I got really good at card games I liked. I enjoyed that. Other things took, like volunteering at the women's centre and the Friendship Centre, that was fun for a while. But mostly I took care of myself. Like I took care of you, I cared for myself like I was as important. And I listened to myself like I listened to you guys. Listening is important. Hearts are like kids, I think. They're loud like kids. They let you know what they need."

Cheryl didn't know what to say to all that. Wanted to say something good. But as she was thinking, she heard the gentle sounds of her mom snoring. Cheryl smiled. Flora letting her know.

Cheryl has never been as generous as her mom, or as gentle. Cheryl has always been rough and desperate, her life has been full of panic and crisis. These last few years, up here in the boring bush, was the first time she's really rested. Simple, exhausted bush rest. Isolated and lonely but also sort of full, at least some of the time. This bush and man and little plywood-sided house she couldn't manage to leave. So maybe she shouldn't. Maybe she should stay put and take care that way.

By the time Joe gets home, Cheryl is curled up on the couch with a glass of water, reading his stupid Buddhist book. Her bag unpacked and back on the shelf. Her mood full of deep breaths.

"What's up? Everything okay?" Joe says, shuffling around her. Handing her the keys.

"Yeh." She looks up and smiles. "I'm not going."

"You're not going?" Joe stammers. "Why aren't you going? What happened?"

Cheryl puts the book down. "Nothing happened. Louisa said not to come. She didn't want me there."

Joe tilts his head, like he does when he's trying to let her know he's really listening. But she's been deep breathing for a while so it doesn't completely annoy her. "She's hurting," he says. "She didn't mean it."

"Yeh she did, but it's okay. I don't have to go. I called Gabe and told him what's going on. He's going to go down and deal with everything. It's his family. I don't have to."

"But I thought you were . . ." Joe drops into a chair. "Damn. I got off early. I rushed back here."

Cheryl looks at the old clock for the first time. "Oh! It's only two."

"Yeh, it's only two. I rushed over. I was going to go with you. Told the guys to finish the roof without me." He leans toward her.

"Oh," Cheryl says, realizing something else. "That was nice of you."

"Well, if you need me, if they need you." Joe shrugs and takes another long breath. An old man who used to be so wild. Now wild in different ways.

Cheryl second-guesses herself for the millionth time, so really millionth-guesses herself, but then shakes her head. "No, Louisa said not to come and I think I should respect that. Gabe can do it. They all can do it. I don't have to."

"Oh. Well, that's big of you. I know that's hard for you." Joe with his definite "in the moment" look on his face. Like he's concentrating on being "in the moment" so hard.

"It is. But that's okay." And she might convince herself.

Joe gets back up. "I got days off now. I guess I could go back to the job."

"No, don't. Let's go for a drive. Go down to the lake awhile. Be all in the moment and shit."

He laughs, that loving laugh he's always been so quick to give her. "Sure."

"I'll make some sandwiches," she says, moving to get up.

"Can we make a thermos of coffee too? I'm fucking dying over here." He smiles like he did when he was twenty. Same eyes too.

Cheryl smiles back. And reaches out her hand so he can help her up.

She won't go far though. Not yet.

And she'll bring her phone. In case they do need her soon.

To be safe.

SHAWN

Shawn has visited every Thursday afternoon for weeks now. Thursdays at three. He's amazed how easy it is. How natural. He hasn't told his wife, Nikki, yet. He really should.

It started innocently enough, how these things always start, with an internet search. His daughter, Cedar, had been looking for her mom and sister for a while and he was helping. They seemed hard to track down, so Shawn figured it would be something like that. But it wasn't. He typed in the name and a yellow pages listing popped right up. Right there. Auguste Rivard. His father.

Shawn had known the name since he was a kid, his mom was very honest with all the details, but he had never looked him up before. There was always something else to do, something else to keep him away. For a while it was because he was out of province, and before that he assumed if his dad gave a shit he'd be the one to come looking. But that excuse, that anger, faded as Shawn got older, as Shawn got to raise his own daughter after not being with her for so many years. He did it quick, and there he was, Auguste Rivard, some address on Taché. Not far at all.

It took him a few more weeks to call.

"Allô!" The voice was loud, an old man.

"Hi, I'm looking for Auguste Rivard."

"You found him." Friendly, gruff. Definitely Métis. "What can I do you for?"

"Um, my name is Shawn. Dupuis. I am Adèle's son. Adèle Dupuis."

"Addie Dupuis? Geez, I haven't heard that name in, what, thirty years?" The voice oddly sounded, or maybe felt, familiar. Maybe not oddly at all.

"More like forty." Shawn's voice nearly cracked.

"Ah." The old man didn't say anything else. Seemed to understand right away. Or maybe he always knew. His mom said she never told him. But as a boy Shawn thought the man must know, must know and didn't want him.

Shawn told him his mom had died all those years ago, and the old man had said he was sad to hear that. But then asked about Shawn. Well sort of. He actually said, "And you, you turn out okay?"

Shawn said, "Yeh. I'm good." Told him about his family, his work. The old man seemed pleased by all that. Asked if the job was union and if he owned his own house. Made a soft grunt of approval when Shawn said yes to both. Told him to call him Gus.

When they hit a silence, Shawn said something like, "I wanted to call and see how you are. You know."

Gus didn't miss a beat. "Oh, I'm good. Fine, fine. Old. Lucky to be old, I guess. It's boring. Lucky to be bored. Haven't been bored my whole life, now I'm old and there's nothing to do."

Shawn laughed, felt put at ease by that.

"I'm glad you called. It's nice. That you called."

Shawn knew the type of guy he was talking to. Knew many men of that generation, like his uncles or other boss types over the years, so he knew that that statement, said short and quick to get it over with, was downright emotional.

Gus was easy to talk to, to say things to. Didn't ask too many questions, or seem bothered by the calling, or anything at all. And the more Shawn called, the more the old man became Gus, the guy Shawn called to ask how he was now and then. They never talked for long. A short check-in and Shawn would ask how he was, tell him about his family. How Cedar was doing so well in university—Gus had a nephew who taught at the university, and his niece Frieda, "she was the smart one of the family, some kind of office person now." Shawn would say how Faith was doing good and working over in Alberta—"Nice country over there." How Nikki was driving him nuts because she was so heartbroken with the kids out of the house—"Never got married. Never able to con a woman long enough to have her agree to it." It was the pandemic and Gus was in a nursing home so there was no pressure to actually see each other. It wasn't 'til this year, when all the fear seemed to finally ease, that Gus brought it up.

"They're letting visitors up now, you know. Over here."

"Oh yeah?" Shawn was outside, getting ready to rake the yard like he'd promised Nikki he'd finally do. Now that she was back at work and anxious all the house chores wouldn't get done.

"Yeh. Nice lawn to sit on, pretty shady. Good place to watch the river go by." Gus seemed to chew his words. Consider them. "Comfortable chairs, those, what do you call them? They're wooden and kind of go back, like. You know the kind."

"Adirondack?"

"Ando—what?" Back to gruff. "I don't know about that but they have footrests."

"They sound nice. Want me to bring you anything?"

"Tea, double-double. Best make it milk to be healthy, but don't be putting that fake sugar in it. That stuff'll kill me faster than the 'betes will."

Shawn smiled at the clear almost-summer sky he was standing under. "Want a donut while I'm there?"

"Naw. Naw. Tea's good."

"Okay. Why don't I come after lunch?"

"Make it three. Not so hot. And I might go for a nap yet."

"Sure. Three it is."

Gus gave quick directions. The kind that assumed Shawn knew where everything was—over the bridge by the museum that looks like a little penis, or if you're coming from the hospital side, go right.

"And hey, maybe, maybe one of those crullers, hey? If it's not too much trouble. I'd go myself, but I can't walk that far anymore."

"Not too much trouble at all. Be glad to."

"I can pay you when you get here."

"My treat."

"Oh, that's nice. That's nice of you, son."

It was the first time he'd said something like that. Even when Shawn introduced himself he'd never used that word, not in connection to Gus. He was Addie's son. Not Gus's. But Gus's.

That first visit, Shawn was nearing the front entrance when a tall man sitting in an Adirondack chair under a pergola clumsily got up with a long arm reached out in a wave.

"Shawn. Shawnie!" he called hoarsely, still trying to stand up.

Shawn put his drink tray on the table and helped the old man back down.

"You walk like your mother," Gus told him right off the bat. "Look like her too." He didn't look at Shawn when he said this. Instead he busied himself with sitting down again.

Shawn sat down too. Not sure what to say, so they sat quiet for a few minutes. Stealing awkward looks at each other. The old man had a lot of hair, all white and thin on top but still in curls behind his ears. His face was gaunt and there wasn't much fat anywhere on him. His clothes were clean and pressed, smelt like fabric softener. Might have even been ironed.

"The river is moving fast today. Still melting. Doesn't look it but it's ice cold in there."

"Oh yeh?"

"Oh yeh, this river stays cold all the time." The old man's chin quivered a bit. "Wouldn't know it to look, but it moves too fast to get warm."

"Didn't know that."

Gus gave a soft grunt, something Shawn had gotten used to on the phone. It was something like the final word on things, a driving the point home, a "that is that" kind of sound. It made Shawn smile.

So then that became their routine all spring. Thursdays at three, hot tea and a honey cruller. A large black coffee for himself. But that first time, Gus sat there, donut in its paper bag untouched for nearly an hour.

"Gonna eat your donut?" Shawn leaned back in his chair after a quiet moment.

"Was waiting for you. Where's yours?"

"Didn't get one. Don't usually go for sweets."

"Oh. Then I shouldn't either."

"No, no, you eat. Please. I got it for you."

"Rude to eat alone like that, if you're not eating. Take it home to your wife." He pushed the bag across the table between them.

"No, you keep it. Eat it later."

"Well, maybe. But only 'cause I can't walk that far anymore."

After that Shawn made sure to buy a sour cream glazed for himself too. When Gus saw that, he seemed more at ease. He'd take the tea with a nod and open the lid, let it sit there to cool and he'd gobble up his cruller almost whole. Shawn found it really endearing. Like it was immediately familiar to him, though he didn't know how or why. Maybe because it became familiar.

He really should tell his wife sometime soon.

He thinks he's gonna tell her every time he comes home from a visit. Every time he learns something new about this old man who is actually his dad, which means he also learns something of himself. Like how Gus worked up north for years, in the bush, running road, as he called it, sometimes back-breaking work paving roads, fixing them. How he liked the quiet of the bush and used to have a crow that'd follow him around and he named him Gilbert, which was the same name Shawn called the cat he had as a kid. There were a few neat coincidences like that. Gus had a home off Lusted for a while, not far from the halfway house Shawn lived at for a bit, though not at the same time. And years ago, when Gus worked construction, he helped build Windsor Park, the neighbourhood

Shawn lived in now. Probably nothing, common things that people who live in a small prairie city would share, but they were neat to Shawn. Every night, he'd wait for Nikki to get home, sure he was going to tell her. She'd come in and wouldn't stop moving and talking, complaining about work, complaining about the mess around the house, complaining. By the time she got to something like "How was your day?" or more often a quiet breath between another round of her talking, he'd be too tired to start. It was big story. It would take up all the air in the room, in their life. Mostly he knew once he told her then Nikki'd take over. She means well but she'd want to meet him, do stuff, plan an event. Apparently Gus's niece Frieda was the same. That's what they were talking about that afternoon, before Cedar called.

"Haven't told her about you yet. She'd make a big deal of it, hey?" Gus shook his head and cooled his tea with a blow. "She'd want to have a picnic. She loves picnics, that one. Calls them family reunions. Has them every year. Don't understand how it's a reunion if you have it every year but she does. Yeh, she'd make a big deal of you. And that girl of yours in university, too. She loves university, that Frieda. I think that's why her kid, Jimmy, kept going to it. Years and years of it. Too much, if you ask me."

Shawn nods, says something like, "Yeh, Nikki's the same. Not the university thing, but she takes any excuse for a party."

"Never partial to them. Never saw the point."

Shawn makes a soft grunting sound in agreement. He is the same. He guesses a lot of people are but it feels good. He's like that, his mom was definitely like that, so is Cedar. It's nice that Gus is like that, too.

Actually he wants to tell Cedar more than he wants to tell Nikki. Cedar wouldn't make a big fuss or be mad that it'd been going on so long. She'd just be happy. That's what he'd been thinking about on the drive over. He was even smiling thinking of it. Blasting Power 97 and thinking about how he'd tell his girl about his dad.

"I think I'll tell C. Think she's the person to tell. The first person, you know?"

"Makes sense to me. Though I don't think your wife will be too happy about that. From what I know of wives."

Shawn nods. Knows. He's nodding when his phone starts vibrating in his pocket. "Speak of the devil," he says, standing up. "I gotta..." He always takes it when Cedar calls, which isn't often and is usually something important she's worried about.

Gus waves him off and continues to blow on his tea.

"Dad? Dad!"

"Hey, what's up? What's wrong?"

"I... The police called."

"Why? What happened?"

"They're holding someone. In the Remand Centre? They..." She's trying to catch her breath, trying not to be as upset as she obviously is.

"Slow down. What happened?"

"Phoenix was missing. Is missing. Oh god."

"What? How did she...?"

"She got out and then got... missing. I thought she took off, you know?"

"Oh C, why didn't you—?"

"I thought she took off but they, like—arrested someone? They think he... They think he killed her, Dad!"

"Why do they—? Who called you? Who said this to you?"

"Some detective, he... couldn't get ahold of Mom. Oh god."

"Okay, don't worry. Don't worry. I'm coming there now. I'm, I will be right there."

"No, Dad, it's okay. I'll be okay. Ziggy will be home soon. I..."

"Don't be— I gotta, give me a couple minutes, okay? I gotta finish something and then I'll call you when I'm back in the truck."

Shawn stares at the screen, trying to figure out what to do next. How to. His and Nikki's wedding picture stares back at him. He never changed the lock screen. Nikki had put it there on, like, his first iPhone and he never thought to change it. It's a nice picture. Smiling, happy, like normal people.

"Gus, I, I gotta go. C's in, well, her sister . . ."

"Sounds like trouble."

Shawn shrugs. Not knowing what to say. "They think her sister died?" He doesn't know if it was a question. "I don't know. I gotta go see her. Figure this out."

"Yeh, go, go then. Take care of your girl. That's what you're supposed to do."

The old man looks right at him, right in the eye, something he hasn't really done yet, so Shawn knows it's important. He feels everything right then. Doesn't know what it all is or what to do with it, but he feels everything between them, all at once before the old man waves his old, long hand again and says, "Go, go."

Shawn jumps then, over the grass to this truck. Forgets his coffee, even. He plugs in his phone before he even starts the engine. Cedar picks up but doesn't say anything. He can hear her breathing, trying to catch her sobbing breath.

"Okay," he says to her. "Start at the beginning. When did she get out?"

And Cedar tells him.

WAABAN

Waaban feels it. He feels all the pain. All the time. That's why he prefers to be out in the bush. Out where Mother Earth can heal him as people hurt him. They don't mean to. They are the ones hurting. They don't know he can feel it. People who are hurting rarely think beyond their own pain. But he feels it. He feels it all.

Out here he has only a few people with him. He stays with a small Circle of helpers and healers, many who don't know they're helpers and healers yet. Elsie is one. She is here, healing and a healer, but Waaban doesn't know if she knows any of that yet.

Out here he wakes up with the sun and feels the cold air on his face. Even in the hot, hot summer it's cool that first time of day. When he can stand here, watch the dew smoke off the grass and trees as the day begins. That's when he starts his prayers, when the sun lights the first smudge.

New age white people call it an empath. Not a bad word, as white people words go. He's never known a word for it in Anishinaabemowin or Michif, but then again, he's never asked. He suspects that all medicine people, all Knowledge Holders, are what they call empaths. Or even more so, that all people are empaths. They're just too busy and distracted all the time. In too much of their own pain to feel anyone else's. But really, we're all supposed to feel each other's pain and anger and joy all the time, and if everyone got their heads out their asses long enough, they would.

This is what Waaban knows. He spent years in pain and didn't know how to feel anyone else's pain. He didn't even feel his own. It was

Ceremony that brought it out, years ago. Ceremony and a good, patient teacher named Ben who helped him. Taught him. So now he helps and teaches others in the same way. The only way. The old way.

"Morning, Waaban." Elsie comes up quiet, holding out a steaming tin cup of coffee.

"Ah, miigwetch. Chi miigwetch." He takes it gratefully. Then raises it first to her and then to the morning sky. "It's going to be a beautiful day."

She nods to him, still shy. Still not herself.

When he met her she was still twitching from her drugs and twisted up in her grief. That first sweat he felt her discomfort. Watched her from the other side of the fire as she couldn't be still, couldn't be with herself, didn't want to be there. Now she is quieter. Getting there.

They stand in silence for a moment longer as he feels her talk come to the surface.

"I got a call from my girl," she says. She holds up a phone as if to show him proof.

"Oh? Everything okay?"

"My other girl. The one that got into that trouble, hey? Phoenix. No one knows where she is."

"I thought she was in prison."

"Just got out." She doesn't really look at him. She still looks at the black screen on the phone in her hand.

"Ah." The sun rises, and both of them wait for Elsie.

"They arrested someone. Think he hurt her."

"That sounds serious. You must be worried." He does look at her, trying to see what there is to see there.

"I am, but . . ." She sighs deep. "She's done this before. Taken off. I think, I don't know."

"We can get someone to drive you to the city. If you want to go find out."

"Naw." Her body, held so stiff, releases a bit. She stretches her arms. "Cedar, my other girl, has her dad. I would get in the way."

"In my experience, a mother is never in the way."

Elsie laughs. Waaban smiles too, though he didn't mean to be funny.

He waits, again, for her to say more. Doesn't want to impose on her thoughts, only sips his coffee. She knows just how much sugar he likes.

"I'm not, I mean, if I really think about it, I am not worried about her. About Phoenix. I feel she's going to be okay. She has, she has a big will. She's so tough, you know?"

Waaban nods. He does know people like that.

"I wish Cedar would know that."

"Maybe you could tell her."

Elsie nods. Holds up the phone that's been clutched in her hand. "Yeh," she says like a whisper and walks away.

Waaban continues to watch the sun. He thinks of the first big, deep conversation he had with Elsie, back when she first started coming to his Ceremonies. Back when she was even more pale and more unsure of herself.

"Waaban, do you think that I could, can I ask you something?" she had started, awkwardly.

"You can always ask," he said, in a coy tone she doesn't catch.

"I, I've been thinking about forgiveness. Do you believe in that? Like, is there such a thing?"

He remembered because it was so big so fast. She surprised him so much he laughed, but she looked embarrassed so he was sorry for it.

"Do I believe in forgiveness!"

"Yeh. Like, is it only a Christian thing?"

"Well, no." He felt tired all of a sudden, felt her tired from her, but he didn't want to stop. He knew if he shut her down now, she might not ever ask him something like that again. "I don't think it's only a Christian thing. I mean, most Christian things aren't even Christian things. Those guys appropriated everything as they went over Europe, over the world, all over here, so that might be one of the things they took, I don't know.

But I think forgiveness is a human thing. Doesn't have rules you need to follow. More of a feeling, I think."

He could see her really thinking, going over a list of questions and trying to pick which one to ask. She decided on, "But how do you get forgiveness, when someone doesn't forgive you? Is there a way to make them see?"

"Naw," he said, too quick, then took a breath. "You can't ever make anyone do anything."

When she didn't say anything he looked over to her. She was so young, forty maybe, but in her eyes she was younger yet. It was like she'd stopped living long ago. Never learned. Never knew. Some people do that. In her eyes, it was like she was still a kid.

"That's the good news. You can't make anyone do anything because they are not your responsibility. You're just responsible for yourself. What you do. What you feel."

He let the last word dangle there, rubbed his hands together and let it sit.

"But I want her to forgive me."

"I want a convertible sports car but it's not looking like it's going to happen this lifetime." He smiled at her so she knew he was trying to be funny, but she was thick in that kind of sad, even as funny as he liked to think he was, and he wasn't funny to her now. So he tried again. "The only person you can make forgive you is you. You're the boss. The one whose opinion matters."

Elsie looked down, thinking more big thoughts and feeling big feelings. "But I've done so many horrible things," she said like a whisper.

He nodded, looked up and away to give her some privacy in her grief. "Most of us have."

After another minute he looked to her again. She had stopped crying and looked like she was trying to see what he was looking up at. He laughed a bit more at that. She was not twitching. It was the first time he had ever seen her not twitching. She was also not moving, like she didn't want to leave.

So he tried to dig up some more wisdom for her. "We just have this moment, really. This moment. Not before. Not even after. Just now. It's what you do right now."

Her forehead wrinkled. "That's never made any sense to me. We're full of the past. We're full of our people, our ancestors, our children. How can we just be a moment? We're all things."

"Yes, every little thing. And every little moment."

"That doesn't make any sense."

"Sure it does. You are everything you ever were, baby, kid, teenager, adult, and everything you will be, Elder, spirit, all at once. All the good, all the bad, if you wanna think of it like that, but it's more like you're never only one thing. You're everything." And nothing, he thought but doesn't say. Didn't think she was ready for that part yet.

Elsie looked up, and the brightness of the light there made her squint. The white hair at her temples, the small dark hairs on her face, and her youthful eyes, almost like a baby's, all lit up there.

"I don't get it," she said.

"Maybe you will one day. Or maybe you won't and I'm full of shit either way."

She laughed. At the silliest joke, not even a good one but the silliest one. He made note to remember that next time he wanted to try to make her laugh.

The sun's higher, and Waaban's coffee isn't much more than grinds when Elsie comes back to him.

"How'd it go?" he asks her.

Elsie looks up at the warm sun, not at him. "She's hurting. Cedar is. But she's going to be okay too. She has a lot of people helping her."

"So do you," he says and sweeps his arms around, the camp behind them, women in the tent making porridge and toast. Men cutting wood for the fire. All of them talking and laughing. Sweet smells and sounds all around.

Elsie looks too. Her eyes wet and a bit red-rimmed but nothing she can't handle.

"I'll call her again later, to check up on her. Check up on things," she says with a nod of determination. Then she takes his cup. "More?"

Waaban nods and puts his newly empty hands together in thanks. "You know, you're the only one who lets me have any sugar in it. Chi miigwetch, Elsie."

She smiles.

Waaban keeps standing where he is. He likes this spot for the sunrise as he stands, waking up his leg muscles. Stretches his torso. Mountain pose, the yoga people call it. Not a bad name for it.

He likes moments like this, ones he can spend by himself. It's hard being around so much pain all the time. So many are filled with such pain. Young women like Elsie who think they're so bad. Old women full of anger. Old men full of regret. Young men—young men are the worst. He feels their pain the most because it is and was his. He remembers it so well. So big he couldn't see past it, through it. He thought that feeling was all there was and ever would be. He thought that was what it meant to be a man. But it's a lie. He didn't know how to be a man, not really, not a good one. Not one who took care of people or loved people, and loved himself. No one around him remembered enough of the Teachings to teach him that he was valuable. That everyone together makes this beautiful Circle and each one of us is so precious and important. No one around him even knew any of that, and everyone else seemed to treat him like he was vermin. Less than vermin. Vermin at least get a role in the world. He never got a role. He thought it was something he had done wrong. That's the worst thing of colonialization, worst in a long, long list of the atrocities and numerous genocides, that it got into their minds and hearts. All those young people who were supposed to be leading, doing, being a part were instead thinking they were wrong. Instead of feeling good about themselves, they believed those lies. So many still believe, like he did, what they said about them, and forgot, because that was taken from them too, how it was supposed to be.

Now Waaban is trying to remember, trying to learn. He's already an old man but still has so much to do, so much to learn. All the things he has to undo. And redo. All at once.

Not a cloud in the sky. He can see the dark blur way up. An eagle, circling high. Circling over him. Good medicine for the day.

The sun is all the way over the short, young trees and he moves his feet, ready to go. Ready for the real Ceremonies. Or at least the other ones that don't belong to him by himself.

PART THREE

NEVAEH

Nevaeh is swiping on Tinder when Cedar texts. Nevaeh can tell the girl is stressed. The girl is forever stressed by one thing or another, but Nevaeh thinks maybe there's more news about her sister so invites her over. Says she'll cook or something. It feels like the grown-up thing to say.

She puts down her phone when Evangeline starts calling from her crib. Her baby loves her schedule, always gets up on time. It's so weird to Nevaeh because she never liked a schedule before. She used to like not knowing what was going to happen or what she was going to do any day. She used to sleep in 'til whenever and do whatever she felt like. But you can't do that with a baby. And all the sites and experts say you have to have a schedule so she made one. Evangeline is the same every day, give or take twenty minutes. She gets up from her nap by three and wants a snack. Then she plays or they go for a walk before dinner. It's a nice day so they'll go over and meet Cedar by her place. It's not far and the baby loves the sunshine.

"Hello, my baby girl." The just-one-year-old stands up on the mattress and bounces against the railing. "Oh you're so happy."

The sites also say to talk to the baby all the time, even before they can talk. That's how they learn. So Nevaeh talks to her about everything all the time. She used to feel silly but now she's used to it. Even likes it. Especially when it's just the two of them, her own voice fills their home so she doesn't feel so alone. The baby can say a few words now too. She does a very clear "bye" and "Mom" and "Dada" and even did a "hi" a couple times. It's pretty early for her to be talking too. Nevaeh is pretty sure she's gifted.

"Are you hungry? You want some num-nums, my baby?" The sites are mixed about whether or not to use baby talk. Most say not to and to use the real words, but Bezhig and his mom use baby talk all the time so Nevaeh started. She often corrects herself too though.

"Do you want apples or grapes today?" She changes the baby's diaper and puts her in the high chair, carefully adjusting the straps. Bezhig sometimes doesn't even do them up. It makes her nervous but he says it's okay. He's the oldest of five so he's used to babies. Casual with their girl, even. Nevaeh knows she should trust him but sometimes she doesn't.

She cuts the grapes super small because she heard they could be a choking hazard and checks her phone while Evangeline eats. She tries to stay off her phone when her baby's awake but today feels like a hard day. A long, lonely day. She's glad Cedar's coming over later.

She got a match on Tinder and the guy messaged. They go back and forth a bit and agree to meet up the next day. Bezhig's mom says she'll take the baby for an overnight. Nevaeh isn't about to tell her baby daddy's mom why though.

"We're going to go see Aunty Cedar! You want to go into the stroller? Maybe we should go to the park."

Bezhig hasn't contacted her for almost three days now. Usually he comes back a few hours after a fight with a "Hey baby" text, but this time she thinks they might have broken up for good.

"Why you gotta do this to me all the time, girl?" he whined when she told him to leave.

"This is my place and if I say go, you go." She folded her arms in front of her and didn't even want to look at him, turned away from him on the couch.

"Why you gotta be like that? Baby?"

But she wasn't moving, so he sighed and swore under his breath but left.

That was two nights ago. He hasn't even called to check up on his daughter. He must be really done this time. Nevaeh's glad, really. Relieved. Really. She is starting school soon and Baby's going into daycare next week, so she needs to concentrate and stay focused. She's going to be a dental hygienist. The program is almost a year long and pretty intense, they said. She doesn't want anything to get in her way.

They're actually early to meet Cedar so she turns down Westminster to go to the Tot Lot. The schoolyard's closer but its play structure is really more for bigger kids, and she doesn't mind the walk. The Tot Lot is small and has those preschool swings so her baby can be safe. There're lots of parks around actually but this is her favourite. It's small and they have it to themselves most of the time. Sometimes there's another mom but the older ones from this good part of the neighbourhood. The ones who own the big beautiful houses Nevaeh dreams of visiting never mind living in. Most are polite to her.

She and Bezhig break up all the time these days. They want different things. Nevaeh wants to go to school and make something of herself. Bezhig is happy to work at a gas station and is not in a hurry to go to school even though he'd get funding if he wants to. He doesn't understand why she wants to go in a program that's so expensive, especially because she can't get funding. She got a student loan, doesn't even care how much it is or that she'll have to pay even more back with interest. She doesn't have to do that until she's making good money in a good job anyway. She might even be able to save up enough money to buy a house one day. Not one of these houses around here but maybe a small one. Somewhere. That's all she wants, really. To live in a place that's really hers and she never has to move from. She likes her apartment. Was super lucky to be able to get into a co-op that's so nice and clean. And quiet. Her rent is subsidized so she just has to pay a little bit now, because of the student loan. But she knows it's not a forever home. For one, if she makes more money she has to pay more. That's how these things work. For two, it's not like it belongs to her. Not really. But it is hers alone. Hers and Evangeline's. She really liked that at first. That she was the one in charge. But now, all these months later, she's pretty lonely when Bezhig isn't around.

Her phone dings and it's that guy again. He's talking pretty dirty already and Nevaeh's getting second thoughts. Does she really want to do this? She hasn't been with anyone else since long before she had a baby. Been with Bezhig for years now. Since she was a kid. It's fun to flirt but it's a big deal to actually fuck another person. This guy seems nice enough and all, but they all do at first, don't they?

She'd talk to Cedar about it but she's pretty sure that girl's still a virgin. And probably a gay one at that. She has a sort of thing with her roommate Ziggy, but Nevaeh is like, 99 percent sure it's a PG-13-type deal. Cedar's even more messed than she is.

Nevaeh texts Cedar when they leave the park. Politely smiles at the mom who was playing with her kid there. The lady kind of nods back. Sometimes Nevaeh thinks she'll get in trouble going to this park, like someone's gonna tell her she's not supposed to come here because she lives across Maryland in the bad part of the neighbourhood. So far it's been okay though.

Cedar looks like she's been crying but smiles and coos at the baby. Nevaeh likes it when people talk to Evangeline. Hates the ones who ignore the baby like she doesn't exist. Especially now that Evangeline notices everything all the time, and likes to wave and smile at people. It seems so rude to ignore a baby. Cedar's not like that. Cedar gets right down in front and greets Evangeline like an old friend. "Hello, beautiful girl. How are you?" She smiles but still looks sad.

"She says hi now, sometimes. Say hi, Baby. Say hi." But Evangeline just looks up and smiles back at Cedar, reaching for her face with her chubby hands. "Well, she does."

"I believe you."

Cedar doesn't say much as they walk. Nevaeh talks about Tinder and how she was going to meet this guy but now he's kinda creeping her out. She talks about Bezhig, complains really. Cedar takes the baby out of the stroller when they get inside and goes and plays with her on the floor while Nevaeh opens a can of sauce and puts some water on to boil. Spaghetti, or any kind of pasta really, is the best thing she makes. She cuts up a green pepper and half an onion to put in the sauce and everything. Fries it first in a little bit of oil so it gets nice and soft. Bezhig taught her that. He can cook all sorts of meals but so far she only knows this and roast vegetables. She's too afraid to cook meat. It's too easy to do it wrong and she doesn't want to give her baby food poisoning.

She feeds Evangeline plain noodles but makes two heaping plates for her and Cedar. She even has sprinkle cheese to put on the table. They're sitting down and eating when Cedar finally says it. Blurts it, really.

"They arrested someone. I don't know how it works. They think he killed my sister."

"Oh fuck. That." Nevaeh almost chokes a bit and coughs. "I'm sorry, Cedar. What do you think happened?" Nevaeh knows better than to trust the official story of anything.

Cedar looks up, her fork rolling around the noodles. "I don't, I don't think she's dead."

"But they're not going to what, fucking look for her now? They arrest this guy and that's that?" Nevaeh also knows enough of the system to be mad at it.

Cedar shrugs. Not like she was dismissing anything, but more like she's trying not to feel it for real. "There was a witness? They said someone saw my sister with this . . . guy. They think he killed her. I guess."

"Fucking cops." Nevaeh's heard this story before. Her aunty went missing a few years ago. They arrested her boyfriend right away, but she turned up weeks later. She had gone off with a friend. Well, there was more drama than that but it wasn't her boyfriend's fault at all. He was completely innocent, but try telling the cops that.

"I want them to keep looking for her. I think, I worry she's in trouble."

Nevaeh leans over. "Fuck, I know. I know! I am so sorry, Cedar. That sucks. Fucking sucks."

Cedar nods, looking like it's all she can do not to bawl. She cries quiet though. Cedar's always been a quiet crier.

They don't eat much after that. Nevaeh's still hungry but it seems wrong to chow down when her friend is so sad so she leaves everything on the cold stove so she can eat some later. The baby's covered with sprinkle cheese so they give her a bath, and Evangeline, as if she knows something is wrong, makes Cedar laugh with her little splashes and eating the bubbles. Nevaeh leaves Cedar watching Netflix while she goes to put Evangeline down. She has to rock her for a bit because she never got really good at sleep training. Couldn't stand the crying. Bezhig wasn't all that better either. Evangeline is such a daddy's girl and he would rock her to sleep every chance he got. So she got used to it. Nevaeh doesn't mind. She likes the quiet time to cuddle with her baby. She doesn't nurse her to sleep anymore though. She knows that's not recommended at all.

Cedar's halfway through an episode of *Friends* when Nevaeh comes back in. "I can go back, if you want."

"Naw, don't worry. I've seen them all before." Nevaeh pulls up her phone. That guy sent a fucking dick pic. What is wrong with people! She blocks him and deletes the app. Again. She just opened this one up again yesterday. Fucking Tinder. She messages Bezhig's mom that she doesn't have to take the baby tomorrow but his mom texts back that she wants to. "Haven't seen my girl in too long," she says. It's only been like a week but she loves her grandbaby like that.

Nevaeh doesn't know what to do with a whole night to herself. She could message people but it's been a while. She doesn't know the last time she went out anywhere. It'd be nice. But then again, it's not like she wants to.

"Need anything? I think Bezhig left a Coke here."

"Naw, I'm good."

"Your sister's hard, Cedar. Hard as fuck. Hard as they come. If anyone can be okay out there, she can."

"I know. I, I can't even remember her face anymore. You know?"

Nevaeh does. She remembers not seeing her mom for so long and she was so young, for like a year she thought she made her mom up. Like having a mom was a daydream and not her real life. When they did finally let Nevaeh see her, her mom looked so different than she remembered. Not better or worse but not the same. Like she changed. Like she was a stranger trying to pretend she was her mom.

Nevaeh also remembers when she met Cedar. When they lived at that foster place and the girl cried all the time. Cedar had lost her little sister then. That's the worst. Losing a little kid is the fucking worst. Nevaeh can't imagine anything worse. Of course Cedar doesn't want to lose another sister. Her last one.

"Has your mom been around?"

Cedar shakes her head. "She knows. But she's out of town somewhere. Not worried, she said. Fuck."

Nevaeh's surprised at the swear and her jaded tone. Little Cedar's growing up. Getting a little hard herself.

She walks Cedar to the door and they make plans to get together the next day. Cedar says Nevaeh should come over and drink wine and smoke weed with the university kids. Nevaeh's never met Cedar's roommates and they sound stuck up but she's curious enough to go. That and she doesn't want to be at home all by herself all night.

She checks on the baby, who's snoring and sleeping on her belly with her little butt in the air. Evangeline does this now. It's supposed to be okay now that she's older and if she moves to her stomach on her own. You're not supposed to put babies on their stomach when they're newborn. Nevaeh's getting more confident about it every day. If she ever has another kid, she knows she'll feel better about everything all the time.

Bezhig wanted to have another kid right away.

"It's nice when kids're all close together. Get them all out of the way, all at once."

"It's not like you have to be pregnant all the time. All at once."

He laughed like it was funny. "We could have a boy. One of each. Then we'd be done."

"I'm not even twenty-one, Bey. I want to finish school at least. Get a house."

He waved his hand at her like he was dismissing her. "We can do all that whenever. We got our whole lives."

He wanted to move in too. Wants to move in. Have another baby. Get married, even, one day. He's always wanted his own kids, wants to do a good job raising them. Nevaeh wanted that too but she wants other things as well. Like a career. She always thought it'd be so good to have a career.

When she filled out the application for school, one of the questions was why did she want to be a dental hygienist. She said because she really believes in good oral health, but that was a lie. Well, not really a lie, she is really good at keeping her teeth clean, and Baby's teeth too. They brush every night. She even flosses sometimes. But she wanted to be a dental hygienist for more than that. The real reason was, when she was a kid, her teeth were really messed. Her mom never took her to the dentist because she was too busy surviving and stuff so when Nevaeh went in care, her first foster took her to the dentist all the time. That one was a decent lady. A bit spineless and her husband was a total ass, but the lady took her to the dentist so that was good. Nevaeh loved the dental hygienists. They were all pretty with full makeup on and important-looking in their scrubs and stuff. She never met one that wasn't nice to her, that didn't smell nice and look like they took care of themselves. That was all she wanted to be when she grew up. To be important, at least a little bit, and look like she knew how to take care of herself. She tries. She never goes out without her hair decent and some makeup on. Evangeline too is always clean, has a bath every night, and her hair is always brushed, her clothes always clean. No one is going to ever doubt her baby is well taken care of. No one would ever try and take her baby off her.

Nevaeh turns off the TV and goes out for a smoke. She never smokes inside or around her baby but sometimes, at night, she likes one. At the end of the day. When she can sit on this little balcony, cross-legged on the cement because she doesn't have any chairs, and she looks out over the back lane, can hear the cars swooshing by on Sherbrook, can even see them through the houses. It's a pretty good place. Better than she thought she'd have. Almost as good as what she's really wants. She doesn't want to lose it. Not for anyone. Not even Bezhig. She wishes there could be a way to have him and have everything she's ever wanted too.

Her phone dings.

She smiles before she even looks. She takes a long drag and knows. The sky's almost clear and everything's gonna be okay.

"Hey baby," it reads.

She leaves it on read and finishes her smoke. He left her stewing for three days, so he can wait another minute.

LOUISA TRAVERSE

I would kill for a large bag of ketchup chips and about four chocolate bars. Maybe a Slurpee. Definitely a Slurpee. Junk food. All the junk food. It's the one thing I do when things go fucked. I am ashamed of it. I do it in secret. I hide around corners, and can inhale ketchup chips like it's my job. Keep m&m's in drawers. Get Slurpees even in the winter. I figured out, the other day, I've done this my whole life. Loved all the food that's so very not good for me. It's been, like, the longest relationship in my life, besides my family. Definitely longer and more reliable than any man I've fallen for, or my kids. Sure, it'll probably kill me. But only if these fucking men don't do it first.

Gabe called last night. "What the hell is going on!" was how baby daddy number 2 started.

"Hello to you too."

"Don't." His sigh deep, knowing. "Don't start, Lou. What the hell is going on? Why am I finding all this out from your mother? Why are you avoiding me?"

"Avoiding" means not answering his texts. "Mother" means meddlesome Cheryl, I should have known.

"It's okay, Gabe. It'll be fine. It's all a big stupid, epic misunderstanding."

"Jake is in Remand!" The words as brutal as the tone.

"It can't stick. This kid, person, must have took off or something."

"Or something," he scoffs.

I know everything he means by this. I know the meaning of every one of his gestures and half gestures. But I still say, "What the hell does that mean?"

"Lou." This guy and his fucking "Lous."

"Do you actually believe Jake"—my voice goes high, then, conscious of Baby in the other room, I lower it to a sinister whisper—"could do this?!"

"No, but, Lou."

Like I can handle his fucking "Lous" right now. "No of course not. Of course not." If I say it enough, it'll mean something too.

"That doesn't mean it's going to go away, Lou."

He knows me too well too. Knows waiting for things to go away is my MO. My own gesture and half gesture. The other thing I've done with absolute reliability my whole life.

I had a counsellor a couple years ago. Started seeing her this one time Gabe went up north and I was convinced he was gone for good. Convinced he should be gone for good and we were better off without him. She said, asked really, for me to think about avoidant personality.

"Not as a diagnosis or a . . . life sentence, but as something to consider."

I looked it up. It was nothing like me. I am excellent in a crisis. I am calm and collected no matter what I do. I can see the practical things I need to do and do them. I skip my usual tendency to overthink, to overanalyze, and get down to business. I can take in an overwhelming amount of information and not get overwhelmed. I take it one thing at a time, and I told her so.

"But what about your emotions? What are you feeling when you are doing?"

"Nothing." Because it's true.

She leaned back like she had made a point and I moved on to something else that was going on. All that shit with Jake then. Jake acting out because his stepdad had taken off again. Jake needing a man and I couldn't keep one. I didn't tell her that feelings aren't facts. That feelings don't really matter. They're sneaky, useless little fuckers that need to be avoided so I can do all the shit I got to do.

I choke through a blueberry muffin as I wait for Shannon. Got to eat something halfway healthy, even though it makes me nauseous. Self-care is so annoying.

Shannon, sharply dressed in a pantsuit, comes in to get me in the waiting room. Not like a Hillary Clinton pantsuit but a suit suit. Well fitted. Tailored, I guess. Zero chip crumbs on their shirt. Polished and pretty. They wear their hair down and it never looks messy. They just got married. Wear diamonds and white gold bands on their finger like you're supposed to. Their wife is also a lawyer. There's a picture of them both on their desk. They both wore off-white suits and light-hide beaded moccasins. Backlit by a sunset and archway of pink flowers. The symmetry as gorgeous as the people.

"We have options," they said. The coffee I brought them sitting there. Steam slipping out of the opening. "I don't want you to think we're out of options."

I didn't say anything. I let them go over all the "options" again. All the things that really involved pleas and number ranges that really meant years. Jail time. Federal. Manslaughter.

Federal means Stony. Mountain. The old institution they don't call a penitentiary anymore but it still looks like one.

It takes half an hour to there from downtown. I'd taken enough clients there. Clients who'd get babysitters, time off, arrange everything as well as somehow manage to look their best. They'd endure the long drive, the seemingly endless walk-through security checks, questions, pat downs, and locked metal door after locked metal door. All this for the chance, the all-too-brief opportunity to be close to the person they loved. Usually they couldn't even touch each other, and if they could it was only a moment while they were watched suspiciously. There was always something put between them—a table, a plastic barrier, jealousy of freedom, misunderstanding of confinement, trauma, pain.

Most would cry all the way back to the city. It was never enough. Never what it was supposed to be.

"What about if this kid shows up again? If she just took off to cause trouble?" I'm not looking at Shannon as I ask. They're too good-looking. They're sitting too straight. Backlit by the sunny day through their big office window.

"What about his story about the blood? Where it came from? Did you find this kid Dug? Well I guess he'd be a man now." I know I'm rambling.

"Lou, I'd really rather not go down that path if we don't have to."

"Why? If it can explain why there's blood on the knife he had. It's whose blood it is!" I try and look at them now, the tall city buildings behind, the sun behind one. Their white shirt perfectly white.

Shannon leans back, swivels in their chair a bit. "The story seems . . . a little far-fetched."

"Jake would never make it up. I remember when he got out of all that. When he was a kid. He was really messed up." The holes of my son's childhood filled up. The things I wish he'd never seen, never knew he's seen. As useless as the rest of me.

"That makes it even worse, Lou. I mean, what if we got forward with this and the kid died since? Or died from that? There are too many unknowns. It'd be too easy . . ."

I get their meaning even before they do. "You don't think? What the hell? You don't know my kid. You didn't see him cry like a baby."

"It doesn't matter what I think. It matters what I can prove." Shannon leans forward again. "And that's on me. They only have to cast doubt. This could cause doubt."

"But can't we do that too? I mean, there's not even a body!" The last word echoes.

"No, but." They sigh deep. "The river's always been a good hiding place. Lots of bodies never come up again. It's a, sadly, too common story."

"But my kid, these people don't know my kid. He could never, would never." My voice shakes so I stop. Look away again.

I am grateful when Shannon doesn't say anything.

I take a breath. Gather. Resolve. But when I look back, their shiny eyes are full of pity.

I take another breath. The silence grows uncomfortable.

"That's a really nice blazer," I say and believe it. "Where'd you get it?"

I check my phone after I leave. After Shannon walks me to the elevator and likely doesn't think of me again. I know the drill. I do the drill. Crisis is so much better when it's not your own. I wish I was at work. I wish I was doing a home visit, dealing with something that required my full attention. But I am not. But I cannot.

When I get outside, cool in the shade between the buildings, I check my phone twice. Once to check for him, and then again for the time. He didn't text me back.

I didn't want to have my parents' relationship, what Cheryl and Joe had. Have. I hated their back and forth and back again. They say kids always want their parents together, but I never did. My parents together meant years of living in the bush, going to that stupid small-town school and hearing them fight when we went to sleep. Stupid fights. Never nasty, but all the time. Their breakups meant going home, back to the city, to Kookoo and our cousin Stella, to the school we liked and the kids that looked like us. Mom was better too, in the city, on her own. Dad was Dad. I never understood what they hung on to in each other, how Mom got quiet 'cause Dad was quiet. How she'd feel stuck and have to escape. How they'd half-heartedly date other people and we'd pretend to care. I thought it was Gabe who took up with other people in between, but now I guess it's me too.

I check my phone again. He didn't text yet, but my friend Rita calls.

"So what's the latest?"

I sip on my half-drunk coffee and smell the pissy smell of the city. I walk slow as I talk.

"He's going to take a plea deal?" she says after I tell her. "That's crazy."

"I know, but it's not looking good."

"They got nothing. Who is this lawyer? Fucking lawyers!" I can imagine her hands flailing with the word.

"Shannon's good. I trust them. They're trying to be realistic, they say."

"Hell with that. Get a second opinion. If he can sit tight then that Phoenix will show up and he can go home."

"But what if she doesn't?" It's so hot already. I need more sugar.

"It's only been what, a week? Not even?" She lets the question hang. I try and stay in the shade of the buildings. Resent the sun.

"This is bullshit," she says. "It can't stick." Ever defiant.

"I agree with you," I say, without clarifying what I agree with.

When Gabe started going up north, it was supposed to be temporary. He was going to take care of his aunt and uncle. They were elderly. He was a good guy. I was busy down here. I had my family down here. Then all that shit with M happened and I was really busy down here, really had my family. He'd come down when he needed to, took the boys to things when he had extra cash. Came down when my Kookoo died. Held my hand through the whole Ceremony and service like he'd never leave. Left the next day.

I didn't want us to stay together. It was more convenience than anything else. I didn't have time to go through his things in the closet or basement. Made more sense for him to stay with us when he came down.

Then sometimes he'd buy me a bottle of my favourite wine. Sometimes he'd cook his specialty lemon pepper chicken we all loved. Sometimes he'd brush my arm so gentle and innocent and I knew I'd move toward him when Baby went to bed. I would take his hand and lead him into my room, our room, and I'd feel whole again, for a while.

Jake's face looks sunken, his skin pale. The plastic between us gives off a glare that blurs his eyes until he sits down across from me. Close enough to touch. But I can't touch him.

"Are you getting any sleep?" A practical question.

He shrugs. His hands under the table. I didn't check if they were still cuffed before he sat down.

"I just met with Shannon."

His eyes widen. "Did they find Dug?"

I try and use the best words. "They didn't think, they're not going to go that way." The certain ones. Or at least definitive.

"Why not? He's a good guy. He'd have my back. Last I heard he was in Saskatoon. Maybe Regina." His turn to ramble.

"He'd be hard to find."

Something passed over him, and he leans back. The glare. The shadows.

"How's Baby?"

"He's good. They take him swimming, like every day. He likes that." I want to be more reassuring than that. "He's okay, Jake. We're all okay."

"I know." It's the crack in his voice, not his red eyes that give him away. He's always been like that. Even as a little boy, even that time his arm broke in two places. He still tried to be so tough.

"You too. You're going to be okay too." I reach out. My hand stretched across the clear plastic. I am just showing him my palm. It does nothing.

When I get my phone back, there's finally a text.

"Sorry, was working. I have some time this afternoon."

Finally something to do.

I didn't mean for it to happen. It was all so inappropriate. Likely that was its appeal. He'd come to the pub I went to. I'd seen him around. He seemed familiar. Sometimes familiar means you should know a person. Sometimes it means you already do.

It wasn't that I stumbled over, but I'd had a couple drinks to get the courage.

I stuck out my hand. "Lou."

He took it with a smile I would come to know so well. "Tom."

I was talking to him twenty minutes when I finally figured it out. Cop. Beat. Just made detective.

"Oh shit, I have met you!" Then when I thought better of it: "On the job. I'm a social worker."

"Yeh, yeh, I thought you looked familiar. Do you remember when?"

I'd had two white wines, a good day, and didn't want to get into it. "Sorry, no. It'll come to me." And smiled. Tried to look flirty. Like I knew what that even looked like.

We barely made it into the car. He said he'd drive me home. He wasn't drinking. He seemed so smooth and I liked that he wasn't drinking.

"I do drink," he explained as we walked. "But I have an early morning, you know."

I did.

We smiled at each other like little kids.

Our hands brushed as we walked and he took mine.

I shivered. It was early spring then.

He put his jacket around my shoulders,

opened the passenger side door for me,

I pulled him in.

We had enough sense to move to the back seat, but not before the emergency brake bruised my back. He held me tight and looked at me long. It unravelled me. I closed my eyes to keep away from him. Thank god he had a condom. I hadn't carried around condoms since I was a kid.

We moved like we knew each other. We fit into that tight back seat like we belonged there. I had never done anything like that before. Not like that.

He kept hold of me even after. When we exhaled and were still and he stayed there inside me. I let my eyes open. The air hot. The windows steamed. And he was looking at me. Looked like he knew me. Like he could love me.

I couldn't get enough. I'd meet him whenever I could. Whenever he got off work early. Whenever I did. We'd go to this hotel in the afternoons. A nice one. Near work so I didn't have to go home. He never pushed. He never asked. He'd pull my hair gentle until my neck was exposed and then kiss wet there. Soft.

Eventually I even kept my eyes open.

I didn't tell him about Jake, Baby, anyone. Didn't tell him where I really knew him from. That horrible day when my niece M was hurt. His uniform at the time. My curtness. I didn't want this Tom anywhere near that one. Or anyone else. I wanted him all to myself. I'd never had anyone all to myself. I was in no hurry to give that up.

Before all this anyway. Now I don't even know what I want.

"I'm sorry I didn't get back to you," he says when I get in his car. I love his car. It's not even a great car. Just a place I like to be. "It's been a pretty intense couple days."

"Tell me about it."

Instead of answering, he says, "How are you? What's up?" It's not that we didn't talk about things. We talked about all sorts of things.

I take the measure of the side of his face as he drives.

"Where we going?" he says with a devilish smirk. If only I was in that mood. I appreciate his generosity though. I didn't even shower this morning.

"You're a cop, right?" I start.

"Last time I looked." He smiles his great smile.

"Can I tell you a case, hypothetically, and get your take on it?" I am figuring out how to ask the big ask. How much he liked me. What rules would he break to get me more information.

"Hypothetically, sure."

I give it all in bite-size pieces. "Okay, it's this kid, like twenty, never been in trouble before. Had an alleged altercation with someone he'd had a history with. Not violent history, but motive, right? Was seen with this person and now this person disappeared. Likely took off but no one knows."

His face looks serious. I like that he's taking it seriously. "Why is it likely this person took off?"

"Because they're like, they're like that. They just got released from prison, prone to violent and bad decisions, likely took off."

He goes slowly over the Provencher Bridge, turns left. Nothing.

"A murder charge can't stick without a body, right?"

He pulls over by the old fort. The park there. I hope he isn't thinking of making out now. I really want to jump into that convenience store we just passed.

My hands are shaking, so I rub them together to make it stop.

"Lou," he starts. Puts the car in park and turns to me. Too serious.

"I sound like I'm talking on a TV show, don't I? 'Sticking a murder charge.' It's all so ridiculous." I try to laugh.

"Lou," he says again, and I can see it in his eyes too. Pity.

I take a breath. A long one. I want to leave.

"I can't tell you anything about Jake's case." The words seem unreal. Like I imagined them. "I'm sorry, Lou."

"What are you . . . ?" I exhale and try to smile. "I was just talking hypothetical."

"I know, but I know. About Jake. About Phoenix."

That name, more than him saying my son's, gets me even more.

I'm crying before I even realize. Tears blur my sight, drip down my skin. I wipe at them hard.

He reaches for my hand but I pull it away before he can take hold. Thinking.

Finally, "How long have you . . . ?" I don't even know what to finish.

"Known who you were? Since I met you. The moment, actually. You're not easy to forget. Even when you're a victim's tough aunty giving me a hard time." Is he actually laughing right now?

"Why?" The word cracks.

"Not my place, I guess." He sighs, rubbing his hands on his legs like they're sweaty. "I mean, if you said it, that would be different, but I didn't think you wanted to, or even remembered me, so I didn't say anything. Either way, it didn't seem like my place."

I thought of these boundaries. Professional. I had done something like that before. Well, not like this.

He looks so vulnerable sitting there. Maybe I did want to make out.

"Why say something now?" I ask him as if I'm brave.

He speaks slowly. Aggravatingly slowly. "Now? Now is different, don't you think?"

And I spit back, "Because you know about Jake. Or think you do."

He nods. "I know about Jake."

"Well then, you know he'd never do this. He's never even been in trouble before." My hand out, pointing at him. Like I have a point.

"Lou." There's that pity again. Fucking pity.

"Fine, you can't tell me, you can't even tell *me*. About my own kid." I slump down in the seat a bit. I want to be anywhere but here.

"It'd be different if he was a kid. And this was official and everything."

Official how? Is he really asking me this right now? And then I realize he means if he was the cop and I was the parent of the accused.

"He's the nicest person. He'd never hurt anyone. Never even been in trouble."

He says nothing. Doesn't have to. Because we both know that isn't true.

Tom drives me home. It's the least he can fucking do. I give directions in short sentences, and fold my arms in front of me as we go. Don't let him get anywhere near me. I think of our hotel nights. I think of lying beside him, the blinds open to the lights of downtown. It felt like we were as revealed as we were hidden, lying there in the dark. Naked with the blankets on the floor. Just us and the white sheets. Not cold at all. He smiled in the dark. He smiled across to me in the dark. He made me feel safe.

We pull up to my little brick house and I look at it awhile. The day still bright out. Baby still at program. Don't have to get him 'til four.

I turn to this man. He turns to me. Knowing.

"Want to come in?" I try on my best let-him-know-I-need-something-but-not-too-needy voice. "I gotta take a shower but you can come in." Best to acknowledge my obvious undesirability at the moment.

"I don't know, Lou." He always plays a bit of the hard-to-get.

"Come on. It'll be fun." As if I'm upbeat. I keep smiling. Not too big. Can't do too big. It's pity sex. We both know that. But I try not to look too pitiful.

He undoes his seatbelt.

I put my key in the lock but the door opens. I hear the beep of Baby's video game and look into the living room. My kid on the floor, head arched up to the screen.

"What are you doing home? How'd you get home?" My arms out behind me, as if shielding this man from my home, my child.

More beeping. The microwave this time. I hear something and see Gabe in the kitchen doorway.

I can only stand there, but poor Tom can't get away fast enough. I don't even think he says a full sentence, just a sort of "Okay, take care," then waves stupidly, like he's a colleague. I watch the door close behind him before I move. Then I kiss Baby's sweaty head and go to deal with his father in the kitchen.

"What are you doing here?"

"Cockblocking, apparently." He gets a cup out of the microwave and blows on it. I can smell the stale coffee he had reheated from what was left in the pot. I hate when he does that.

"Fuck off," I whisper. "I told you not to come."

"Well, so sorry to interfere with your poonch, Lou, but our son is in fucking jail." His matter-of-fact fuck-you tone.

"My son, not yours, mine." My gesture like claws in front of him.

He leans back, makes himself taller somehow. "Oh don't do that. Don't try to pull everything away 'cause you're scared. I'm scared too, Lou."

"What the fuck do you even know? You haven't even fucking been here." My voice struggles to stay low. But still be cutting.

"Evidently," he mocks.

"Fuck off. I can do whatever I like." I point at myself now. Trying to convince us both maybe.

"Even cops, hey?" His trying-to-be-funny annoying tone.

"I can." Then I think. "How'd you know he's a cop?"

Gabe just shrugs. I know, cops have a walk. Social workers have a smell. We're all so fucking obvious.

If only that was my biggest problem. If only this was.

I sit down hard in the chair. Stretch my arms in front of me and rest my head.

Gabe comes behind me, hand to my shoulder. Almost a rub. More gentle.

"Want some coffee?" He offers his cup.

"Yeh," I breathe. "But not that nasty old shit. Make fresh."

He pushes an unopened bag of chips across the table to me before he goes to the sink. Old Dutch Ketchup. Big bag.

I inhale for real, for what feels like the first time all day.

DETECTIVE TOM SCOTT

When Tom heard the video game, he knew something wasn't right. Then he looked over and saw the big guy, this tall, beefy man standing in a doorway across the room.

Tom took an immediate step back. He would have kept moving out the door but Lou turned, gave him this apologetic smile. Her hair was greasy and she looked haggard but still somehow hot. Still Lou.

She didn't say anything but looked like she was pleading with him to, so Tom had to think fast.

"Oh, you know what? I think I forgot that . . . thing, report," he stumbled and then gathered himself in his best sympathetic professional tone and posture. "Why don't I go and get that and I'll come back later."

She had nodded. The large man over her shoulder across the room didn't change his expression. He wasn't convinced at all.

Tom backed out quickly, hands up at his waist in case of any sudden moves. As soon as the door was closed he booked it back to his car.

He didn't know the whole story, obviously. There could be an explanation. How the hell would he know? He went over it all in his head as he drove, knew she had a younger kid, never talked about the ex except that he was gone. Tom didn't think they were still together. But you never know. Maybe Lou had her reasons and didn't say anything. He didn't worry about Lou. Why the hell would he judge her for that? But the guy, he had a good foot of height on Tom. His hands made the mug he was holding look tiny. The last thing Tom needed was a beating from some jealous ex, or current partner.

He went back to the station. Back to his desk with reports still to write. It'd been a hectic time. He was going to make the big arrest. The case was strong. He did a good job, might even get a commendation, or at least a pat on the back by those who matter. He'd made detective a year ago. It was a big deal. He wished he could have shared it with Lou. Wished he could have told her how good he was doing, how impressive. But even he wasn't that cruel.

He'd known who she was immediately. Weeks before they actually met. Fridays at the pub. He wasn't surprised. The place was downtown, and both the child welfare office and the public safety building were nearby. Lots of social workers, and he remembered she was one. He remembered her well, the good-looking, tough aunty who stood all of her five four right up against him. He was so green back then, so earnest and trying to do good with all that. He's almost embarrassed to think of it, how scared he was of everything. At least he's grown a pair since.

She was so hot, of course he noticed her. Back then, even in all that craziness, she still was halfway put together. Like a sexy, cocky librarian with these gorgeous eyes that seemed to see right through him. She was hard to forget. So, when he saw her across the pub, walking like she did, with purpose and so unselfconsciously, he knew who she was in an instant. She didn't move like some women who walk like they expect everyone to be looking at them. Lou didn't give a shit if anyone was looking at her. She was somehow confident and shy at the same time. He didn't talk to her. Didn't want to start anything. But kept going there at the same time, Fridays, in case she was there, too. In case she wanted to talk to him.

It was a few weeks before she came over. Had gotten into the wine and smiled at him invitingly. Tom felt her all over, instantly. Like not felt her up but felt her as she stood in front of him, as she moved just inches from him. He sat on a stool. She leaned one hand on the bar. They moved toward each other in small increments as they talked, moving closer but moving away at the same time. Like dancing or swimming or something. Tom's head felt light. He was completely sober.

He offered to drive her home, and it seemed innocent enough. He took the risk of taking her hand once they turned down Princess, out of sight of the busy street, and she grabbed hold eagerly. He could barely walk he was so hard. She leaned in as they went, tilted her head toward him, close enough he could smell her, feel her warmth, a small gesture that would come to drive him nuts. When she pulled him into the car after her he almost came right there. She was wild the way people are supposed to be. Not like how some women are, the ones trying to be wild to seem wild. Lou was truly wild. Tom could not get enough of her.

"Hey may-tee, I heard about your good haul."

It was his old partner Christie, a sack of shit of an old guy who should have retired years ago. They finally made him run dispatch, so now Tom has to see the asshole almost every day.

"Yeh, looks like it." Tom feigns modesty. He knows the old fart is eating his hand with jealousy. Christie never made higher than beat cop.

"Looks like it. Shit. I wish you worked so fast when you worked with me." He laughed his guttural, fat-man laugh.

Tom smirks and keeps walking. The best way to deal with guys like Christie was to know you had something better to do.

It was a good haul and people were taking notice. He did basically solve a murder case in like, a day. Everyone knows things like this are pretty cut-and-dried but that doesn't mean they're easy. Gangland stuff is obvious, it's a small world really, same guys doing different things in rotation, but try proving that, try connecting the dots and getting all your ducks in their rows. But he did, he did that. He was proud of himself. So proud. He wishes it wasn't so plagued by the idea of what would happen if Lou found out.

As if she reads his mind, she texts right then.

"Hey sorry about that. The ex comes down whenever he feels like it. Never a warning. Next time?"

Tom knows she's trying to distract herself. Obviously she's worried about her son, and her family. He doesn't want to take advantage or anything but doesn't want to say no either. "Friday?"

"Sure," she gets back right away. No games with this one. When she wants something, she goes for it.

He's really glad the guy is an ex. Even if that's bullshit, he wants to believe it. He's glad she said it.

They mostly go to this hotel, nice place, discreet. A place none of their chirpy colleagues would frequent. It's their place, their time. The rooms are clean and the king-size bed soft and warm. Or that was Lou. Or both. It became this addictive sanctuary where they got to leave their lives and be together. They never talked about anything big. Until today Lou never asked him for anything. Most times, they'd start kissing as soon as they saw each other. Like they were pulled by ropes and strings until their bodies pressed together. Until there wasn't any space between their skins. They'd fuck intensely, sometimes quickly, that first time. Then they'd hang out, order room service, do it again. It was like they had to, they couldn't help it.

Sometimes he'd pick her up, and when she'd get in the car her hand would go right to his thigh. So quick he didn't even see, but he came to expect it. She touched him as soon as she could. Her hands belonged on him, moving slowly, slow enough. She'd run her fingers up and down his leg, walking them softly until he was so fucking ready, it was work to drive. She wore a G-string because he'd joked that he liked them, she waxed herself and said she did it because she liked the feel of it. She started working out because he said some bullshit about being healthy and she told him he was right. Honestly, he didn't care what she did. Why would he? Everything about her tasted good no matter what.

They never got routine. As predictable as their meetings became, the fucking was always new, different, like something to find. He didn't tire of her yet. And that was saying something. It'd been months.

He knew it was her kid right away. The case unfolded easily. Like a map in front of him, a place he knew really well. Phoenix Stranger, just released, didn't check in to her halfway house on day 2. Tom didn't need to look anything up to remember everything about that girl. All her assault charges didn't surprise him. She was a real piece of work. They only let her out because they had to. Kids like that usually either go right back in or get in trouble. For Phoenix, it was trouble.

The list of possibles seemed like it could be pretty long. Tom was going to interview her uncle first, this equally messed-up piece of work who went by the street name Bishop. He'd obviously know something but say nothing, but Tom had to start somewhere. No one was thinking of the family, the original victim's family, Lou's family. It's not like he wanted to be thinking of them either. But it was an obvious question. And Lou's kid, he knew Jake had been in trouble before, had a connection with some banger named Threat who ran a crew. He'd looked it up after this one time she mentioned her eldest "turning his life around," which meant trouble. He had to look it up to be sure. He couldn't be fucking some banger's mom. It's not like him and Lou were anything other than hotel mates, really. But still. So really, when this went down, Jake was the first person he thought of. Instinct. Right place at the right time, but Lou wouldn't think so. He put it off, is what he's getting at, he didn't mean to, until that witness called it in.

He couldn't ignore that. A matching description, a reliable account, the old lady could be sure it was Phoenix. It was strong.

He should have passed the thing off right there, on conflict of interest, but it was so easy. Tom knew all the connections he made were from the previous case and not because of his relationship with Lou. It's not like it looked bad or anything, just that he had a good memory. No one knew about Lou, so as long as that didn't come up anytime soon, he'd be good. For the moment, he could get some good credit on a bigger case, and he really needed to make an impression these days. Jake had motive, means, opportunity, and when they picked him up, the idiot even still had the knife.

Tom didn't want to go to his place of work, didn't want to do him that bad, but picking him up at home was too risky. His apartment building was a three-storey walk-up, lots of exits, too many things could go wrong if Jake decided to run. So they chose to go to his work. It wasn't an arrest, only a "come with us," and Jake did. Didn't say a thing, walked out with his head held high. Nodded at this other worker, a couple young kids. Tom felt bad for all of them, all too young to deal with all this crazy shit. He got the uniforms to take names for later interviews, but yeh, felt bad about it.

Once they got Jake in, he wasn't talking. Didn't say shit about the knife. They could have charged him on that alone. When it came back with blood traces, he came up with this stupid-ass story of his friend getting stabbed and not by him. Tom looked up the name and the story, but there was nothing. He followed up on Jake's far-fetched idea of this person being in Saskatchewan, thinking he might get more charges out of it, never know. But there was nothing there.

In the end, Jake sat in Remand to sweat it out, and Tom did the boring work of writing the reports. Part of him wanted to get it all over and done with, but he also knew he'd never be over with it. Even if he got away with this part, if it went to trial he'd have to testify. One way or another Lou was going to find out. Sooner or later. Likely sooner.

Tom goes home early. It's a slow day, a weekday and too hot to do much damage, so nothing new comes up. It's different on the weekends. Weekends in summer are like full moons, anything can happen, and most of the time anything does. It's best he rest up now. Summer's just getting started. He thinks about texting Lou again, checking up, being a good guy, but figures she'll be busy. Figures he should really start making his exit now, wean himself off of her before things get really fucking messy. Not that this isn't all messy, but thus far, Tom can at least keep his hands clean. He doesn't want to let it get so bad that he can't. Doesn't want to have to answer for this. And it's not like he did anything wrong. He was doing his job. The law is clear, the evidence irrefutable. If he didn't think Jake did anything wrong that would be different, but he knew he did. He felt it. He had good instincts on this kind of thing, after all. He felt bad about it but he also knew he was right.

So he didn't call Lou. He'd see her on Friday. He'd get their hotel room and spend some time in her arms, between her legs. He'd make her feel better too. He was all about making sure she had a good time and knows she always did. She wasn't exactly quiet about those kinds of things. Not like some.

Maybe then he'd stay away from her. Maybe then, after one more time, he could say goodbye. Or maybe her situation would get unmanageable and she'd end it. He wasn't opposed to that. He'd feel bad, sure, but he'd totally understand. He'd miss her. He is going to miss her like fucking crazy. One day. Probably soon. No helping that.

Tom pulls up in his driveway and pulls his thin wallet out of his jacket pocket. He likes to spend a moment, when he gets home, looking at his house. The curtains are open but he can't see in. The sun's still out. It'd been a while since he'd got home while it's still light out. He looks forward to the evening ahead. Olivia would still be up and he could play with her awhile before she went to bed. Hannah was so crazy about their daughter's bedtime so Olivia was usually asleep when he got home. Hannah was like that about their daughter. Hannah was like that about everything.

Tom reaches into his slim leather cardholder to get his ring and slips it back on his finger. But he doesn't get up, not just yet. He's not ready to be husband and father yet. He wants to sit in his shut-off car another moment, trying to breathe. Trying to breathe it all out of him, first.

'SHIP/ALEX

'Ship picks up the phone and listens to his own Uncle Toby's raspy desperation.

"Have you heard anything new, Alex? I'm starting to get real worried over here." Uncle Toby's old voice choked like he was gonna cough. His old-man cough getting worse. "I haven't been able to get ahold of Elsie for weeks. Like over a month, maybe."

'Ship thinks of his sister with his usual anger at her uselessness, didn't think it was a mystery where she was. "Don't worry about Elsie, Uncle. You know she figures herself out."

"You say that but she struggles. She's struggling, Alex. Especially now with all this? Hate to think what she's going to do." Uncle Toby no doubt shaking his head back and forth like he does. Worrying about his family 'cause he feels like it's his job. 'Cause he's the only Elder left to worry about those who come after him.

'Ship scoffs but not loud. Toby'd been getting upset a lot since he went to the home. Like somehow being around all those other old people made him realize he was really fucking old, too. But 'Ship didn't give a fuck about his waste-of-space sister. He knew what she would be doing. "It's gonna be fine, Uncle. Wasn't Elsie getting all spiritual out in the bush somewheres?"

"Yeh, but she came back in. And then was gone again. You know I think the worst."

"She'll turn up."

"Hopefully they'll both turn up," Uncle says, thinking of Phoenix, their other missing family.

"Yeh" is all 'Ship can say. Slowly, quietly. More like a breath than anything. "Listen, Uncle, I gotta go."

"Sure, sure. I'll let you know if she picks up the phone."

"'Kay, 'kay." 'Ship clicks off probably too fast but he has stuff to do.

'Ship'd always been a good man. He looks to and strives to be like good men. Strong men. Men who get things done. He's read all the biographies and autobiographies of those men he admires. His favourite is *The Autobiography of Malcolm X*. The way ol' Malcolm articulates the struggle and puts things together in ways no one had ever done before. Malcolm showed the line between nothing and something, between racism and oppression in a way 'Ship had never seen before. He rereads it now and then. It makes things clear for him. He's read all the others too. *Monster*, about Sanyika Shakur, was decent but sounded like the ghost writer didn't know what he was talking about half the time. At least ol' Alex Haley knew his shit and obviously respected the fuck out of Malcolm. Like who wouldn't. Of course *The Ballad of Danny Wolfe* was exciting 'cause it was 'Ship's own town and his people, but again the guy writing it didn't know, didn't know what it was like, didn't know what he was talking about. White gaze, they call it. Uppity classist privileged-as-fuck gaze is what 'Ship calls it. People who take choices for granted, who really don't know what it feels like when you don't have any.

They knew though—Malcolm, Sanyika, Danny. They knew it all, a hell of a lot more than 'Ship for fucking sure. They knew they did what they had to to protect their own, to keep their own. No one should ever doubt that. 'Ship never would.

Not that he can write for shit, so who the hell is he to talk. But still. If he ever gets a book written about him, he hopes to hell the person writing it will at least respect the shit out of him. That he is a man worthy of respect. Even if they don't fucking know, they should know that.

'Ship is a good man, has been taught to be a good man. Had a good dad, a scary-as-shit mother, and a bunch of great men along the way who told and taught him what was most important in this life. Family. However and whomever. Family. End of fucking story.

Kyle's down. Of course Kyle's down.

They meet up where they meet and break it all down. They were gonna get the boy outside but hadn't moved fast enough.

"Threat said he'd move aside. Kid ain't nothing to him no more." Kyle smokes a lot when he's working.

'Ship leans back, nods. He never liked Threat but this feels like respect. "Good, good." He sees it all out in front of him. He likes to do that. Visualize. Kyle knows 'Ship so well it's like he sees it all too.

"I'll go in tonight. Get a look around tomorrow. You sure he still in Remand?"

'Ship nods. Doesn't have to tell him how he knows.

"'Kay, den," Kyle says and lights another smoke.

'Ship sticks his chin out to get one too.

"Thought you quit, man," Kyle says but hands the pack over.

"Twelve long fucking hours." 'Ship inhales long. "Nicking out'll kill you faster than cancer."

"Or you'll kill someone." Kyle laughs, like he does. Out loud with his head back.

'Ship tries not to think about that. "Something like that."

Kyle looks, like he does, a little too long. Anyone else would get punched for a long look like that. Anyone but Kyle. "It's all good, man. No worries. No worries."

"No worries," 'Ship says like he's somewhere far away. But then he remembers. Kyle. His brother. He doesn't trust anyone more than he does Kyle. "None," he says, resolved. "None at all."

Family means different things to different people but for the most part it's all about who you love and who loves you back. Who you gotta take care of and who takes care of you. People think gangs aren't family, friends aren't brothers, but those are the fuckers lucky enough to have whole families who take care of them. Truth is when you come from less, then you need, by definition, more. People who have it all, the privileged, it's like they have the whole world helping them—institutions, systems, schools, businesses, they're all theirs. When you don't have that, you can either fight your way in or make something new. That's what gangs do. They make something new. It ain't perfect, it ain't pretty most of the time, but it belongs to those who work it. It was built by those who need it, who didn't have anything to begin with. And it stays where it was made. If you really think about it, is it any different from, say, the big businesses destroying Mother Earth or banks destroying poor people every day? Shit's dirty, but it's all fucking dirty. Don't look down on those who do it on the street 'cause you're doing the same fucking thing in a fancy boardroom.

'Ship turns up Aerosmith on his way home. Likes that old stuff. It makes him homesick for his dad's old shop and all the old guys he was brought up with who taught him how to do. How to say things without saying them, how to know just by knowing. That was how he learned. His dad, Sasha, was hard as they come when 'Ship was a kid. No one ever crossed his dad and got away with it.

This one time, this guy, who knows the guy's name, some old punk tried to rip off his dad with a piece-of-shit car. But Sasha never even got mad, only got the guy back to his shop and kicked the living shit out of him. Didn't ask for help even though he'd get it from any of his boys standing around looking. Didn't even look mad, just did it.

And the guy, bleeding on the ground, yelled up, "Who the fuck you think you are? God?"

It was a stupid thing to say. Sasha, face red from giving all those kicks, looked down at the guy and said, "I'm your fucking God. I'm the Pope, me," he said and laughed.

All those guys called him the Pope from then on. Laughed about it and told the story over and over about what happens when you cross Sasha. What happens when you cross any of them. What you do.

Fucking Pope. Sasha loved it though. Made the most of it. Called everyone around him Cardinal or Bishop, shit like that. It was a laugh. But for 'Ship it stuck. Bishop to everyone. Even his girl called him that. Street names are like real names. Like those given-in-Ceremony kind of names. Names that become who you are and what you're supposed to do. His dad naming him, that gave him a job. A person to be.

His dad's all retired now. Spends his time going wherever he wants. Passed on his legacy to his son, like you're supposed to. And 'Ship does it. 'Cause he's supposed to.

"Did you get those pictures I sent you?" Angie yells from the kitchen. Not even a hello or nothing.

'Ship slams the door too hard and his kids jump on the couch.

"Sorry, guys." He laughs and goes up to hug them both, together. They squirm and moan but he does it anyway. He needed that.

He walks up to his woman but she's on him right away. "Did you get those pictures?"

"All's I got was four pics of yellow. That what you talking about?"

"For the bathroom. I can't decide. Which one do you like?"

"They're all yellow."

"They're different shades of yellow."

"Look the same to me."

"Well, I'd like your opinion. You're always like 'whatever, I don't care' and then you complain you don't like something."

"Whatever, I don't care." But he smiles and reaches around her, bringing her whole body in. He has loved this woman since he was basically a child. It's like they've always grown together. He couldn't ever fit this good against anyone else.

"You're such a fucker," she teases with a slap on his arm.

"Promises, hey?" He inhales her. He wants another cigarette but inhales her instead.

"'Ship, I wanna talk to you."

"Mmm." He could sleep here, against her. He could sleep right now.

"'Ship!" She moves away, turns to face him. "I really want to talk about this. I think we should go see your brother."

"Why the fuck? I haven't seen him since he left."

"Because he's your brother. Because he reached out. Because—"

'Ship moves away from her, far away. This was the last thing he needed right now.

"'Ship. He's family. What do you always say, all the time? 'It's all family, family.'" Her stupid mocking him all the time. "Shit, 'Ship, you're like a *Fast and Furious* movie or something. Well, he's family."

That was fucking it. 'Ship has enough to deal with. And he's so tired. "Jesus, Ang, he's not family. You think that fuck is family? He isn't. He left, took off the second he was eighteen. He left it all to me. With our fucking parents. Fucking Margaret. I had to deal with fucking Margaret, by myself. And everything. Fucking Joey didn't take anything fucking on. It was all me. Family ain't just blood, Ang, you know that. Family is who acts like family. Joe only acts for himself." He knows he's yelling so he stops. Knows his kids were gonna be still as statues on the couch waiting to see what happens next. He remembers being that kid, waiting for your dad to stop yelling. So he got quiet. Has nothing left to say.

"'Ship." Ang reaches out, but he moves his arm so she can't touch him. "'Ship, I know he hurt you . . ."

"Hurt me? Fucker *wishes* he hurt me. No, he didn't hurt me. He destroyed anything I have for him though. I don't care if he sends my kids blankets. Blankets don't make up for abandoning your brother when your brother's still a kid."

"He wanted to find his own way. Your mom, you know your mom was such a piece of work. None of you guys turned out all okay. I mean, look at your sister."

'Ship scoffs. He really doesn't want to think about Elsie in all this. Right now. Fuck Elsie.

"Think about it, okay? I think it'd be fun. We can make a road trip out of it. Show the kids the mountains. Hell, I've never really seen the mountains."

'Ship scoffs again, doesn't want to start anything else. Let her have this. He doesn't need this today. Shouldn't've gotten into it at all.

Ang seems satisfied with his silence and gives him a kiss on the cheek. Like she's won. She does that sometimes.

It's not a bad idea, getting a camper or some shit, taking his kids across the mountains. Ang has some holidays coming up, summer is getting started, and the kids are bored already. Maybe they can do that anyway, fuck his waste-of-space brother.

His mom was tough, it's true, but how both his siblings ended up so selfish, he'll never know.

Family is business and business is family. These things don't have a line between them when you're fighting every day. 'Ship will be sad about Phoenix one day. He will mourn his niece. She was fucked up and gave him nothing but grief but she was family. More than blood—blood and then some. She was messed by the system and some sick fuck and then the system again, and again. As much shit as she caused, it wasn't her fault she ended up like that. She shouldn't have been taken out like that.

But more than that, that little uppity fucker Jake shouldn't have stepped so far out of line that he thought he could get away with doing that. That is a problem. Because if he thinks he can, then others think they can. If he does, others could. It's that Jake fuck who's made this fucking mess and 'Ship's gotta clean it up now. Simple as that. Eye for an eye. Those who say the thing about everyone being blind don't understand that reciprocity is simple. You do good, you get good. You do bad, you get worse. There are rules and there are ways, and this Jake stepped out of those. You can't do that. 'Ship can feel for him. Seems like he's just a stupid young little shit. But 'Ship also knows he has to do something about it. It's a system. A business. And that only works if you do your part. If 'Ship let it go, it wouldn't just hurt him. Threat knows that. They all know that. Because it's true. Because if everyone'd protect their own then everybody'd be covered, and we wouldn't have to worry about any of this shit anymore.

The kids went to sleep before ten, and Ang was looking fine in his old sweats and no bra. A good night. 'Ship is feeling good by the time he goes out on the back step for his middle-of-the-night smoke. He likes it out here, smelling the old cedar tree and looking out into his small backyard. He loves that fucking tree. The reason he bought Ang this house, really. Could've bought her anywhere, she liked everything, but that tree was killer. It was probably twenty feet high and wide and it sprays cedar sprigs everywhere. Some Elder sometime told him those sprigs the trees drop are gifts. For smudge or baths or stuff like that. That those are the ones you're supposed to use, not pick them off the tree. He taught his kids that. Alexandra picks them like it's her job. And it sort of is.

Uncle Toby calls then, late, but Toby sometimes wakes up after an evening nap and can't go back to sleep.

"Heard from her. Heard from Elsie earlier. Thought you'd want to know."

"Yeh, sure" is all 'Ship gives him. Gives her. Fucking Elsie.

"She's still out in the bush. She knows what's going on, that Phoenix is still missing anyway. And the kid they caught."

"Oh yeh?"

"She said she thought Phoenix would just show up someplace, hey? Like she was hiding out."

"Oh yeh." 'Ship flicks his smoke away and rubs his hands together. Kyle'd be in by now.

"She thinks it'll pass so she's staying out there. Really sounds at peace, that one. Really taking care of herself. That's good, hey, Alex?"

"Yeh, yeh, for sure." Kyle'd be processed and out in gen pop by breakfast.

"I think I'm going to think like that too, be optimistic. I was really looking forward to seeing that Phoenix, haven't seen her since she was a kid. I told Shawn to bring by the other one, a while ago now, but he hasn't yet. I haven't seen that one either."

'Ship gets the hint. "You want me to bring the kids down tomorrow, Uncle?"

"Oh no, no, don't waste a whole Sunday coming to this boring place. No."

'Ship knows what that means too. "We'll pick you up. Take you to Skinner's by the river or something."

"Oh! Oh, that'd be nice. Haven't had a real ice cream cone in a while. They just have that fake soft-serve bullshit here."

"All right, then, we'll come by around lunch, okay? Now you should go to sleep."

"Okay, okay, thanks, Alex. You know, you're a really good boy. Your mom always said, 'That Alex, he's the good one.'"

"Yeh yeh, Uncle. Go to bed." But he smiles as he hangs up. As he looks up at the tree and inhales its medicine scent.

He lights another smoke. Kyle'll be in by now.

KYLE

Kyle was sorry
for all he'd done

for all he'd do

one time this boy told him
everyone is new
every day
every day is an opportunity
to be a whole different person
but that fuck was a fucking jackass

Kyle holds things
holds on
holds in
keeps his things close
knows
doesn't

he thinks of his mother
she was never well
he never realized how much
she wasn't until he was older
that not all mothers
nap all day
not all mothers
scream for nothing
she was not well
he forgives her
even if she doesn't forgive herself

Kyle hasn't seen his mother
in years
he looks for her
whenever he goes downtown
whenever he sees
a limping woman with dark hair
but it's never her
even if it is

Kyle lives simple
small apartment
weights bench
bed
couch
TV
that's it
Kyle gives his mom money whenever he sees her
even when she doesn't know him
which is always
she says thank you
holds the cash up to the sky
the old way

lockup is never different
same guys
different faces
not that different
same sounds
bangs
buzzes
they should make it all soundless
keep the lights low
everyone'd get a lot more chill
if it were quiet

someone gives it to him
to say he's not going to say
who
is an understatement
Kyle holds on
holds in
you don't say
you don't tell
just do

someone gives it to him
plastic
light
sharp
was once a toothbrush
or a serving spoon

someone else gives him
a bag
plastic
bread bag
smells like
sanitizer and
the kitchen

Kyle gives his little cousins money
whenever he sees them
he knows they buy shit
then don't have enough again
but at least they're happy
for a minute
a break in this life
a bit of what everyone else
seems to have so fucking easy

and all the time

Kyle sleeps
on and off
dreams of his mother
when he does
dreams of when he was little
and she was smiling
warm
doing well
she would hug him
all the time
walk him to school
hold his hand
across the street
be there
when he came out

the noises of lockup
get into his dreams
a bang
a scream
the motor of the air conditioning
going off
going on

breakfast
everyone bleary eyed
coffee basically piss
the boy didn't even look up
at first

it's a series of movements
seemingly connected
but also
not

bag around blade
in
up
down
out
warm

bag covers blade
sleeve covers bag
passed
passed
gone

Kyle's grandmother
used to speak Michif
only Michif
his dad answered back
in English
Kyle understood
the long French sounds
twanged with Cree
recognized them
after she died
when he heard French
when he heard Cree
but never heard them
together
anymore

the kid died
they heard by lunch
Kyle was sipping tea
that was basically piss
he was also very high
bleary eyed

one time he was at a pen
he's not going to tell you which one
they took a boy out
with a beating
about 7 of them
after lights-out
after the boy's cell was left open
each took their kicks
their part
no one did more
no less
boy took it
lay there
didn't make a sound
died by morning
was found
alone and cold
3 of them went down for it
4 of them didn't

the kid had looked up
when he felt it
was too late
already

kid was shook
didn't see it coming
obviously
not that hard
definitely
out of the game
didn't know any better
Kyle felt sorry for him
then

kid looked long enough
to see Kyle's eyes
to show Kyle how
it felt
kid looked
then
nothing
not even a sound

Kyle is sorry for what he's done
sorry
for what he will do
sorry

Kyle dreams of a house by a river
someplace out of the city
quiet
the only sound the wind
maybe a dog
an old one
trees

but he never goes
his family is here
his guys
his mom

and what the fuck he do out in the bush anyway

JOE STRANGER (MONIAS)

Joe got off work early 'cause of the rain. It was letting up but they needed to pour concrete today so there was nothing to do but wait. He didn't like losing out on a couple hours' pay but was glad to be away from the crew and all their yapping. Like chickens, those guys, never shut up. Joe's happy to get in his truck, blast some AC/DC, and get the hell out of there.

It's too early for Bree and Maisie to be home so he thinks he'll get the dogs and climb up the mountain. What he calls a mountain. Bree says it's a hill. But Joe grew up where the ground was flat flat flat, as he tells Maisie, and she thinks it's amazing. "So flat you can't even see above the trees, you never even knew what was on the other side," he told his four-year-old and her eyes widened. Maisie can't imagine this. She only remembers this place, their house trailer on the side of the mountain/hill. The view out her bedroom window is the long slope down and all trees. Her drive to daycare goes up and down and around and into town. She knows the prairies as much as he knew the mountains before he came here, which is not at all.

He unlocks the door and Rufus and WhiskeyJack bolt out like they know what he's thinking. He takes them up whenever he can, unless he's really beat at the end of the day. Sometimes in the morning too. The air is so thin up here, cold even in the middle of summer, when it's not on fire, that is. He inhales deep, the thick pine and soggy muskeg. The path isn't all that muddy 'cause it's covered with overhang, so their way is easy. WhiskeyJack cuts off Rufus to take the lead. She needs to be the first in line. Rufus lets her because he's younger, but also because he's a boy and boy dogs are ruled by girl dogs.

Joe doesn't know where this path came from. He thought it might have been an old mining path, or better yet, an ancient one from the real keepers of this land, but Bree thinks it was probably made by the hippies in the trailer park on the other side. Or the boomer ranchers who rent out this corner of their massive plot of land. Fuckers bought in in the seventies too. Crazy to think how much it's worth now, and how much they paid for it. How some people have all the luck.

Joe really likes it here. It's the longest they've been anywhere but he's happy to stay as long as he can. His job's kind of crap but it's regular at least, and Bree likes hers answering phones at the clinic. Maisie can even start school next year and there's the baby coming soon. It's wild to think Joe's setting down some real roots. He never thought he'd do that.

He left home a very young man, never looked back. Never went back either. Not when his grandma died. Didn't even think about it when his mom died. No need to go back to a place that had nothing for him. He barely took anything, an old duffle bag with clothes and some CDs, a few pictures and some old IDs from an old dead uncle. They shared the same first name, or rather, Joe was named after him. The one long dead before he was even born. The one who was the better Joe, the real Joe. He was just Joey. He took those cards so he could leave. Wasn't supposed to leave, was supposed to be on parole. But with the old cards, he could be Joe Stranger, if he needed to be. At least as long as no one looked too careful.

He met Bree in Edmonton. A friend of his buddy Shawn's new woman. The woman Shawn and Nikki set him up with so he'd leave them the hell alone. Bree wasn't even a close friend of Nikki's, never even liked her actually, but had been bored that night. Lucky for him. Bree's as crazy as he is, as moody as he is, and was motivated to get the hell out of Edmonton too. They'd been moving ever since. Taking jobs, her at resorts or offices, and him in construction, all through the mountains. Small towns with good views, she said. Quiet places with no neighbours, he agreed. Before now, they stayed places a year or two, at most. Even after Maisie—they lived in a converted van the summer she was born. Then Bree's cousin got her a job in Golden and she always liked this town, so here they went. Joe's ready though. The van's still in the driveway ready to go, just needs to be stocked and insured. But this is as roots as roots get for Joe.

There's a part in the trail, about half an hour in, when things get rocky and the ground gets a bit loose. Rufus slips but WhiskeyJack picks over the ledge like a goat. Joe's gotten better at scaling it. What he calls scaling, what Bree would say is walking on an incline. But right after, it gets to a nice landing where he can look out over the trees. Dark evergreens in every direction, up ridges and around corners. Joe feels so small here, thinks of how humans are really so small and unimportant after all.

His first ever view of the mountains was near here. When he first came out West he took the Yellowhead up to Fort Mac. He thought those hills up there were mountains, even went so far as to call them something like that out loud, and got laughed at. How the hell was he to know? Basically mountains, he thought. He couldn't get any work up there, but heard Calgary was looking for construction workers, so he took the bus down. Then one day, he was getting a ride to the worksite on the west side of town and he saw them, from a distance, sitting like monsters on the edge of the world. Mountains.

He wanted to go a bit further, even asked to, but the guy he hitched with didn't have the gas so they never went further than the site.

He kept looking over though, seeing them just out of reach for a few weeks while he waited for his first cheque. They seemed dark, shadowed somehow. They were luring him in. It made him excited, nervous. Reminded him of spooky basements in horror movies. The ones the characters have to go into even though no one watching ever thinks they should.

As soon as he could, he bought a bus ticket to Banff for no reason but to see it. Not it, but them. He was not disappointed. The closer they got the happier he felt. First one rose up beside him, then another. Soon he was surrounded by them, enveloped by them. He felt covered, protected somehow. It was a crazy thought. Not like anyone was chasing him, but if they were, they'd never find him in there.

He never wanted to leave, but jobs dry up, or crews change companies and need more ID, information. That's when he suddenly has to go somewhere else. He went back up north, more west, then east again. Edmonton, Grande Prairie, Prince George, and there around. The ground was his gauge. He never went anywhere totally flat. He stayed with the mountains at most a drive away. When he met Bree, she was already perfect, then she told him she grew up in there. Born in Hope, raised in Haida Gwaii, she's been all over. Her parents were real hippies, like still-get-high hippies, like damn-the-man hippies. Her full name is actually Breeze, and the van is her parents' old one. Joe might have fallen for all that as much as he fell for her. But she's also really beautiful.

They still take the van out on weekends, when they can. When he has no work or she can get holidays. They go out to the coast, camp in beach parking lots. The ocean a whole other mystery, all the untapped places Joe has yet to know. He wants to try surfing. Bree thinks he's full of shit because he's too afraid to even ski, but he'd totally try it. And he's not afraid of skiing, thinks sliding down the side of a mountain is a stupid-ass idea only good for a concussion. Nothing like the smooth glide that surfing must be. Out there on the water. That quiet, sunny, salty quiet. Maybe. He hasn't yet. But maybe.

For now, he hikes mountains, even if they are just hills. He works shit jobs with low pay but Bree is happy. Maisie's happy. The dogs are panting and ready to run downhill so Joe races them through the cedars.

Bree said she's going to get a maternity leave with this one. She finally has that kind of job. They've talked about taking off then, going along the coast a while. Maybe even driving down to Mexico. Joe would even go north a bit, along the islands and up into Alaska. Beautiful country. North feels free of people somehow. Even though people are all around there. But up there they know how to let the world be the world and not mess with it too much. Same couldn't be said for going down through the States, but at least it'd be hot.

"And you could go surfing," Bree had said with a smirk. If it was anyone else, he'd think they were making fun of him, but she was never like that. Never acted like that one bit. After years of loving her, he might even believe she loves him back.

He feels happy and content, fresh air in his lungs. He thinks of the stewing meat Bree took out of the freezer and even has time to get something on the stove before his girls come home. He could make biscuits. Maisie loves his biscuits.

It's Rufus who barks first, once as a warning, but then WhiskeyJack sniffs the air and bolts out in front barking up a storm. Rufus follows close behind. Once through the trees, Joe sees it too. Someone is at his door, sitting on the steps and a bit too at ease for the dogs still circling and barking. Joe slows down and assesses. A young person, black hoodie up and shadowing the face, grey pants. He can tell they're dirty from here. They're smoking a cigarette like they don't have a care in the world. Joe figures all his moves as he walks, rifle under the bed in the van, accessible from the open back door. Baseball bat behind trailer front door. One of the few good things his mom taught him. Knives in the kitchen, of course. He thinks of their stuff and how long it would take to get everything together. They have so much stuff now, Maisie stuff, baby stuff. It's amazing how quick it adds up. They can't just throw duffle bags in the back of the van anymore. It would take a while to get out of town. Or maybe it should be him on his own. If he knew his girls would be all right if he had to go away for a while, for sure.

When he gets closer the person stands up. They're wide, curvy. Joe realizes it's a girl, with a start. Young. Something isn't right.

He slows even more and comes toward her from the side, closer to the truck, whose extra keys are under the seat.

"Hey," he says simply. "Can I help you?"

"I'm looking for Joey."

"Who's looking?"

"You must be Joey, hey? You look like Grandma Margaret. Anyone ever tell you that?"

Joe gets cold all over. The mountains can be so cold, even in summer. "Who are you?"

"I'm your niece." The kid smiles. Hand in her pocket. Stays hidden. Her smile widens, but not like it's sincere. "I'm Elsie's girl. Phoenix."

"ROBERTA"

Her Uncle Joey looks fucking nervous. He's a tall, skinny version of her other uncle, 'Ship. And looking at him, looking him up and down, it's the first time she thinks about this guy being on the run, for like, years. 'Ship told her all about how he had skipped out of parole, took off and never came back. Not for anything. She thought it sounded awesome. Going off, never getting caught, like some old-fashioned exile or some shit. Real old-school shit. But this guy, he wasn't old school. Wasn't even new school. Just looked like a working guy who didn't eat enough. An old hippie van in the yard. Nothing much in it. She had a look when she realized no one was around. The truck too, and pocketed the hidden keys. Never know when you're gonna need some keys. But still she sat here, waiting for him, curious.

He stared at her like he was some crazy guy in the woods, which he basically was. At least the dogs had stopped barking.

"Yeh, you really look like Grandma Margaret. That's so funny."

"What's funny about it?" He walks past her, dangling his keys at the trailer door. "I mean, you've met her, haven't you?" She knows it's unlocked and he was faking. She hadn't gone inside though, didn't want to be disrespectful or anything. "You best come in then." His words all clipped and short. Not fucking friendly at all. Maybe he wasn't as soft as he looked.

The dogs follow him in and one goes to town on his water bowl. The other pants and waits. The trailer is older but clean, plain grey furniture and girl toys in the corner. A baby car seat by the door with a full plastic bag on top. She didn't think he'd have kids, a whole fucking family. She didn't know what she thought he'd be but not this.

"Have a seat." He turns on the tap. She sits at the dining table. Upright and in the corner, but close to the door. He fills a glass and drinks long, and not offering her anything. But after a long pause, and when the other dog finally gets his turn at the almost empty water dish, he finally asks, "What can I do for you?"

She wasn't expecting a party but fuck. She wonders if her story had turned up before she did. She didn't think 'Ship still talked to this guy but who knows. Joey had sent him a package. Or at least, had sent Alexandra something. And she'd been inside a long time, maybe something had changed.

"I was, you know, passing through." She's never said anything like that before. She laughs, it sounds so funny.

He comes a bit closer, leans on the counter. Folds his arms in front of him, even. "Last I heard you'd gone inside. Raped a girl."

She scoffs. Wondering who'd tell him and like that. "It wasn't rape, it was." She thinks on it, straightens her back. "Assault."

The guy laughs. This fucking guy.

"When'd you get out?"

"Tuesday."

He fucking laughs again. Then looks down at her, suddenly hard as fuck. "There won't be trouble here."

And then she knows. Is even a bit impressed. "I won't be no trouble, Uncle," she says with her best niece-like smile. Guy might be a part of her family yet.

He starts to say something.

"Daddy!" A little curly-haired girl bounces through the door, followed more slowly by a very pregnant pretty lady. Seeing her at the table, the little girl gets suddenly shy and burrows into Joey's side.

"Who's this? Hi!" the lady says, her eyes moving back and forth between her and her uncle.

"This is, my sister's kid," Joey stammers.

"Phoenix," she says for her own fucking self, then smiles again.

"Hi, Phoenix. It's, this is a surprise but it's nice to meet you." The lady bows like a little, with her hands in like a prayer in front of her chest. Definite hippie shit. "I'm Bree. And this is Maisie. And this"—she rubs her huge belly—"is we don't know yet." Then laughs all nice like.

"Hi." Then sensing she should explain more, or pretend to: "I was . . . travelling and remembered you lived here." Such bullshit.

"You've seen Alex, then?" Joey puts things together at last. Must be smart like Grandma Margaret was.

"'Ship? Yeh, I saw him, few days ago."

"You've come a long way," Bree pipes in, putting her stuff down. "What brings you out West?"

"Oh, you know, wandering." Because she knew this one would dig shit like that.

"Oh, I get it. I get it. You should stay for dinner, then. It's just a stew but I think we can talk Joe into some of his famous biscuits." Bree hugs Joey, gives him a long-ass kiss, and he fucking melts in her hands. This guy's not hard at all.

"Cool. Thanks. I'm going to go out for a smoke." She needs to think about her next move.

"Can I go outside?" she hears the little girl ask.

But her dad comes in with a too quick "No!" followed by a more gentle, "Not now."

She can hear them start to talk as the door closes behind her. Whispers. Unsure. She won't be able to win him over, but doesn't have to. She only has to win the lady over and she'll be fucking fine.

'Ship gave her a couple hun as fuck-off money. He didn't want her around, like even a little bit, so he pushed a couple bills at her and told her to fuck off, basically. She didn't know she was going to take off at first. First thing she did was go to the school her son went to. It was summer, she hadn't thought of that, and cursed herself when she realized it, but she walked up and down Polson awhile wondering if she could tell what house they lived in. Then a bunch of little kids ran out to play in the schoolyard. A few tired workers behind them, one with a bag of soccer balls. One of the kids had a messy braid and even ran like her baby sister had. She thought she knew, then doubted herself. Couldn't get close enough to know for sure, but stood at the fence awhile, hands hooked in the chain-link, stupid smile on her face. Watching. Imagining. A worker clocked her and she backed the fuck up, moved down the sidewalk, ready to take off.

That's when she saw him. Over to the side but right on the sidewalk, all heat score. Pretending he was looking at his phone. Fucking guy.

She looked down at her old iPod. If she needed to, she thought, she could pretend to call someone, too. An old lady across the street was like pruning her roses but not looking. The kids were still screaming and running but didn't notice anything. Why the fuck would they.

Then, when he finally looked up, she smiled at him. To her surprise, the guy didn't back down at all, he came right the fuck up.

She didn't think he had it in him.

"You Phoenix?" he said like he's all that.

She laughed. "Who the fuck are you?"

"I'm someone you're going to listen to," he said all like that and showed her this little fucking shank. Pathetic little knife all wrapped in hockey tape. This kid looked like he was in high school. Like he was late for class or some shit.

He motioned for her to go that way, and she went because what the fuck else was she going to do. Not that she was scared or thought this guy was going to cut her right in the street, in front of the kids or anything. She was curious enough to go along with it a fucking while.

She walked slow though and took a long last look at the school field, at the boy, pretending it was hers. Pretending she was here to pick him up for the day. Did that until she got to the end of the fence. Then they crossed the street and she couldn't see anymore. She still walked slow, past the houses, looking at the yards even, like she cared. She even lit a smoke to be chill, and it seemed to fucking annoy this guy so she smiled, too.

She crossed Scotia and went into the little park along the river. She'd been here before. It's a nice place to go, to smoke or sleep, if you need to. There's an old bench, a plaque for some scientist guy, and a little path down to the mucky edge of the river. Small, lots of trees.

She went to the edge of the river and lit another smoke. Even offered him one but he shook his head. He just stood there, his little knife out but not up. She shrugged and put the pack away. Looked at the river while she waited.

Finally he said: "I'm M's cousin."

"Who?"

"M. Emily."

She looked at him and shook her head. This fucking guy.

"The girl you raped."

She cocked an eyebrow. Yeh, didn't think he had it in him.

But then he really got going. "The girl you and your friends held down and raped and fucking left to bleed to death."

She took it like a blow and leaned back. After a long drag and this guy not doing anything, she said, "Not really how it happened but whatev."

"How the fuck did it happen, then?" He was angry, heated. Not calming down, rising up.

"Bitch was trying it with my man," she said and winced. Didn't mean to but remembered.

"So you fucking raped her?!"

"I didn't fucking—"

"You did! That's exactly what you fucking did. Just admit it at least." His voice cracked. He was too fucking emotional. "To yourself at least."

She flicked her smoke into the water and took a long breath. "I didn't"—useless fucking words—"didn't mean to."

"Didn't mean to? What the fuck use is that to me? To her. Didn't mean to doesn't mean fuck all."

He raised the knife a little. Maybe he would. She took a long breath. "Listen. Listen. I was a fucked-up kid. It was years ago. I was a fucked-up kid." She kept her voice even. As even as she fucking could.

"We were all fucked-up kids. We didn't go around raping people."

She nodded and looked at her shoes. The mud on the ground was mostly dry but still soft. Her cheap-ass issued shoes still mostly clean. She wished she had a new pair, something decent. She wished for a lot of things.

"You fucked her up. Bad." The knife was down again. He looked away. Stupid of him. Not much fucking fight in this one.

But she didn't have much fight either.

"I'm sorry." She didn't think it before she said it. Or more like, she thought it all the time, but didn't know she was going to say it. And when he didn't say anything, she said it again. "I am. Sorry."

But that got him all riled again. "What the fuck good is that to me, huh? To her. Huh? Your words are fucking useless." The knife was up again. He might actually fucking do this.

"Listen, listen." She put her hands up a little, trying to show him she wouldn't do anything. Then she realized, all the way through her she knew, she didn't care. Why would she care what he did to her? She dropped her hands, took another deep breath, as deep as she could, and turned to look out to the river again. "Do what you need to do," she said, more to the river than to him, or even her fucking self. "Do whatever you need to fucking do."

He rubbed his eyes with his other hand and gave out a grunt. She saw, didn't look all the way but saw. Fucker was crying.

"Fuck," he spat. "Fuck."

Then she understood. He wanted to. He would have. He couldn't.

It wasn't that she felt sorry for him. She fucking envied him.

"I'll go," she said to the river. "I'll go away and I won't bother you or your family. You'll never have to see me again." She said it all before it was even a plan.

He kept looking at her like he was trying to gauge if she was bullshitting or not. Like he was trying not to cry again. But she looked out, the brown water, the trees, the cankerworms all over, the sun blazing. She grew up on the other side of the river. The brown house with her whole family. Just over there.

"Fuck!" he spat like he was all frustrated with himself. Then she heard him stomp back up the path. When she looked, he was gone through the trees.

Right then, her body shivered with it, all of it, how close she was. For a minute she convinced herself she'd just said sorry to keep him from stabbing her. For a minute she thought she really hadn't wanted him to do it, was only saying that.

But he didn't. No one was fucking gonna kill her today.

She lit another smoke and thought about walking into the river. Thought how easy it would be to get her feet stuck in the mud and let the water do what water does. But she didn't move. She stood there as if the mud held her. She stood and smoked for a long time.

It was almost dark when she came to. It was like suddenly she had to piss, was thirsty as hell. She moved her stiff legs slowly. Through the little park and to the street, she turned quick, headed to the store.

She didn't know she was really going to leave, but she was about at her curfew so if she wanted to do something she had to do it now. Sure, she could wait another day, but another day she might feel different. So, she went. Got the first bus out of town. It was only Yorkton but at least it was in Saskatchewan so almost far enough. The next bus was Regina and then Calgary. She ran out of money there and lifted a purse in the depot. Hadn't done that since she was a kid but shit like that's basically fucking muscle memory. She hitched to Banff and stayed there awhile. It was nice out and so beautiful there. She got a few more purses and some stuff from the store. Blended in with all the tourists. Even ate caramel popcorn and took a few bad pictures of the mountains with her fake phone.

If anyone asked, she was going to say her name was Roberta. Even had the ID card from her ex-friend on her. It was in her stuff her uncle gave her. Her old bag was mostly a rag. She left it in a dumpster but pocketed the ID and the pictures. Old family photos she liked. Kept her feeling close to a bunch of people she barely knew.

The next bus was Golden. She asked at the post office about the address. She knew that much. There was no RR 2. Not really. She walked the rest of the way. Two hours along the highway. To the rundown trailer, hippie van and family. Her family. Blood.

Her uncle and his woman are still talking when she finishes her smoke. She stands out in the chilly wind awhile longer, waiting for them to stop. She'd make nice to the wife and be fine. If they kicked her out she'd come back for the truck. Or the van if she could get it started. The van would be a sweet place to live. She could go anywhere she wanted.

Or she could stay here. Nice little family. Space. Wilderness, basically. How great was this here. She would enjoy living with a little family. A sweet little girl. A new baby, even. Like a fresh start. Like a fucking home of her own.

That Joe wouldn't put up with much. Would be a grumpy old fuck, for sure. She'd known enough of her family to know they're all assholes. No loyalty. Not to her, anyway. No one ever'd been all that fucking loyal to her. Except maybe her little sister. But Cedar's better off. She missed her, and her son, Sparrow, named after her sister who died, but she's been missing them forever.

She'd call Cedar sometime soon. Once she got somewhere. Maybe she had. Gotten somewhere. Maybe they'd let her stay. Or maybe they wouldn't even let her in again.

They stop talking in the trailer. She had heard the sounds of moving and clanging from the kitchen. The mother called to the little girl, "Wash up. We're going to eat soon."

Phoenix keeps standing there. Keeps her face neutral. Like nothing is wrong at all. She's only looking, the darkening mountains behind the trailer, the yellow windows of the home, people moving inside. She is as still as she can get, and would never admit it, but she is really hoping, fucking wishing, they will invite her back in.

EPILOGUE
ONE YEAR LATER

ZIGGY

Ziggy and Cedar get to the Sundance late in the morning, and things are already well underway. Ziggy slowly manoeuvres the car over the bumpy field to find a place to park.

"Is it bad we're so late?" Cedar asks, obviously anxious.

"Nah, it's fine," Ziggy assures her. "People come and go. Visitors don't have to be here at any set time."

Cedar nods, and Ziggy looks her over. She's okay, Ziggy thinks. It's Cedar's first time meeting Ziggy's family, her first time at a Sundance, and she's a pretty anxious person at the best of times. Ziggy's gotten used to being gentle around her.

"Wanna grab that bag? I'll get the blanket," Ziggy says as she opens the trunk. She keeps her voice light but looks a little longer, wants to make sure her friend is really all right. "We can put on our skirts here."

"Like right here?" Cedar takes the crumpled skirts out of the bag.

"I put mine over my shorts." Truth is, Ziggy doesn't feel right wearing a skirt anymore. Not that she thinks she's changed her gender identity but more like she bristles against the binaries. She's tried talking to her mom about this but she doesn't quite get it.

"I just don't see why we have to wear something different," she told Rita. "I mean, guys don't have to wear anything different."

"Males do so have to wear their own thing, you know that. Skirts are about the sacredness of women."

"It feels . . . othering. And all those Moon Time rules, they don't sit right with me."

"Moon Time is its own Ceremony! C'mon, Zig. These things are pretty simple."

"Exactly. Kinda too simple. They have a whiff of the colonial, you know? Patriarchal. If women are supposedly the ones in charge and all sacred, I am pretty sure they wouldn't've inconvenienced themselves so much."

"If you feel so strongly about it, go talk to your Moshoom."

"Moshoom won't know. He may be an Elder but he's still a boomer."

"It's just a skirt."

"It's funny that we criticize other countries and cultures for making women wear particular clothes, but we don't even recognize it in our own communities."

"No one is *making* you wear anything. It's tradition. It's respect."

"I am pretty sure that's their argument too."

"Just put on the damn skirt, Ziggy!"

Ziggy walks Cedar over the flattened grass and waves to her aunties, who are hauling cases of water bottles out of a car.

"Hello, Miss Zegwan," one calls with an exaggerated wave. "Who's this?"

Ziggy gives a cheeky smile back and keeps walking. She knows they're teasing. Or going to tease. She's used to it, but she's not sure how Cedar will take it. Ziggy wants to get her comfortable a bit more before she has to meet all the relatives and their jokes.

Of course they only go another few feet before Sienna steps into their way. Makwa on her hip and Memegwa at her hand. "Hey, Aunty Zig, nice to see you," she says and immediately passes the baby over to Ziggy's arms. "Who this?"

"This is my friend Cedar."

"Cedar, hi. I'm the sister-in-law. These are the niblings. Where you from?" Sienna was never one to take her time.

"Um, Winnipeg. I guess. I'm Métis," Cedar stammers.

Ziggy wants to reach out to her but the baby squirms and needs two hands.

"Oh yeh." Sienna gives her the once-over with her chin and doesn't say anything more.

"How's Sunny doing?" Baby Makwa slaps Ziggy in the face as she talks.

"Okay so far. It's supposed to be like thirty-five degrees this afternoon. I am already tired. Imagine him."

"They start dancing at sunrise," Ziggy explains to Cedar.

"Which is like, what, four a.m. these days. He's been gone since Wednesday setting everything up. And your mom's been working. I'm sick of these kids." Sienna says this with a laugh.

Ziggy knows she's joking but she's also hinting. "Uh-huh" is all she says, putting the baby on the grass. The chubby guy immediately gets up on his feet and takes off through the cars.

"What'd you do that for?!" Sienna gives her little daughter's hand to Ziggy and races after the baby.

"Sorry, I didn't know he could run!" Ziggy calls after her. She looks down at her niece. "When did he start running?"

The three-year-old shrugs.

"This is Memegwa," she says to Cedar. "Meme, this is Cedar."

The kid just looks. And then finally, "Can I play a game on your phone?"

Cedar laughs.

Ziggy smiles. She loves it when Cedar laughs. "It's my only babysitting trick," she explains.

They stretch out the old blanket and settle in. Meme beeps away Ziggy's battery and Cedar looks at everything so intently. Ziggy sees Sienna hand the baby off to the aunties and help with food.

"I thought the dancers weren't supposed to eat," Cedar says.

"It's for the guests. The others. Us, if we want some." Ziggy knows it's probably all red meat. She believes in taking what you're given and respecting people's rules. So even if she doesn't like it, she's wearing a skirt, and even though she doesn't like eating meat, she'll eat what's served at Ceremony. She's about to explain this to Cedar when Rita pops up.

"Hello, girls. Nice to see you." Her tone a barely subtle criticism.

Ziggy groans. "Hi, Mom." The woman has a way of making her feel thirteen like instantly.

"Is this the famous Cedar?" Rita sits and curls around her little granddaughter.

"Hi," Cedar says with a shy smile. She's so shy.

"Hi, Cedar. Nice to meet you. Welcome here." Of course, Rita doesn't criticize her.

"Thanks."

"Have you been to Sundance before?"

Cedar shakes her head, and ever the good host, Rita starts to explain the finer points of what's going on.

Ziggy zones out. She sees her brother. True to his name, Sundancer has become a very committed dancer. He started as soon as he could and goes every year. The dance is hard, especially the way Moshoom does it. It's a long, arduous physically and mentally demanding process, but they all do it, every year, because their efforts help others. They do it for the people they love. Their communities, their families. It's a great sacrifice and something people are called to do. Ziggy has never been called. And weakling that she is, she thanks Creator she hasn't.

Sweat pours down her brother's face and she could cry. Every time she sees it, she appreciates it a bit more. The sun gets high. Rita finds a shade tent for the babies and makes Ziggy and Cedar set it up. They eat and talk about nothing, and slowly, slowly, Cedar talks a little bit more. Rita, of course, knows who she is. Ziggy told her last year when she found out.

"I can't believe I didn't know. I can't believe . . ." Ziggy was so upset.

"What? That Indians would know other Indians? You know what they say, small world, small Winnipeg."

"I . . . I don't know. I don't know how to feel about this."

"About what? Your friend? She didn't do anything wrong."

"But now this sister is gonna get out and I don't want this person in my house. Around me. I don't want her around Cedar, even."

"Well, you can't do much about that. But if you don't want her around you, that's a boundary you make. That's it."

"Mom, you always think things are black-and-white. It's not that simple."

"It really is, Zig. But it's not black-and-white. It's boundary or no boundary."

"But what if I say she, like, can't come to our house but then Cedar moves out?"

"Then that's her boundary and you gotta respect that."

And in the end, it didn't come to that. The sister took off and was presumed dead. And then it all became so much worse than Ziggy thought it would have been. So much worse than what she'd been dreading, what they'd been fighting about. But at least they stopped fighting.

Their roommates were going to come to the Sundance too, or at least talked about it. Izzy ended up taking summer courses so had to read something. Wynn and Phil were going to come but Phil felt there wasn't a place for them.

They're not wrong. She's brought it up to her Moshoom, but the old tried-and-true binaries are really instilled.

"Moshoom, you know some people are LGBTQ2S+, right? They should have a place in Ceremony too."

"I never keep anyone away from Ceremony. I would never discriminate."

"It's not that you're not letting people in, it's that they don't feel they have a place. It's only male or female. There are no other places."

"I know people can change genders. I don't care about that. Not my business what's in your pantses."

"It's not just either-or, Moshoom. Sometimes people aren't either-or."

Moshoom nodded like he understood, but Ziggy wasn't so sure.

That was confirmed when Sienna texted a bunch of laughing emojis, telling her Moshoom made this long speech one day, saying anyone could go wherever, no matter what was in their pantses. It wasn't quite right, but good for him, Ziggy thought, wishing she could have been there.

Ziggy and Cedar had stopped fighting and started crying, and now, a year later, they've barely stopped.

Ziggy was over visiting M, finally visiting after Jake had been arrested. Zig should have gone sooner, felt like she didn't belong as she walked through the house. As a kid, she practically lived at M and Paul's place, but it had been so long.

Little Gabey was there and looked so big. He leaned into the TV screen with a controller, beating his uncle at whatever game they were playing.

In the kitchen, Paul and Lou sat at the table in front of going-cold teas. They weren't even talking.

"Hi, Aunty. Hi, Aunty Lou," Ziggy greeted them. Unsure.

Lou's face brightened. "There she is! How's school going, Ziggy?"

They talked a bit about courses. Ziggy was taking a lot of conflict resolution and Indigenous studies, like Lou had back in the day.

"So you gonna be a social worker like your mom, then?" Lou grinned. Trying as she was, her sadness was all around her. Her worry. She somehow looked older and greyer. Too old for how old she was. Zig wanted to hug her and keep hugging her.

But instead she gave a scoff and a "She wishes!" so they could all laugh at her mom, Rita, at Ziggy, at how they were both as headstrong as each other. How everything might be okay after all.

After that she went down to see M. They hadn't seen each other in way too long. It was awkward, for that long minute things are awkward with old friends you haven't seen in too long. And then Ziggy offered a quick joke, something small and inside, so M, too, could laugh and everything could seem okay.

Ziggy pointed to the colourful drawings across the table. "So tell me about your book."

It was easy for M to talk about her book. "That's the Animikii, Thunderbird. He's the hero. He's trying to do so much good, trying to do the right thing. Kind of an anti-hero, like no one understands him, but he's really the hero. A good guy. He takes care of everyone, his family."

Ziggy smiled. "The best kind of guy."

M looked down at her work like a proud mama.

"You hear from Jake, then? How he's doing?" How do you ask after someone who's locked up?

M shook her head, saddened to be brought back to earth.

Ziggy was trying to figure out what to ask next, what to say to bring her back to something happy or even laugh, when she heard it. When they both heard it. It was a sound Ziggy will never forget. A howl. Like an animal's howl. And it was right upstairs, inside the house. Both of them looked at each other for a moment of knowing and then ran up the stairs.

Lou was on the floor, on the floor in the kitchen, and Paul was draped over her sister as if shielding her from a bomb. Or keeping the bomb in.

"No no no, Paul, no!" Lou cried. Her phone on the floor in front of her.

Ziggy came to know it all slowly, in pieces.

"What's going on?" M knowing too.

Gabey and his Uncle Pete stood in the doorway.

Paul motioned for the boy to be taken away. To be shielded from this.

Pete said, "Come on, kid. Let's go for a walk."

Gabey didn't want to, you could see in his face he knew too, but he was too young to say it.

And when the front door closed, whatever Lou was holding in, barely holding on to, was let back out again.

"No no no no, Paul! He can't be gone, Paul. He can't be." Her voice cracked and faded.

M fell to a chair.

Ziggy called her mom.

The details came out slow. Ziggy made more tea. M didn't move. Lou got quieter, then louder again, in waves.

Pete took Gabey to get some pizza, and brought back boxes that nobody touched.

Lou went upstairs to lie on Paul's bed.

M went back to her room and didn't want Ziggy to follow.

Rita arrived with a paper tray of coffees and a large box of muffins. She held Ziggy for a long time before going upstairs to hold her friend.

Eventually, Paul sat next to her nephew and told him in short, simple sentences. "I am so sorry, Gabey. Your brother got hurt. Jake got hurt in jail. Jake's gone to the spirit world, Gabey. He's going to go be with Kookoo Flora and she's going to be so happy to see him."

It was simpler than a kid that old needed, and though not intended for her at all, Ziggy appreciated hearing it like that.

She finally called Cedar that evening.

"Where are you?"

"With my dad."

"Good. Good. How are you?"

"How am I supposed to be?"

Ziggy didn't know how to feel either. It was a mess. Ziggy's truly dead friend, Jake. Cedar's uncle she didn't even know was arrested. Everyone thought her sister must be dead then. Life is like that sometimes. Stupid.

Then, months later, Phoenix called her sister. Was alive after all. Just took off, like some had said.

Ziggy doesn't know what they talked about, never heard another word about it. Cedar told everyone that her sister was okay and that was all. She stopped crying and got anxious for a while. Ziggy remembers the night Cedar sat next to her on the couch and just said, "I'm sorry," over and over. She held Ziggy and stroked her hair until she stopped crying because it was her turn to cry.

Sometimes, Ziggy thinks that it's so hard to be an Indigenous person. That all they do all the time is mourn. Grieve losses. Lose. Take turns crying. Stumbling from one tragedy to the next. She knows it's not like that, only feels like that. Sometimes. Tragedies, trauma, happen, are dealt with, and they move forward. Forever forward. They've become experts in it but also out of it 'cause if anyone knows how to get past it, to deal with it, it's Indigenous folks. They sure have had the practice.

Meme lays her head on Ziggy's lap and lets her aunty comb her fingers through her hair. Sienna nurses the baby and Rita dozes like a cat in the corner. Cedar wears a soft smile and watches the dancers like she's mesmerized.
"Pretty neat, hey?" Ziggy whispers.
"It is. It's so"—Cedar searches for the word—"soothing?"
"Healing."

They've kissed once. One night a few months ago. It was tequila and mushrooms and they took a break from being sad to laugh and party. Practise joy, Izzy had called it, and they laughed and kept saying it. Making jokes about it but really wanting it.
Cedar put her hands on Ziggy's cheeks and pulled her close. She kissed as gently as the girl walked in the world, so light it was like she wasn't even there. And in it, Ziggy tasted something she had forgotten.
The next morning and after, they never talked about it. They talked about everything. But that.

Cedar hasn't heard from her sister again. And she still barely hears from her mother. The world has let Cedar down a lot, but Ziggy won't. Even if they'll only ever be friends, Zig will love her.

Though hopefully they won't just be friends.

Ziggy watches her brother as the sun sets and the trees grow grey. His face is the same face he used to make as a kid when he was so pissed off. Sunny was real easy to piss off as a kid, and Ziggy did it often, just for fun. But now, his angry face seems to serve him. He's pouring all that anger, that rage, his own mourning, into his work. All of himself into the healing. Into the carrying. For others. The moving forward.

Ziggy doesn't know if she'll ever feel called to dance. She's only ever been a helper. She shouldn't say "only," she's been told enough times. Helping is a vital part of the whole. She knows that. She has great respect for the Ceremonies, even though she knows they aren't perfect. They have so much Power. Like the people who hold them and go to them and all those who don't, they all have it. To her, Ceremonies are a manifestation of what's inside of them all the time. Even after all this bullshit, all that's happened to all of them, it is still inside of them and coming out. Always coming out. Never stopping. Moving forward.

Some call it strength or resilience or whatever. She calls it Power.

Beautiful.

Fucking.

Power.

ACKNOWLEDGMENTS
(A VERY INCOMPLETE LIST OF ALL THE HELP I HAVE RECEIVED)

Marilyn Biderman, agent
Nicole Winstanley, editor
Jennifer Griffiths, book designer
Shaun Oakey, copyeditor

All the other fine folks at Penguin Random House Canada:
Kristin Cochrane (CEO)
Dan French (marketing)
Bonnie Maitland (sales)
Alanna McMullen (managing editor)
Meredith Pal (almost everything else)

KC Adams, artist (her art adorns the covers of both *The Circle* and *The Strangers*)
Vanda Fleury
Chrysta Wood
Anna Lundberg
Reuben Boulette

The residencies that have helped me write for the last few years:
Centre for Creative Writing and Oral Culture at the University of Manitoba
Simon Fraser University
Athabasca University

All the other warriors, helpers, and teachers—traditional or otherwise—I have learned from over the years.

My kids—all of 'em.

And, you, reader-friend. It is my honour. Maarsii mille fois.

© Vanda Fleury

katherena vermette (she/her) is a Michif (Red River Métis) writer from Treaty 1 territory, Winnipeg, Manitoba, Canada. Born in Winnipeg, her Michif roots on her paternal side run deep in St. Boniface, St. Norbert and beyond. Her maternal side is Mennonite from the Altona and Rosenfeld area (Treaty 1). Her first book, *North End Love Songs* (The Muses' Company), won the Governor General's Literary Award for Poetry. Her novels *The Break* (House of Anansi), *The Strangers* and *The Circle* (Hamish Hamilton) were all national bestsellers and won multiple literary awards. Her work for children and young adults includes a picture book, *The Girl and the Wolf* (Theytus), and graphic novels, *A Girl Called Echo*, Vol. 1–4 (HighWater Press)—a special omnibus edition of the series was released in Fall 2023. She holds a Master of Fine Arts from the University of British Columbia and an honourary Doctor of Letters from the University of Manitoba. katherena lives with her kids—fur and human—in a cranky old house within skipping distance of the temperamental Red River.

katherenavermette.com